the GRAY CHAMBER

GRACE HITCHCOCK

BARBOUR BOOKS
An Imprint of Barbour Publishing, Inc.

Print ISBN 978-1-64352-235-7

eBook Editions:
Adobe Digital Edition (.epub) 978-1-64352-237-1
Kindle and MobiPocket Edition (.prc) 978-1-64352-236-4

Published by Barbour Books, an imprint of Barbour Publishing, Inc., 1810 Barbour Drive, Uhrichsville, Ohio 44683, www.barbourbooks.com

Our mission is to inspire the world with the life-changing message of the Bible.

ecpa Member of the
Evangelical Christian
Publishers Association

Printed in the United States of America.

PRAISE GRACE HITCHCOCK

"With beautiful description and shiver-worthy scenes, Grace Hitchcock has penned an incredible fiction story based on true history. *The Gray Chamber* is a fascinating and chilling read. Edyth's story had me glued to the pages. But as I journeyed with the heiress and her eccentricities, the greed of her family which saw her locked up in an asylum against her will made me grateful for the freedoms I have today. And made me pray that my voice would never be silenced. The nightmare was brought to life so vividly that I found myself holding my breath and then cheering on Bane as he never gave up on Edyth. This is a story that will stick with me for a long time. Well done, Ms. Hitchcock. Well done."

–Kimberley Woodhouse, Carol-Award winning and bestselling author of more than twenty books, including *Miss Taken Identity*, *The Express Bride*, *The Golden Bride*, *The Patriot Bride*, and *The Mayflower Bride*

"In 1893 Chicago, the World's Fair brings excitement to residents and visitors, and danger to a group of young ladies in this rousing solo debut novel [...] Hitchcock keeps the pace quick and tension high as the characters face dangers both physical and emotional. Readers will enjoy the snappy dialogue, vivid depictions of the famous World's Fair, and the surprising historical details."

–*Publishers Weekly*

Dedication

To Daddy, my kindred story-weaver.

Yea, though I walk through the valley of the shadow of death,
I will fear no evil: for thou art with me.

PSALM 23:4

Chapter One

*When once you have tasted flight, you will forever walk the earth
with your eyes turned skyward, for there you have been,
and there you will always long to return.*
~ Leonardo da Vinci

New York City, Fall 1887

Edyth Foster's limbs burned as she pedaled down Fifth Avenue, her white skirts whipping in the wind while she wove around pedestrians and carriages, ignoring their shouts of protest. Rounding the corner, she slowed her velocipede and overheard two women gasp and comment on her lack of chapeau and corset. Biting her lip, Edyth lifted her hand to her curls, realizing that she had once again forgotten her hat. *Oh well. That is the least peculiar thing about me.* She giggled at the thought and parked her bicycle at the side of the building before hurrying up the steps to the fencers' club, her heart pounding with anticipation of seeing Raoul Banebridge.

Pausing in the small women's dressing chamber, a room which was seldom used by any other woman than herself, she fitted her padded buckskin plastron over her chest before donning a matching buckskin gauntlet to protect herself from the thrust of a blade. Adjusting the burgundy sash over her skirt, she grabbed her wire mask, exited the dressing chamber, and stepped into the fencing area, scanning the room for her handsome instructor. The familiar scent of leather and sweat greeted her, but the men continued their exercises, no longer turning in shock at her presence as they had a decade ago when her father first brought her as a girl of fourteen. She had been a rather plump child, but the years of fencing had turned her muscles lean and strong.

Tucking an ebony wisp of hair behind her ear, she swung her arms across her body, stretching her muscles, and met the dark gaze of Bane. The clanging of steel against steel dulled as he strode across the room.

"You're late again, Edyth." Bane tossed her a foil sword, which she caught with ease. "When are you going to surrender your velocipede and take your perfectly respectable carriage to class?"

Whipping her blade into position, she grinned. "Never. Besides, cycling warms my muscles to save me from stretching forever. Now, if you will be so kind, *en garde!*"

He shook his head and, with a laugh, assumed a defensive stance and gave her the signal that he was ready. "*Pret.*"

"Let's fence. *Allez,*" she responded, and lunged.

Bane parried, his eyes twinkling. "Come now, Edyth, is that the best you've got? Were you up past the wee hours painting again? Perhaps you should heed your instructor and warm up before jumping into a bout with him."

Ignoring him, Edyth stepped forward on the narrow piste as Bane darted backward on the marked-off area, once again blocking her attack that was aimed between his shoulder and blade. He made his counterattack, which she parried, proud that she could hold her own against New York's finest fencing master. But of course the moment she had such a thought, the tip of his blade met her waist as the timekeeper called the three-minute mark of their first round.

Grabbing a towel, she dabbed at the light sheen on her forehead, the weight of her request pressing down on her. "So, what did you decide about coming to the dinner party tonight? Uncle Boris has informed me on multiple occasions how rude it is of you to keep us waiting so long for your answer to our invitation."

He groaned and raked a hand through his shoulder-length blond hair that boasted the most delightful curl at the ends. "You know how much I hate those social gatherings, Edyth. Mothers never fail to present their daughters as a marriageable option, and

I'm too busy with the fencing club to be distracted with taking care of a female's tender emotions."

"But you understand that I *must* attend, and as it is hosted by my uncle's new wife in honor of her daughter's return from living in Paris for the past four years, I won't know any of Mrs. Foster's society friends and it will be *excruciatingly* dull if you aren't there," she said all in one breath. "Please? If you do, I'll have the cook bake that lemon poppy seed bread that you enjoy so much and send it home with you tonight."

His lips curled in a grimace. "Fine. But this is the last time, Edyth, and I want two loaves."

She dipped her torso down, flipping her arms behind her in an exaggerated bow. "Done. Thank you, kind sir, for your gracious acceptance of my invitation."

"What are friends for except for attending boring parties in exchange for food? Minute break is up." He motioned her back onto the piste.

Friends. She gritted her teeth. He had been a friend to her since she had started coming to this club when he, at eighteen, was a champion, a man poised to purchase the club, while she was still an awkward girl. Their families knew of one another from society's intimate circle, and with Edyth's lessons, dinner invitations soon became a common occurrence between the two families and the pair found they enjoyed one another's company. And when her parents died the following year, he had become her closest friend, but Edyth couldn't help but feel that he still saw her as that pudgy girl of fourteen, not a woman of nearly five and twenty. She shook her arms to free herself of her morose thoughts and loosen her muscles. She sent him what she hoped was a brilliant smile and bowed with her foil before stepping onto the piste once again to finish their bout. As usual, Bane won, but closing the gap between the scores always made Edyth feel like it was a success no matter how many points he bested her by.

After an hour-long lesson, she slipped out of the fencing area and spied her wild hair in the looking glass of the women's area. Edyth cringed and ran her hands over her braid that had tumbled from her coiffure before smoothing her white fencing gown, its loose structure feeling more natural to her than any day gown. *Maybe that's part of the problem of why we are only friends.* But even if she did relinquish her comfortable gowns for the more stylish ones, Bane still might not see her as a woman. With a dismissive shrug, she decided not to change her clothes or adjust her hair, as she was certain cycling would undo whatever she managed to fix.

Leaving her gear on her designated shelf, Edyth hopped onto her velocipede and pedaled home, reveling in the crisp air, her long braid whipping behind her back. When the snow fell, she would have no other choice but to take her carriage to and from the fencing club, but as soon as it melted, she would be back on her two wheels. She was used to the wide-eyed stares from women as she passed by, the shocked expressions of men, and the gleeful pointing of the children as she cycled around them. She didn't necessarily care whether or not she fit into society's idea of the perfect gentlewoman. She was one of the fortunate ones, one of the few women who had her future secured without needing to put on a facade to secure a husband's pocketbook. And she was aware enough by now that any man who did attempt to woo her was, in fact, after the significant inheritance left to her by her parents.

Not a day went by that she did not long to be in her father's and mother's embrace or think of that horrific accident. She was supposed to have gone ice skating with them that day. But she had caught a cold and stayed at home. Shaking her dark thoughts, she focused on the fiery foliage of the sugar maples and scarlet oaks and the purple and golds of the green ash trees, attempting to enjoy the fall months while she could, when something gray stirring in the bushes to her left caught her eye. Catching her foot on the sidewalk, Edyth slowed her velocipede and hopped off, wheeling her bike beside her.

Passersby complained when she parked her bicycle against the tree and stooped down to the bush on her knees to find a bedraggled, mewing kitten. "Oh, you poor little dear." She scooped the kitten into her arms and cuddled it to her neck, offering the little one warmth as its frantic mewing increased. She looked about for a mother or siblings, but seeing none, she held the kitten in one hand and wheeled her bicycle home with the other.

Slipping through the side iron gate that was left open for the staff and deliveries, Edyth parked her velocipede and used the service entrance. Waving to the staff who, by now were quite used to her strange comings and goings, did not even blink at the sight of her below stairs.

"Miss Foster, what is this? *Another* stray?" The butler's graying wiry brows stooped along with his deep voice.

"Harrison, how could I not take him in?" She lifted the kitten up to her cheek and nuzzled him, her nose crinkling at the putrid smell clinging to his fur.

"Because you have already taken in two strays this year and one last. I do not know how these kittens keep finding you, but this has to stop at some point, miss. Four felines are simply too many for one household. Where are we going to keep them all? They will destroy the furnishings."

"Well, I suppose we can adjust one of the guest rooms to suit them, don't you think? Perhaps we could pull some old items from the servants' quarters to furnish it and replace the worn things with new ones that are more to the servants' liking?"

He sighed and rubbed his brows with his thumb and forefinger, causing the wild hairs to stick out every which way. "We wondered when you would get to the point of giving your cats a room, but we had hoped you would be fifty and have a few gray hairs before it happened."

She rose on her tiptoes and pressed a kiss to Harrison's withered cheek. "I am a spinster, so four cats in total really isn't all that much, now is it?"

"Will you ever reach a number that is too many?" He smirked, making him look far younger than his sixty years.

"I think perhaps nine would be too many. Please see to it that Katie gives Michelangelo a bath." She deposited the kitten into his hands. "Thank you, Harrison," she called over her shoulder, and darted up the tight, winding staircase to her bedroom on the second floor, nodding and smiling to any maid in passing.

Her leather fencing shoes padded on the lush carpet of the hall leading to her chambers, but before she reached her suite, a shrill voice came from the library that could only be her new aunt expressing herself as she was known to do on occasion. *Was wedding a beautiful woman worth enduring such antics, Uncle?*

"What do you mean? You have put up with this nonsense for *years* and the answer was right here in front of you this whole time and you did not even see it?" Mrs. Foster's high-pitched shriek pierced Edyth's ears from behind the mahogany door.

She sucked in her breath, tempted to continue on to her rooms when another stream began. But while she and Uncle Boris had never been as close as she would wish, Edyth didn't feel right about leaving him to fend for himself if she could distract his new bride from unbridling her wrath. With a soft knock, she opened the door to her father's dark study that she rarely used. Father had kept it well stocked with books from generations of collectors, but she couldn't afford the fascination. Books were too quiet a pastime. She needed to be in motion or fiercely concentrating on something, else her thoughts would come knocking.

"Uncle Boris? Is everything well?" The man who looked so much like her father rose from a leather wingback chair facing the crackling fireplace with a stack of official-looking documents gripped in his fist.

"Everything is fine, Edyth." His gaze traveled over her wild hair and fencing ensemble, his thin lips pressing into a firm line.

Edyth shifted uncomfortably. He had never looked at her like this before he brought Mrs. Foster home last summer. *And now for the protest in three, two, one—*

Mrs. Foster gestured to Edyth's attire and heaved a sigh. "Really, Boris, is this not all the proof you need? Your niece is *cycling* about the city dressed in this outlandish gown for all the world to see when she could have the latest of fashions shipped in from Paris and be driven in one of her many carriages like a proper lady."

Uncle Boris lifted his finger to his lips and quirked a brow at his bride. "Too much, dear. All in good time."

Edyth surveyed the room to see if a half-empty crystal decanter was near at hand to make sense of why they were both behaving so oddly.

"But your aunt is correct, Edyth. It is hardly appropriate for people to see you in such attire. Upon your velocipede, your ankles are certainly in danger of being exposed with every turn of the wheel."

Mrs. Foster pursed her lips. "It is bad enough you wear that ensemble at the fencing club, or that you are a member at a fencing club for that matter, but you *flaunt* your lack of regard of fashion and etiquette to the entire city."

Edyth swallowed back a reminder to her new aunt that she and Uncle Boris were only living on Fifth Avenue because they were residing in Edyth's mansion, not her uncle's. She had never begrudged her uncle a generous allowance from her trust, but his bride was making it rather a burden to house them. *Four more months and I will have the right to my fortune and the ability to set Uncle up in his own apartment and be free from his so-called guardianship.* She ran her fingertips over the calluses on her palm and drew a deep breath. *Lord, give me strength to be kind.* "I apologize if I have caused you embarrassment."

Her aunt gave a short laugh and was about to say something when Uncle Boris placed his hand on her shoulder, halting her onslaught. Mrs. Foster pinched the bridge of her nose, mumbling something about it being all Boris's fault for not doing his due diligence. She lifted her palms up and twitched her lips into a sharp smile. "Well, I'm hoping Lavinia's influence will smooth out your *many* rough edges, Edyth. Your cousin is to arrive within the hour, so I suggest you leave us to our own business and change into something appropriate. Your uncle and I have too much to discuss to stop and address your many faults."

Edyth clenched and unclenched her fists, swallowing her smoldering response. As Mother used to quote, a gentle answer turns away wrath. She dipped into the lowest curtsy she could manage and answered dutifully, "Your wish is my command, oh my queen."

❧

Raoul Banebridge adjusted his worn inverness coat, his focus on the floor-length windows ablaze with candlelight, and braced himself against a gust that whipped his umbrella nearly inside out. *If Edyth wasn't such a good family friend. . .* He cleared his throat and pushed aside the discomfiture of not knowing many in attendance for the chance of a fancy meal. Having spent all his hours and small inheritance on his fencing club, he had little time to spare for dinner parties. In the beginning days when he was building his number of students, Bane attended every party—those he was invited to and those he wasn't. He had managed to procure invitations through Edyth until she had sworn off high society events and could not be persuaded to change her mind. But now that the fencing club had grown in popularity with the elite set, it required all his attention, and parties had become things of the past.

Strolling around the other guests' arriving carriages, he nodded to the doorman and handed his black umbrella, top hat, and coat to the young butler who stood just inside the marble foyer. Sounds of laughter flowed out of the front parlor followed by the clinking of glasses when Edyth flew around the corner in the most outlandish blue-and-green plaid dress he had ever beheld. While he didn't mingle too much with his set anymore, he knew most women chose to wear more demure gowns. This tartan was something new altogether. Bane's gaze went to her hair and he saw that she was trying something different with her coiffure, but the curls, which he assumed she had attempted to tame, had become quite frizzled.

"You're here! I've been watching for you," she breathed, snatching his hand in hers before remembering herself and dropping it and executing a perfect curtsy.

"Of course I am here. You begged me to attend. What kind of teacher would I be if I disappointed the one student who has attended every single one of the fencing club's expositions, demonstrations, and whatnot?" His little friend was nothing if not supportive of his fencing school, but he did not wish to tell her how much it meant to him, lest more invitations follow now that the Parisian stepcousin had come to the city.

"Your hair looks dashing pulled back into a queue, Bane." She reached out and brushed off his coat, her fingertips lingering for a second, then two before she folded her hands in front of her skirts.

"Thank you. And you look. . ." He motioned to her attire and settled with, "Uh, very clean."

She rolled her eyes and smirked. "Thank you. I am certain it took a lot out of you to give me such a lovely compliment." She flipped her hand, beckoning him. "Come, let me introduce you to my new cousin. She is every bit as fashionable as a young lady returning from Paris should be." Edyth threaded her hand around Bane's elbow and pulled him through the french doors into the gilded parlor where he spied a regal creature with an hourglass figure and blond hair curled to perfection, dressed in a heavenly gown of white with a low neckline trimmed with pink roses. His mouth gaped as his gaze rested on her picturesque rosy cheeks and laughing eyes of blue.

Edyth paused in front of the lady, who was a good six inches taller than her. "Bane, this is my cousin, Lavinia Birch. Miss Birch,

I would like you to meet my fencing instructor and dear friend, Mr. Raoul Banebridge, or Bane as he prefers, since he claims Raoul is a name for a dandy."

"And Bane is a much more intimidating name for a fencing master," he added, bowing to the beauty. "It is a pleasure to meet you."

With a pretty smile, she extended her hand. "The honor is all mine, sir. In the few hours I've been here, Cousin Edyth has told me much about you."

Bane fumbled for an answer as he lightly kissed her surprisingly large gloved hand, but thankfully, she continued. "And in order to get to know my new cousin better, I thought, what better way than to have her closest friend as my dinner partner to tell me all about our dear Edyth?"

Bane disliked leaving Edyth in the lurch, but he couldn't refuse an invitation to sit with the guest of honor, nor did he wish to refuse. He looked to his friend and cleared his throat. "If Miss Foster is agreeable?"

Edyth's smile faltered for a moment before she sent Lavinia a confident nod. "Of course. You'll get along famously. Bane has always managed to capture my attention." Her cheeks tinted. "I—I mean, oh, never mind. Go along, and I will make certain the dinner cards are rearranged accordingly." She darted away without another word.

Bane assumed his place beside Miss Birch, who turned to him with an expectant smile. Any thought of making conversation fled with the parting of those full lips into a smile, which was now beginning to falter with his silence. But thankfully, Edyth returned from instructing the butler and, true to her nature, she filled the gaps in conversation with questions and laughter.

Just as the dining room doors were being opened for dinner, three gentlemen that he did not recognize joined their party, two of middling age with short, pointed beards, and the third, a clean-shaven red-haired man who appeared to be around Bane's own age.

Mr. Foster greeted them and nodded toward Bane's corner of the room. He felt Miss Birch's attention drawn to the young man, her obvious interest in him causing Bane to turn to her.

"So, tell me about your time in Paris, Miss Birch. How long were you there?"

"For four years." Her gaze flitted back toward the young man.

"It must have been quite lovely to keep you for so long," he ventured, hoping to pull her attention from the fellow.

"Quite." She replied without looking at him as the gentleman approached her and bowed, sending her fan to flapping and Bane to realizing how quickly he could be forgotten.

❧

Edyth couldn't stop herself from noticing Lavinia and Bane waltzing onto the floor yet again while Bane had failed to ask her even one time to dance. She sighed and attempted to keep time with her current ancient partner. *Well, the night is young. And Lavinia did ask Bane to take care of her.* She swallowed back her growing resentment toward her cousin, determined to give Lavinia the benefit of the doubt.

"Miss Foster?"

She blinked and returned her notice to her own partner, a middle-aged gentleman with a well-groomed graying beard. "I am so sorry, what was your question, Mister. . . ?"

"*Doctor* Wentworth," he replied, blinking in return as if it were obvious.

Edyth murmured his name and earned a scowl, but she had a tendency to forget names as soon as she heard them if she did not repeat them back at once, a practice no one seemed to appreciate.

He cleared his throat. "I was saying that I spoke with your uncle earlier today and he mentioned that you enjoyed a rather *peculiar* hobby."

"There is nothing peculiar about painting. My father was quite the artist, and I hope one day to have my own work displayed," she replied, praying her uncle had not spoken of her fencing. While she adored the sport, she greatly disliked it when others questioned her, for no good came from their judgment, and unfortunately, she was usually moved to respond in kind. She feared she would never learn to control her tongue as long as others did not extend her the same courtesy.

"Of course not. Painting is a most appropriate pastime for a woman of your standing. I was speaking of your taste for fencing."

"It has been around for centuries, sir." She lifted her head, her temper sparking. *Why does he think he should have an opinion on how I choose to spend my time?*

"Well, perhaps not for a man, but for a *woman* it is entirely another matter." Doctor Wentworth twisted his mouth and simultaneously scrunched his nose.

Edyth gritted her teeth and refrained from giving in to the temptation of accidentally stomping on the doctor's toes and waited for them to complete another turn before responding. "And why would that be? *Women* need exercise too, *Doctor* Wentworth, as I'm sure *you* are well aware." She couldn't help herself from adding, "These fashionable corsets are squeezing the life out of girls in the name of beauty, and then men express astonishment at feminine frailty." She shook her head. "If more girls took their constitutionals at a fencing club, I guarantee you would see fewer of them as patients."

"Really, Miss Foster. One should not discuss unmentionables with a gentleman." The doctor's voice lowered to a hiss, his eyes narrowing to slits.

"But you are not only a gentleman, but a physician, sir. Surely the mention of the contraption cannot test your fortitude?" *Or I fear you may be in the wrong profession.* At his blustered state, she cleared her throat and tried again. Her uncle would be furious if he discovered her sharing her outlandish opinions with a gentleman. She turned the conversation to the doctor. "So, where do you practice?"

He pressed his lips into a thin line as if contemplating whether or not to answer her after her scandalous comment. "Blackwell's Island."

"Oh?" This piqued her curiosity. She should have led with this question and avoided the tedium of explaining herself and her interests to him. "For which building? I've heard they have quite the collection of almshouses, hospitals—"

"The lunatic asylum in the Lodge building."

She nearly stumbled, never expecting that answer. She had just finished dancing with another doctor who worked at the island's asylum as well. Why on earth would her uncle have two doctors from the lunatic asylum at his stepdaughter's welcome home party? Her gaze darted to her aunt. *Well, she may have erratic moods.* "But she's not *mad*," she mumbled, and then chuckled.

"What was that now? Have I said something humorous?" His brows shot up at her laughter.

She shook her head. "My apologies, sir, I was merely talking to myself. What is this lodge building? It sounds rather like a place to take a holiday retreat."

He clicked his tongue and sighed. "The Lodge is the asylum's violent ward just down the road from the asylum, and beyond that building is the Retreat, which houses our overflow patients."

Well, that's deceptive. Edyth chewed the inside of her cheek, and the two finished the rest of the dance in blessed silence, both eagerly parting at the conclusion of the waltz.

Edyth moved toward Bane, who was guiding Lavinia from the floor for the third time. "I hope you are enjoying your dancing more than I am, Cousin. I have had the exceptionally bad luck to have been engaged by two ancient doctors in a row. . .neither of which seemed all that eager to dance with me in the first place."

"Mr. Banebridge has been a delight, but I'm afraid I mustn't take another turn with him for fear people will talk. After all, I've only been in New York for a day, and I must allow Mama to introduce me to the rest of the guests." Lavinia sent Bane a sweet smile as a handsome young man with a flash of red hair approached them.

"Excuse me, Miss Birch a—and Miss Foster." The young man politely included Edyth in his greeting, giving them each an elegant bow. "My name is Doctor Roger Hawkins. I must beg your forgiveness for not waiting until we have been properly introduced to request a dance, Miss Birch, but your mother was telling me so much about you and your accomplishments that I had to see for myself if all her claims were true."

Lavinia's round cheeks tinted with obvious admiration. She snapped open her fan and dipped her head. "It is an honor to meet you, Doctor. And I'm certain that since my stepfather invited you and you have spoken with Mama, it is permission enough for you to request a dance with their daughter."

And with that, Doctor Hawkins held out his hand to Lavinia and led her out onto the dance floor without so much as another word to Bane or Edyth.

Edyth drew in a breath through her teeth, feeling Bane's ire over her cousin's obvious attraction to the doctor. *Perhaps Lavinia will be spoken for before the night is over after all, and I won't have to challenge her to a duel for attempting to make off with Bane's heart when she knows good and well my feelings on the matter.* She curbed her thoughts. As much as she might wish it, Bane was not hers and most likely never would be. Why wouldn't he look for a wife if he did not see one before him now? "Do you think my cousin is attractive?"

Bane rolled his eyes. "You never know when to stop asking questions." He offered her his hand. "Come on. I'll dance with you."

Edyth wished she had the strength to refuse his glib offer, but the thought of being in his arms propelled her forward. He pulled her into a waltz and she lost all thoughts but those of Bane. . .and of losing him to another.

Chapter Two

I saw the angel in the marble and
carved until I set him free.
~ Michelangelo

Edyth tossed under her feather comforter, convinced that he was smitten. Seeing Bane fawn over her cousin last night had been excruciating. He hadn't even mentioned the anniversary party for the fencing club at this week's end that she had been planning with him for a month. "How am I to compare with the Parisian Princess?" She sighed and stroked Michelangelo's soft fur that had turned out to be pearl white and not gray. "Lord, help me bear it if Bane chooses her."

She couldn't deny that Bane deserved the best. If he chose to love Lavinia, then she would have to learn to support him and pray that, in time, she would love him as a friend. . .as he evidently saw her. At the gentle tap on her door, Edyth rolled out of bed to find Lavinia in a rosy, ruffled dressing robe, bearing a tray with a steaming porcelain chocolate pot and two matching cups.

"Good morning, Cousin. I hope you don't mind me coming in early after such a late party, but in Paris I always started my morning off with a cup of chocolate. And I was hoping you would join me, or rather, allow me to join you." She laughed, lifting the tray.

Edyth motioned her into her chamber and removed her mother's worn silk robe from the back of the settee. She slipped it over her plain cotton nightgown, watching Lavinia set the tray atop the French-style writing desk with a clank, the dishes rattling against one another before Lavinia crossed the room and threw open the heavy curtains. Edyth held up her hand, squinting in the morning light and coughing at the dust lifted from the windowsills.

21

Lavinia gushed over the handsome men of the night before as she poured the chocolate. Edyth dug her thumb into her palm, massaging against the envy settling over her anew at Lavinia's state of perfection even after a short night's sleep. She shuddered to think how wild her hair must appear, what with the storm from last night adding a bit of dampness to the air. She dared a peek in the gilded looking glass above her vanity and suppressed a shudder. She discreetly wiped at the corners of her mouth, removing any trace of having drooled in her sleep.

Settling onto the settee beside the dwindling fire, Lavinia wrapped her hands around her yellow teacup and sent Edyth the brilliant smile that had captured Bane's attention. It wasn't Lavinia's fault that she was so fetching. What else could Edyth expect, seeing how Lavinia's own mother had captured Uncle Boris's attention by her well-preserved beauty?

"So, you didn't tell me how *handsome* your friend was or that he owned the fencing club. I think he will do nicely for you."

Edyth jerked her head up, upsetting her teacup and sloshing the hot liquid. Sucking in a breath, she wiped her hand on her nightgown, not minding the brown stain it left behind. "But I—I thought you were interested in him for yourself."

"Surely you did not think that I would attempt to steal away the one man you mentioned to me on the first night I was staying under your roof?" She laughed and set aside her cup to scoop up the kitten, stroking behind his ears. "I am not one of *those* girls. I may be searching for a husband, but I think it is important for us to start off on the right foot."

Edyth's ears burned from her assumptions of her cousin. *Forgive me, Lord.*

"And I believe the right foot is to help you capture Mr. Banebridge's heart, so that's why I was asking him so many questions about his friendship with you, to see where his heart might lie concerning you."

The room had grown far too hot. Edyth pulled at the frayed collar of her robe. *Dare I ask what he thought about me?* She could fence grown men and ride better than most, and yet the idea of Lavinia speaking of Bane as if Edyth and he were a couple sent her body into profuse perspiration. "And?" she managed to croak.

"And he respects you." Lavinia settled back triumphantly, sipping her chocolate.

The air went out of her. "Oh, that's lovely."

"Come now, Cousin. That is *high* praise indeed. Not once have I heard a man say that about a female who was not his wife, and even then, it was not often."

While Lavinia's reassurance cooled Edyth's frenzied heart, it wasn't only his respect that she craved. "I think I'd rather be admired."

Lavinia leaned over and rubbed Edyth's knee. "Nonsense. If he respects you, I can push him across that thin line to loving you. It would be a great deal harder if he did not think of you at all, but Mr. Banebridge considers you to be his respected friend."

While she adored Bane, Edyth didn't wish to be the cause of his unhappiness if his admiration of Lavinia was returned. "Are you certain that you do not have feelings for him? Because it sounds like you respect him too."

Lavinia laughed. "Of course I respect him, but I find that a certain young doctor has captured my thoughts and may soon hold my heart."

Edyth pressed the back of her hand to her heated neck. *How could I have so vastly misjudged her?* After Bane finally requested a waltz, she had stopped watching Lavinia and so had missed Lavinia's interaction with the young doctor. Regretting her harsh judgment of her cousin, she retrieved the chocolate pot, topped off both of their cups, and returned to the settee, curling her bare feet under her legs. "I have begun to wonder if maybe dressing the part of a lady might assist my cause? I didn't think it was an issue because, well, men try to pay me calls often enough. Though I am fairly certain it is only for the sake of my inheritance and nothing else."

Lavinia ran her finger around the lip of her cup as if she was measuring her words. "I am glad you brought that up. I do not mean to be rude, but that plaid you were wearing last night is not exactly the height of fashion in New York."

Edyth looked down at her nightgown's collar and cuffs, devoid of the frills that Lavinia's displayed. She had much to learn if even her nightwear was so simple. "Could you help me select a few gowns to have made? Uncle Boris never employed a governess to guide me in such matters and, well, I am afraid I didn't request one. I ceased caring about clothes after the accident." She ran her fingers over the threadbare cuff of the silk robe. "My mother always took care of everything I wore."

Lavinia grasped her hand. "I would be happy to aid you, Cousin." She smiled over her cup, inhaling the steaming tendrils before taking another long draft. "Now, do you know Mr. Banebridge's schedule outside of the fencing club?"

Edyth blinked. "What does that have to do with anything?"

Lavinia giggled behind her hand as the kitten wriggled out of her arms and landed with a plop on the settee. "Everything. When planning to wage a war for the heart, one must know where to strike first."

"I don't wish to battle him," she mumbled, but at Lavinia's pointed stare, she sighed. "Bane always begins his day with a ride through Central Park. I know because I take rides there most mornings as well if I wake early enough to avoid the crowds."

Lavinia set aside her cup and clapped her hands. "Oh, that's the perfect place for our first coincidental encounter."

"But don't you think it a bit forward of me to ride after him and *pretend* to happen upon him?"

Lavinia raised her brows, crossing her arms. "But don't you normally happen upon him?"

Edyth gave a shrug, still uncomfortable with the charade. "I suppose so, but—"

"Then of course it is not forward." Lavinia pulled Edyth up and strode around her, tapping her forefinger to her full lips. "Yes. I have *just* the thing, straight from Paris. Against your hair, it will be sure to catch Bane's attention. He will think you are heaven-sent. It's a good thing we are about the same size in every area besides height and uh. . ." She twisted her mouth and lifted her brows in a telling way. "Well, we can stuff your bodice if we need to, and as for the length of the skirt, it won't be much of a problem with you being mounted, but be certain to stay atop your saddle lest you trip over the hem and betray that the dress was not made for you."

Still transfixed on that alarming detail, Edyth's cheeks burned. "I hardly think it will be necessary to pad—"

Lavinia tugged her out into the hallway and down three doors to her rooms. Within the hour, Edyth's hair was puffed into an elaborate coiffure, perfectly coiled, her torso squeezed into a whalebone corset and thrust into Lavinia's stylish crimson riding gown. The bodice was a great deal looser on her than Edyth thought it would be, and even though she repeatedly refused the scented powdered puffs that Lavinia insisted on stuffing into her gown, she eventually gave in to her cousin's demands. She turned in front of the floor-length looking glass, her cheeks heating at the sight of her tucked and puffed figure. Lavinia deemed her a work of art and sent Edyth off to the park on her favorite horse.

Perched atop her mount on a sidesaddle in the cumbersome gown, Edyth felt utterly ridiculous wearing something so fancy while riding, not to mention a corset and the unmentionable powdered puffs. If it were up to her, she would be wearing her split skirt even though it caused people to stare more than when she wore her fencing costume. She guided her horse across Fifth Avenue to Central Park, where she casually glanced about for Bane along his favored route. Spying his giant, dapple-gray stallion, she gave her gelding enough of a nudge to kick up his heels into a trot to catch up with Bane. She reined back a bit as her mount trotted up next to his. "Good morning, sir."

"Good morning, Miss—Edyth?" His voice was full of astonishment as he openly gawked at her.

Edyth couldn't help but laugh and toss her head flirtatiously as she had seen others do, thankful that Lavinia had secured the frilly riding hat in place. Undeniable admiration sparked in his expression. And she reveled in it. *Finally.*

❧

Bane glanced at her sideways again. He had always thought of Edyth as the young girl who had been sparring with him since she was fourteen years old. But, studying her profile, he was shocked to find that his friend was a beauty.

She turned to him, her eyes alert as if she had heard his thoughts, causing him to feel more than a bit foolish for thinking of her as anything other than his longtime friend, especially after how he had behaved last night.

He had showered Miss Birch with his attention at dinner and, at her sweet smiles, hope had begun to blossom in his heart of finding *the one*, but he quickly realized that Miss Birch gave her smiles freely to any face she deemed handsome. He felt his embarrassment keenly after seeing her waltz with that young doctor fellow and, of all things, allowing him to whisper in her ear at the end of the evening and press a possessive kiss atop her hand. He didn't particularly think a lady should allow a gentleman such liberties after only knowing him for a single evening, or so it would seem. . .perhaps she knew him from before? But she didn't betray their connection when introduced, and in his heart he knew the truth. A doctor was a far more desirable catch than a fencing master.

Bane desired a lady who thought he was everything. That he was her world. He wanted to take care of her, to be needed. Once he'd had the foolishness to admit his longing to his older brothers, and they had mercilessly mocked him for sounding like a novel-reading woman, but after hearing of so many unhappy marriages from the men in his fencing club, he was even more determined to wait until he found that one person before proposing.

"So, what did you think about my new cousin?"

He cleared his throat and pulled at his neckcloth. Of course Edyth would bring up the one subject he didn't wish to discuss.

"You seemed quite taken with her last night," she ventured, adjusting the brim of her little riding hat.

"You thought I was taken with her?" he replied, trying to garner enough time to explain away his actions even though she was right. He had behaved like a schoolboy.

She laughed, her dark eyes sparkling. "How could I not? I have never seen you so animated at one of my uncle's parties."

"Well, sometimes I cannot see what is right in front of me until it is too late."

She tilted her head at him before smiling and moving the conversation to the safe ground of fencing.

He felt like a traitor for having shown Miss Birch such attention last night and effectively ignoring his best friend, but with the morning sun flowing over Edyth's raven hair and immaculate gown, he began to see her in a new light. Edyth shared his interests, which was more than Miss Birch had shown. When the second course had arrived and Miss Birch learned that he was merely a poor gentleman who *must* work at his club to support himself, her interest had waned, and she had brought up Edyth's name multiple times before turning her attention to the doctor who was seated to her left. And though Miss Birch had danced with Bane a few times, he suspected it was only in recompense for her actions at dinner. Edyth would never be so callous or shallow. But, he could hardly blame the girl. Who would entertain a poor gentleman when a rich doctor was close by and would make for a fine husband?

"You're brooding again." Edyth poked his shoulder with her

riding crop. "Come, shall we race around the bend? It is early enough so that we won't trample any pedestrians along this path, and open enough to spot them should they appear."

For his answer, Bane kicked his horse into a gallop, racing down the dirt path. Rounding the corner, they came upon a fallen tree from last night's storm. He managed to slow his mount in time as Edyth soared over the lean tree, but her horse's front hoof caught on a stray branch and stumbled in his landing, sending Edyth sailing over his head, a splash sounding.

"Edyth!" Panic seared through him as he leapt off his horse, leaving his reins dangling to the ground, and vaulted over the log to find that she had landed in the pond. "Edyth, are you hurt?"

She pushed herself back onto her knees and laughed, wiping her sleeve over her face and streaking the mud speckled across her cheeks to her disheveled hairline. "Poor dress never stood a chance with me," she muttered. She moved to stand but at once slipped to her elbows.

"Hold on. Let me help you." Bane yanked off his jacket and tossed it over a branch. Wading into the murky water, he inadvertently stepped into a hole and drew in a sharp breath at the biting cold seeping in the top of his boot. He would have to make this quick or risk freezing. He dug his heels into the bank and held out his hand to assist her. She gripped his forearm, but when she tugged to pull herself free from the muck securing her to the pond floor, his heel slipped and he plummeted to his side, the scum sloshing over them.

"Bane!" Edyth squealed, flicking her hands free.

Bane chuckled as he looked at Edyth. The perfection of her ensemble had vanished, but the unfamiliarity of knowing his friend was beautiful remained. He reached out and smoothed a lock of hair from her dark eyes and smiled, but a bit of mud met his tongue and he gagged, sending him spitting to the side and giving Edyth an apologetic grimace. "I suppose we should go ahead and submerse ourselves completely to rinse away the mud?"

Her teeth chattered behind her smile while she rubbed her hands over her soaked sleeves. "If it were summer, I would say I'm all for a nice swim in the duck's retiring room, but I think I'd rather be muddy and partially dry than drenched in scented pond scum."

"Well, when you put it like that it doesn't sound better." He laughed as she hiked up her skirts, exposing a well-turned ankle, and stepped toward the shore, slipping despite her caution.

He averted his eyes and took her elbow. "You had best allow me to assist you, else you risk taking another tumble from your water-logged skirts."

"I suppose it was rather foolish to wear something other than my split skirt." She gave him a sheepish smile.

Bane shrugged. "I found your new gown rather charming."

"Oh?"

"Found as in *past* tense." Bane laughed and wrapped his arm about her slender waist. He hefted them to shore while a woman parking her pram watched them with pursed lips and two gentlemen caught their escaped mounts. Once safely ashore, Bane released Edyth and retrieved his jacket and the horses with a nod of thanks to the gentlemen. Returning with the horses in tow, he draped his jacket over her shoulders and whispered, "Judging from the shocked faces in this group, we are going to get some marvelous stares on the way back to Fifth Avenue."

"Good thing I am impervious to them by now." Edyth laughed as the sound of hoofbeats caused them both to turn and find Miss Birch riding up with Doctor Hawkins at her side. Edyth lifted her gaze heavenward and mumbled something that sounded like, "Why, Lord? Why must You call my bluff? I admit it! I actually do care what some people think of me."

He ran a hand over his jaw to suppress his laughter at her utterance and Lavinia's expression.

Lavinia gasped. "What on earth, Edyth?"

Edyth busied herself with wringing out her hem in what he believed was an attempt to ignore the question, so Bane stepped forward. "It was entirely my fault, Miss Birch. I goaded her into racing at such a breakneck speed."

Lavinia pressed her lips into a thin line, looking remarkably like her mother. "I'm sure it did not take much coaxing for our dear Edyth to be convinced that it was indeed a sound idea." She tugged at the reins as her mount threw back its head, stamping its hoof and snorting as if eager to be on its way. "But, despite your current circumstances, it is fortuitous that we happened upon you two. Roger invited me to dinner with him, but as I had already made my mind up to dine with Edyth tonight, perhaps you, Mr. Banebridge, could join us for a fourth at Delmonico's?"

"I would be honored," Bane replied, extending a hand to Edyth. "If you are willing?"

She gave him that smirk again and nodded, creating wondrous flutters in his stomach. "You know I am always in the mood to eat, especially at my favorite restaurant."

~

The servants' entrance was unusually busy with deliveries of massive crates marked for her aunt, so despite the mud caking her person, Edyth decided to take the main entrance. She paused in the marble foyer to hand the ruined riding hat to Harrison, who merely shook his head. "Oh miss. I'm afraid your aunt has company and will be most upset—" He snapped his mouth shut and bowed as her aunt exited the parlor and gasped upon sight of Edyth.

"Gentlemen, do come out and see what we have to deal with on a daily basis, and please, tell me my arguments are not valid."

Edyth's jaw dropped, and with widened eyes, she ran her hands down her skirt, whacking in vain at the dirt clinging to her gown. "Why on earth would you call people to come see me when I look like this? I'm hardly ready to receive guests. If you would only give me a moment to change—"

But she didn't have a moment. Two middle-aged gentlemen, one with thick-rimmed glasses and one with a pencil poised above his notepad, stepped into the foyer from the parlor. *The two men from the party? Why are they here again?*

"Does this look like a healthy young woman of sound mind to you?" Mrs. Foster threw her hands in front of herself, gesturing to Edyth's gown.

"What are you talking about? Why are these men here and not at the asylum?" Edyth resisted the urge to cross her arms over her chest as the men's stares roved freely over her.

"Because they, as my personal friends, came as a favor to me. I could not trust anyone else with something so sensitive." Uncle Boris appeared from the parlor, his fingers tugging the end of his mustache. "Well, gentlemen, I believe you now have enough proof to support what my wife and I have been saying. Shall we adjourn and discuss the diagnosis?"

Diagnosis? Edyth stepped forward, her heart hammering with concern. She was in perfect health, but she had noticed her uncle's ever-present cough had grown steadily worse in recent weeks. While she had never been close to her father's brother, she did not wish to lose her last remaining link to her father's people. "Uncle, are you unwell?" Why else would he summon doctors from Blackwell's Island when he had access to the best of care in the city?

Mrs. Foster pressed a hand to the back of Edyth's soaked gown, nudging her toward the stairs. "This is not the time to discuss such things."

"She does show signs of erratic behavior. I mean, look at the state of her," one of the doctors mumbled.

Edyth cringed, feeling her temper rising to the occasion. Gripping her riding crop in both hands, she breathed in before slowly turning and planting a fist to her corseted waist, the wretched thing making it difficult to draw a full breath. "Excuse me? How dare you come into *my* house and address me so rudely?"

The men twisted their lips, and the scrivener of the pair jotted down something.

"What on earth are you writing? I did not give you permission to quote me." She moved to snatch the notebook out of his hands, but her uncle lifted his hand, stopping her.

"I think you must agree with me, Doctors. She is as mad as they come." Mrs. Foster clasped her hands in front of her pristine skirts, a gleam in her expression that Edyth had never seen before.

"Mad?" Edyth clenched her jaw and turned to face Mrs. Foster. "If anyone is mad, it is you for bringing doctors into *my* house to accuse me of being out of my mind."

Uncle Boris placed a hand on his wife's arm and drew her behind him as if Edyth would use the riding crop on the woman. "Now, Edyth, you mustn't grow hysterical."

"You have to admit that it is rather strange for *you*, who have never shown any interest in gowns, to suddenly dress in a Parisian riding ensemble," Mrs. Foster piped up from behind her husband's shoulder. "Which you have now seen fit to ruin in one outing. Madness!"

Edyth ran a hand over her eyes in an attempt to squelch her growing agitation lest she prove their claims true. "That's because Lavinia dressed me this morning. Really, it is absurd that you would make such wild accusations because I have taken an interest in something as simple as a fashionable gown."

Uncle Boris patted her on the arm. "Of course. Now, why don't you change, and we can discuss this more in private." He leaned forward and whispered into her ear, his breath reeking of port. "These men are not here to evaluate you, my dear. They are here for your aunt, but please, do not say a word to anyone until it is time for her to be taken. I would hate to cause Lavinia any undue stress if Mrs. Foster is found sane. . .and if she is not, I do not wish her to become violent."

With those words, Edyth's anger turned from the doctors and

toward her uncle as she peeked at the wide-eyed woman behind him. She lifted her lips to his ear, keeping her voice low. "Uncle, don't you think you are being rash? While she may have a temper, she is as sane as you and I, and to even contemplate such a thing is not only unwarranted, but utterly ridiculous and cruel."

His gaze narrowed. "This is obviously not the time to discuss this. Promise me you will not create a scene?"

She quirked a brow. "Of course not, Uncle, but we *will* discuss it?"

At his nod, she stepped back and gave the group a smile. "My apologies, gentlemen and Auntie. If you will excuse me, I have an engagement and must retire to dress. Please enjoy some refreshments before you depart."

Chapter Three

The sight of the stars makes me dream.
~ Vincent van Gogh

Dressed in a gold gown that fairly sparkled in the candlelight of Delmonico's, Edyth held herself just so, aware of her padded front as she took a seat beside Bane at the small round table in the corner of the narrow restaurant. Since the powdered puffs had remained firmly in place even after taking a fall from a horse, she was a bit more confident in her enhanced figure and even added more powder, as the scent was delightful.

Aching from her bruises, Edyth perched on her seat and eagerly awaited the soup to warm her body from the lingering chill from this morning's soaking. And as Lavinia kept the conversation flowing, Edyth's mind kept drifting to her odd encounter with her uncle and aunt.

In her hysteria, Mrs. Foster had revealed that she considered Edyth a nuisance, even though she was living under Edyth's roof... well, it would legally be her roof on her twenty-fifth birthday. Until then, Uncle Boris still had control of her assets and her home, but with only four months to go, one would think that her aunt would want to be a bit friendlier considering Edyth held the entirety of the family's fortune in her hands. As the second son, Uncle Boris only inherited a small portion of the family's wealth, and while he had not shown any bitterness over that fact, it seemed that Mrs. Foster did harbor a great deal and was set on poisoning any love Boris felt for Edyth. But why would he try to have his wife committed? *Does he truly fear I will turn him out once I have access to my wealth because of her dislike for me?* It was the only reason she could come up with that explained her uncle's wish to commit his bride

34

of only six months. At first, Mrs. Foster had seemed to have a fondness for Edyth, yet, in recent weeks, she had grown excessively rude. Despite her aunt's hostility, Edyth wouldn't forget the man who raised her. He was family, and while Uncle Boris had never told her that he loved her, she hoped that he returned her affection.

Edyth tore off a chunk of a dinner roll and absentmindedly spread a generous amount of butter on it and popped it in her mouth. When her father and mother had passed away, Uncle Boris had continued to allow her to fence despite his misgivings, thinking it would be a good way for her to move past her grief. And when she had started ignoring fashion and avoided wearing a corset at all costs, he had merely shaken his head at her choice. While he approved of her painting, a pastime that sprang from the art lessons her father had endeavored to teach her throughout her childhood, he had never shown Edyth animosity for her other unconventional choices, and she loved him for it.

Bane leaned over to her, whispering, "You haven't been this quiet in all the time I've known you. Did the fall cause you great discomfort? Do you need to see a doctor?"

She shrugged, thinking she would have to tell Bane about her encounter later when Lavinia was not present. "I'm just hungry." *And bruised and confused.*

"Well, 'tis a good thing, because the first course is on its way." Lavinia clapped her hands as the tomato basil soup arrived, and turned her attention to Doctor Hawkins, speaking in low tones, giggling, and leaving Edyth to fend for herself.

How on earth was she supposed to *flirt* with her best friend? He would notice it at once and most likely tease her mercilessly. The very thought of him discovering the admiration she had harbored since she had met him sent her stomach roiling.

"I think we are all set for the anniversary celebration," Bane commented, unaware of her tumultuous state. "And I have you to thank for that."

"You know I would do anything for my friends," Edyth replied, fixating on a wrinkle in the tablecloth under the flower arrangement.

"But aren't I your *only* friend?" he asked, his brows rising, a teasing lilt in his voice.

"No." She gave him a light kick under the table before she could remember it was unladylike. "Your sisters-in-law and I get along famously, as you very well know."

"You need more friends than just the Banebridge family, but I approve of your taste." He added a wink that softened his words.

She ran her fingers along the perimeter of her napkin. "I have never really been one to make friends easily, so I am thankful to have your family. But, if you should ever forsake me, I have Lavinia now."

"Well, that is a comfort." He reached into his pocket and withdrew a small, narrow black box and, to her utter astonishment, slid it across the white tablecloth toward her, drawing Lavinia's attention at once as Edyth sucked in a sharp breath. "But the reason I brought the anniversary up now is that I want to give you a small token of my appreciation for all you have done in planning the event. I could not have done it without you."

Edyth sent him a smile and wished she could tell Bane how much she adored him for everything he had done for her and continued to do. "You didn't have to give me anything, Bane. You know how much I love the fencing club." *And its headmaster.* She popped open the box and exhaled, not even realizing that she had been holding her breath. Laughter bubbled up inside of her at the sight of a stickpin shaped like a miniature silver rapier with a single crimson stone set in the handle. She stroked the ruby and giggled in delight.

"You hate it," he said as Lavinia sighed in open disappointment.

"No! I *love* it. It's absolutely perfect." Edyth removed the rapier from its velvet cushion and pinned it to her bodice above her heart. "I will wear it every day," she promised. Her gaze found his, and she had never wanted to kiss him more—more even than the time when she was sixteen and first fell for him, or rather, into his arms during a fencing bout that had gone terribly wrong. Bane had lowered his face to hers to be certain that the blade had not left a mark. She could still remember the touch of his calloused thumb stroking her neck. The tiny scar at the nape of her neck was worth the concern and tenderness he showed her in cleaning and bandaging her wound. In that moment, she fell irrevocably in love with Raoul Banebridge.

He grinned. "Well, I won't hold you to that, but I am relieved you like it. I have never picked out anything for a woman besides my mother, but the shopkeeper insisted that ladies love to wear stickpins as brooches these days, and when I saw the sword set with the stone in your favorite color, I knew it was made for you."

"What a lovely surprise to see you, Miss Foster and Mr. Banebridge." The buxom Miss Heather Finley appeared on the arm of a rather stout gentleman and fluttered her eyelashes at Bane, flirting as always.

Heather. She gritted her teeth at the arrival of her former friend, waiting for her to simply walk past them to her own table. Heather and her mother were the reason she had been kicked out of New York's Four Hundred, and she did not care to relive the painful memory of her disastrous debut season.

The gentlemen rose and bowed as introductions were exchanged, and small talk ensued until Heather flicked open her fan and curtailed the conversation, stating, "Well, we must join the rest of our party, but may I say what a charming couple you two make, Miss Foster and Mr. Banebridge." Heather directed her smile at Edyth as if knowing Bane's protest was imminent.

Edyth sighed and waited for Bane to correct her as he had every time throughout the years when someone assumed they were a couple.

"Thank you. I quite agree," Bane replied, taking a sip from his glass and ignoring Edyth's gaping mouth.

Nestled in the open carriage beside Edyth with Miss Birch and Doctor Hawkins seated across from them, Bane kept thinking over his revelation of Edyth being more than a respected friend. After all these years, he found it strange that after seeing her in stylish clothing once, his view of her had shifted, and it excited him to discover what that shift could mean for them. He wasn't even certain Edyth wished to court, not with her weekly gentle rejections to would-be suitors. She loved her independence, that he was certain of, but wasn't she also much more attentive to him than anyone else? He shook his head to free it from his churning thoughts.

The carriage rolled to a halt, and Bane waited for the other couple to disembark before stepping down and offering Edyth his hand. Her fingertips pressed into his palms as she hopped out, and a spark ignited in him. Bane knew he had to explore this new feeling for his old friend without her knowing in order to protect their friendship.

"Thank you for a lovely evening and my sword pin," Edyth said, brushing her fingertips over the piece and giving him a smile.

She moved to follow Lavinia inside, when he grasped her elbow, staying her, "Edyth, wait—"

She turned abruptly as he stepped toward her, and her face met his chest in a cloud of powder that shot up his nose. Edyth jumped back as he sneezed before wiping his hand over his cheeks and jaw to find a film of white powder that smelled like the scent Edyth was wearing. "What on earth?" he coughed out.

His eyes trailed from her mortified, pallid expression and the bits of powder flecking her face to the front of her gown, but she whirled around and dusted off her bodice and the bow at her throat that secured her cloak. "Good heavens," she mumbled.

He sneezed again, and with her back still facing him, she handed him a handkerchief over her shoulder. He accepted, his fingers wrapping around her wrist and turning her back to face him.

But she wouldn't look at him. And then he spotted the source of the powder, sending his gaze dashing aside and mirth swelling in his chest. He couldn't contain it, and threw his head back and laughed. "Why would you—?"

"Raoul Banebridge. It is *not* humorous in the least. I have never been so embarrassed in all my days. I never should have listened to Lavinia. This is one of her gowns, and the maids only had time to hem it, so, well. . .I won't say it, but it was *necessary*, I assure you."

Checking his laughter until his eyes watered from the suppression, he rubbed his finger over her cheek to wipe away a trace of powder. "Edyth Foster, you never cease to astonish me."

She looked up at him sharply, as if to read his meaning, and her lips quirked into a half smile. "So, before we were distracted, was there something you needed to tell me?"

He glimpsed behind them to find that Miss Birch had already stepped inside with Doctor Hawkins. Now was as good a time as any, but his words stuck in his throat. Perhaps he should wait. Yet, one look into those dark eyes, and he knew he could not. How had he missed noticing that enchanting light all these years? She really was his dearest friend, and the thought of another gentleman laying claim to her heart sent him a much-needed burst of courage. "Would you like to keep walking? There is a coffee shop down a few blocks that might be nice."

"It sounds lovely, but don't you have a private session with me first thing in the morning?"

"It's not far." He grinned and held out his arm to her. "Besides, when have you ever been concerned with getting enough rest?"

"True." She laughed and wrapped her hand around his arm and stepped beside him, waving to her doorman to let him know not to hold the door for them any longer.

They walked in silence for a couple of blocks until he pointed to a shop on the corner with the warm glow of candlelight spilling from the windows. "There it is, but, uh, so about what I wanted to ask before. . ." He ran his fingers through his hair as music from somewhere nearby drifted out onto the street and enveloped them in the sighing strains of violins. This was harder than he thought. "What are you doing tomorrow?"

"I do believe we have a party to attend in the evening." Edyth sent him a smile and rolled her eyes. "First you forget the morning lesson, and then the party. I hope you will remember to attend."

He cleared his throat. "I meant to ask what you were doing during the day. I was hoping to attend the new exhibit at the Metropolitan Museum of Art."

"The Metropolitan? You?" she asked, her brows lifting.

"Well, with you, after our lesson, that is. One of my students mentioned that a Cephas Thompson donated almost two hundred drawings this year and uh, they are on exhibit now." He ran his fingers through his hair again. "Mostly Italian works, I believe."

She blinked. "But why? You have never expressed an interest in art before."

"Because"—Bane thought quickly—"it's the other half of your thank-you present. You are always going on about your art and, well, I think it would be nice to see why."

She squeezed his arm, her cheeks a pretty pink in spite of the lingering bits of powder. "I would love that, but I believe your sister-in-law mentioned you are practicing your dancing with her tomorrow afternoon?"

How does she know my schedule better than I do? "Well, perhaps I could cancel that appointment if you wouldn't mind a slow waltz now?" His pulse thrummed in his ears as he halted, turning her to him and grasping her hand, sliding it to his shoulder.

She laughed and glanced about. "Out here on the sidewalk?"

He shrugged. "No one is around, and besides, I don't want to embarrass us when we open the dancing."

She smiled, rested her hand in his, and stepped close to him as he placed his hand against the back of her slender waist. "You should know by now that few things embarrass me."

He waited and counted to three with the music before slowly turning with her, and he was surprised to find that dancing with her felt natural. While he had stumbled over his feet in lessons as a boy and avoided the dance floor as a man, he found that dancing was not completely unlike the fencing patterns on the piste. But with the moonlight bathing her face and dark features, all thoughts save of kissing her vanished.

Ending the waltz, he drew her closer, and the air charged between them. He leaned down, pausing a breath, then two, when a figure lingering by a lamppost caught his attention. Not caring for the man's leer directed their way, he regretfully twirled her out of his arms and extended his hand. "I think it might be best if we head to the coffee shop before you regret accepting my invitation to accompany me, a man who cannot draw a star, to an art gallery."

Chapter Four

In my deepest troubles, I frequently would wrench myself from the persons around me and retire to some secluded part of our noble forests.
~ John James Audubon

Edyth paused inside the Metropolitan Museum of Art in front of the stunning piece by Edward Burne-Jones, simply entitled *Head of a Young Woman.*

Bane turned his gaze from her and back to the portrait. "This woman looks a great deal like you, or is that the first sign one is dealing with an amateur art critic?"

"It is my mother." Edyth smiled at his slack jaw and stepped aside to allow a couple to pass them. "My grandfather and the artist were friends, and Edward Burne-Jones asked to practice his sketching with her posing. As Mr. Burne-Jones had already painted the one of Grandmother that hangs in our parlor, Grandfather eagerly agreed."

Bane rubbed the back of his neck. "Pardon me for asking, but if this is your mother, why is her picture here? How did the museum get ahold of it?"

Edyth fanned herself with her museum literature pamphlets against the stifling air brought from too many bodies in one building. Tucking her sketchbook under her arm, she removed her lace-trimmed handkerchief from her beaded reticule and dabbed at her temples, remembering Lavinia's statement that gentlemen do not find a perspiring lady attractive. *Too late for that.* Fencing was not a sport for the delicate. "This piece wasn't meant to be locked away. I have kept it to myself for the past decade even though my parents had intended to donate it following the example of Cornelius Vanderbilt II, who donated nearly seven hundred of the old masters' drawings. But after the accident I couldn't bring myself to let it go and selfishly kept it until last year."

"No, not selfish. You were grieving." He took her gloved hand in his, sending a pulse radiating through her arm.

She stepped away from the artwork, and to her surprise, he didn't release her hand. *What is he about?* Certainly, it was nice to have his comfort when speaking of her parents. Nothing had been the same since their passing. She shook her head, willing away her thoughts lest they turn from happy memories into shards of pain as they usually did. She lingered in front of the recently donated black chalk work of a colonial couple by an unknown eighteenth-century French artist. "Tell me what you think about this piece."

"*Figures in a Landscape.* That doesn't give a fellow much to go on," Bane muttered. He sucked in a breath through his teeth and cleared his throat before tilting his head, squinting at the lines, and releasing her hand to step back. "Well, it's certainly interesting."

"That's all?" She wanted to laugh but did not wish to discourage him from returning to an art museum. "Why do you think the artist chose to sketch *this* couple? What of the execution of the lines?"

"Well, I think it's rather overly simple to be anything special and on display." Bane stuffed his hands into his pockets. "But, in its own way. . .you could say it is beautiful because the couple looks like they are in love, and one could argue there is nothing quite as beautiful, nor powerful, as love."

"Raoul Banebridge has taken me to an art museum and is now speaking of love?" she teased to distract herself from the hope blossoming inside her that, with all his talk of love, maybe, just maybe Bane was beginning to notice her. Why else would he have brought her here and be saying such strange things?

"After all, didn't one of your favorite artists say that 'a work of art which did not begin in emotion is not art'?"

Her mouth fell open. "Now you are quoting Cézanne? Who are you, and what have you done with Bane?"

"Bane has been listening to your art ramblings for years." He chuckled and nudged her playfully with his shoulder. "Maybe one day your sketches will be displayed next to this artist. Yours look just as good and not nearly so simple, so I suppose that makes them better than this piece."

Still shaken from his comments, she couldn't help but giggle at his summary that an artist in the Metropolitan was not as accomplished as her amateur drawings. "Thank you for your vote of confidence, but the only way I could get my work to appear here is if I give the museum a rather sizable donation on the condition they display my work for a short period." She drummed her fingers over her sketchbook cover. "My style is not exactly what the critics would call classic."

Bane nodded to the sketchbook she was clutching to her side and reached for it. "May I see?"

She reluctantly allowed it to slide from her fingers and into his calloused hands. "I suppose, but only if you promise to look at the back half and not the front. I have had that sketchbook for quite some time and my artwork has changed. I only brought it in case you grew bored and left me—"

He immediately flipped through the first few pages, a gleeful smile reaching his ears as he hooted. "What are all these sketches of me that I see here? Edyth, there are dozens upon dozens." Bane lowered his brows and grasped his chin between two fingers in the brooding expression she loved to capture, but he could not hold the stance for laughing.

Edyth felt a rush of heat to her cheeks, and she snatched the book out of his hands, snapping it shut. "I told you not to look, *Raoul*!"

"You should have made me promise beforehand, Foster." He snorted. "Besides, I thought you were being modest, but it seems that someone finds me quite the model." He ran his fingers through his hair, allowing it to cascade down onto his shoulders and, pursing his lips, attempted another favored brooding pose Edyth had sketched.

"Of course you are. Your exercise keeps you in the peak physical condition that most artists find—" Edyth dropped her ramblings with a grunt when his smile kept growing. She was always revealing too much of herself to Bane, but this was the one thing she had managed to keep hidden from him for years, and she would not allow her infatuation with him to become known now and ruin whatever ground she had managed to capture.

"If you ever need me to pose in my fencing costume, just let me know." He sent her a brazen wink.

She swatted his arm with her reticule. "You best watch yourself, lest I take you up on your offer and start a whole new craze of sketching fencing masters. The artists will never leave you or your club alone, and then you will be sorry for disregarding my conditions for allowing you to see my work." She tugged his arm, pulling him down the hall, weaving around groups perusing the famous pieces by the old masters. "Now, we don't have much time, and as this was your gift to me, I suggest you cease your teasing and enjoy the art for this last half hour before we must head back." She stepped away from him and at once felt the precious sketchbook slide from the crook of her arm as Bane darted away, earning scowls from passersby. "Raoul Banebridge, you stop that right now," she hissed.

He stepped into a small vacant corridor and flipped it open again, but this time closer to the back. "Another sketch of me? Come now, Edyth, am I your study for the entirety of this book?" He used his thumb to riffle through the pages.

She had forgotten that particular portrait was there. He was so often in her thoughts that she must have absentmindedly sketched him after she had sworn she would not do so again for the rest of the year. She could not help it that Bane was the perfect model, with such a gorgeous nose begging to be sketched. Edyth crossed her arms, thinking it best for her if he had his teasing out all at once and then hopefully never spoke of it again. "Go ahead. I can see plainly that you are aching to ask me your questions."

He scanned the pages again, viewing her other work more closely before closing the book and handing it back to her. "Edyth." His voice adopted a tone she had not heard before. "How often do you sketch me?"

"I don't think that is a question you should be asking a lady," she murmured, pretending to study the painting in front of them of a cottage in a wood by an unknown artist.

He grasped her elbow and turned her to him. "But I am not asking any lady. I am asking you, Edyth Foster, my good friend."

She dipped her head, feeling as if she were about to deliver the worst confession of her life. Could she lie? Was that permissible in such dire circumstances? She glanced at her watch pin. "Oh, would you look at the time?"

"Edyth?"

She lifted her gaze to meet his and forced the shameful word out. "Often."

"Good, because now there is a chance you might say yes to my next question, and I would like it very much if you would say yes." A grin played at the corner of his mouth, that delightful dimple materializing in his left cheek.

She regarded him, wary. "And what would that be? I already told you that, no, I cannot get an ice sculpture of two swords crossing in time for the celebration tonight. You should have requested it weeks ago, but—"

Bane lifted his finger to her lips, the pressure halting her words, and slipped his other hand from her elbow to her fingers. "I was hoping that maybe I could escort you to the party?"

Lavinia had instructed her to be coy and not to accept an invitation right away if he asked. . .but Lavinia had not been waiting for this invitation for as long as Edyth had. Her lips parted to say she would think about it, but she couldn't keep her smiles at bay, nor her heart. "I would like that very much."

"You would? Really?" His seeming insecurity took her by surprise. Bane was never uncertain, not on the piste, not anywhere.

She squeezed his hand, reveling in the closeness of him. "Really."

His grin overtook his features as he rubbed his thumb over her hand. "And what about the following day? May I escort you on your ride through Central Park, and perhaps we can go boating afterward?"

Her eyes flitted to his lips and back to him. "Are you asking as a friend?" she whispered before she could take back the words.

He stroked a loose curl from her face. "As only the dearest sort of friend. . .as *my* Miss Foster, if you will allow it?"

"Then I accept," she whispered and, with a little twirl, stepped out of arm's reach and into the back of a gentleman. "Oh! I am so sorry—Doctor Hawkins? What on earth are you doing here?" She bit her lip, worried that he might have overheard her conversation with Bane.

He blinked his focus from the painting before him, from behind a pair of wire-rimmed spectacles that she had never seen him wear, and gave her a short bow. "It is my day off, so I thought I'd come to the museum for the latest exhibit."

"Ah, lovely. Will you be stopping by later today to see Miss Birch?" she asked as Bane greeted him with a nod that Doctor Hawkins returned.

"Ah, no. I stopped by and spoke with Boris this morning, and he said Miss Birch had departed on a spontaneous trip to the Manhattan Beach Hotel with a friend for the week's end," he replied.

"Oh? I wasn't aware."

"Which, I suppose is the nature of spontaneity," he replied, swinging his walking cane as if ready to take his leave of them.

"*Boris*, is it? I didn't know you were on such good terms with Mr. Foster. That must be nice for your pursuit of Miss Birch." Bane grinned at him.

Doctor Hawkins's cheeks dipped in color and he sputtered, "I, uh, I suppose."

Bane laughed and clapped him on the shoulder, giving him a friendly shake and sending the spectacles sliding down the bridge of the doctor's pointed nose. "I'm only teasing you, good fellow. But truly, if you have a position of friendship with Mr. Foster, you had best keep it. The man can become extremely ill-disposed should he set his mind against you."

The doctor looked to Edyth and back to Bane and gave a short, uncomfortable cough. "Good to know. Well, I best be on my way. Enjoy your afternoon. I shall see you tonight." He tipped his hat.

"At the fencing club party?" Edyth asked, her voice rising in surprise, not recalling ever having sent him an invitation.

"Oh dear. You were not aware that your uncle invited me." He dabbed at his forehead with the sleeve of his jacket.

"I did not even know *he* was planning on attending, but any invitation given by my uncle will be honored," she said with a smile of reassurance, elbowing Bane. "Isn't that right?"

"Y–yes, of course. You are most welcome, and we are looking forward to seeing you, sir," Bane replied as Doctor Hawkins bowed and vanished around the corner without another word.

"Odd fellow," Bane said, taking Edyth's hand and threading it through his arm, guiding her into the main hall toward the exit.

"Not really. Uncle sometimes doesn't follow the rules of society." Edyth paused under the metal arches supporting the sloped glass roof and readjusted her chapeau before they stepped outside into the fresh air.

"Ah, I wondered where you got your lack of rule following from," he teased and tugged at the single curl that was left intentionally out of her intricate coiffure. . .but strangely enough, it felt more like a caress than a pull.

She gasped, feigning annoyance, and stepped away from him. "And for that, Mr. Banebridge, you owe me something sweet. I do believe there is a pie shop nearby."

"Fair enough." Bane laughed as he shook his head. "You know, I've always admired your ability to devour pie."

She suppressed a giggle and pulled him down the path to the pie shop. "Well, thank goodness someone appreciates my talent."

Chapter Five

I would kiss you, had I the courage.
~ Édouard Manet

Bane's breath caught as Edyth descended the stairs in a crimson gown that caressed her slender form. Her raven hair, arranged in an elaborate, braided coiffure, was framed with a row of crimson roses that created the effect of her wearing a crown. The single curl trailing down her shoulder touched the ruby pin fastened to a neckline that dipped far lower than he had ever seen her wear before. He averted his eyes as she lifted her billowing skirts to descend unhindered, revealing dainty satin slippers. The transformation of his friend caught him off guard once again. "You look. . ." He gestured to her ensemble and settled with, "lovely."

She dipped her head in thanks, running her hands down the front of her gown. "Lavinia had a dressmaker design this especially for tonight. I hope you like the color."

His gaze flowed over the short sleeves cuffing her flawless shoulders as he rested her gold cloak upon them. "I would say keep having her design your gowns, but I fear I will not be able to leave your side ever again lest every unattached gentleman within a hundred miles should attempt to steal your heart." He held out his arm, her once familiar touch causing his pulse to pound in his ears.

"I don't wish to sound conceited, but I think my odd dresses of the past have acted as a deterrent to my fortune's lure. And now that the deterrence is gone. . ."

"They will be relentless tonight, despite your best efforts in the past to evade matrimony," he finished.

"Then you best be en garde to protect me." She sent him a tentative smile, her sweet lips calling to him.

Always. "Pret," he replied with a bow.

With a laugh, Edyth picked up a wrapped box with a gold bow atop it from the foyer table and bid the butler good night before they slipped out the door, the cool night air whipping through her curls. Bane was glad that he thought to borrow his family's closed carriage, for though the drive would be short, he did not want Edyth's coiffure to be ruined due to lack of foresight on his part. He took the box and deposited it onto the carriage seat before offering her his hand.

"This is an important night for you and your fencing club with your introducing a private fencing room for women. I'm hopeful that once the women get used to the private sessions, they will want to join the fencing classes in the main hall though," she said as she mounted the step into the carriage.

"Yes." Why was it so hard for him to come up with intelligent responses? He shook his head free from the enchanting fog that had descended upon him. "I mean, I hope they are agreeable to the idea of joining the club." He peeked out the window at the gaslights flickering in the night as Edyth filled the silence on her own, shifting the mysterious box on her lap.

"So, are you going to tell me what's in there?"

She smoothed her fingers over the jade paper wrapping. "It's for you, actually."

"Me? Why?"

Her eyes sparked with excitement, raising his curiosity. "I ordered it weeks ago, and it came just in time. It's a gift to celebrate a successful business."

"How kind of you." He moved to take it, but she hugged it to her knees.

"It's for you to open *after* the party and not a moment before." Edyth gasped, grabbed his forearm, and pointed up at the windows of the fencing club where the glowing light poured out onto the street. "Oh! I knew it was going to be dazzling. Aren't you glad that you followed my instructions and placed a candelabra in every window and corner of the hall? Anyone passing tonight will take notice."

"You are a visionary." Bane grinned as he hopped out of the carriage and lifted his hands to her waist, happy for any excuse to be close to her. Judging by her smile, she felt the same way about him.

Edyth wrapped her hands around his arm and allowed him to guide her up the steps into the great hall of the fencing area, which, save for one piste in the back for the exposition later, had been transformed into a candlelit ballroom. Queen Anne chairs lined the walls, borrowed from the Banebridge family estate, and long tables were bedecked with appetizers, desserts, and beverages, served by Edyth's footmen. He nodded to his elder brother Bertram and Bertram's fiancée and his eldest brother Tom and his wife, Sylvia. Bane was grateful that all five of his brothers were happily partnered so that the fencing club had more women than the sprinkling of spouses who arrived on the arms of their husbands, most likely against their wills, judging from the expressions on their faces.

"Why haven't the musicians started?" Edyth muttered under her breath, shaking her head. "If you will excuse me, I need to see to this." Her heeled slippers clicked on the hardwood floors as she rustled over to the string quartet, gesturing toward the door where the guests were arriving. Nodding furiously, the head violinist tapped his bow, nodded to the group, and began playing.

In between greeting his guests, Bane watched his mother and father approach Edyth and embrace her as if she were their daughter. She would fit into his family perfectly if she chose him. Witnessing the gathering of the unattached gentlemen in attendance around her, he ached to be near her instead of encouraging his students to continue their attendance and invite their friends. He couldn't keep from glancing over at Edyth every few minutes. He knew now that they had seen Edyth in this gown, the single men of the club would never allow her to step into the fencing hall without plying her with requests for calling. He needed to ask Edyth to allow him to be her only beau, and the sooner the better.

"It seems your student has had quite the transformation since her delightful cousin came to the city," Jasper Wentworth murmured, pausing at Bane's elbow to throw back his punch. Bane caught the lingering scent on the man's breath and knew Jasper had taken the liberty to add something to his drink. The uncouth man licked his lips, his eyes devouring Edyth like a raspberry tart.

Bane clenched his fists at the man's leering but attempted to keep a civil tone. "It's a party. What did you expect her to wear? Her fencing costume?"

"Come, man. You've seen the outlandish gowns she has worn in the past. It's her pretty cousin's doing." Jasper shook his head and snatched another glass from a passing footman, depositing his empty cup on the silver tray. "If I wasn't already practically engaged to an heiress, I might be tempted to make an offer despite her grating personality."

"And by grating, you are referring to how she bests you weekly?" Bane retorted.

Jasper gave a short laugh, rolling his eyes. "I am a gentleman. I allow her to win."

Hardly. Piqued, Bane sank his teeth into his tart to hide his disgust with the man. Edyth took that moment to find him in the crowd, her smile faltering at his expression.

"Bane, why are you scowling? Go enjoy yourself. This is your night. I'm here to help with whatever you need," she said, laying her hand on his arm.

"I *need* to see to you," he replied, his thoughts flicking to the scoundrel.

She squeezed his arm and said in a low voice, "You *need* to mingle with your guests and secure the next decade of your fencing club's success. Do not worry about attending to me. I can look after myself for one more night."

With a wary glance to Jasper, he patted her hand and left her to join his most influential patron and his wife and three young sons.

≈

"What if he needs for you to look after me?" Jasper lifted a brow at Edyth, openly gawking at her neckline as he lifted his drink in salute.

Edyth's neck flamed, and she glared at Jasper and stepped forward, smelling the liquor on his breath. "For shame, sir. How dare you address a lady so?"

"Please. We all know, Edyth, that you are one of the boys. No need to pretend you don't hear worse, but it is a shame that you don't dress up more often." He continued to leer at her. "I may have to let you win more often if you continue to wear gowns like this one."

She should have never allowed Lavinia to coerce her into showing off what little décolletage she possessed, not when men like Jasper roamed about. "Ball gown or not, I can still best you. So, it would be in your interest to mind your foul tongue before you lose it in a fencing accident."

At that, he threw back his head and laughed, making an unforgivable comment. Without blinking, she yanked off her glove and slapped him, leaving red, angry marks across his cheek. Jasper held his cheek, and the guests murmured so loudly that the musicians quieted.

Bane appeared at her side. "Mr. Wentworth, it is time for you to take your leave," he growled, stepping in front of her.

"You are a coward, Edyth Foster, to strike me and then hide behind the fencing master. You always rave about wishing to be treated as an equal, but I guess now we know the truth, don't we?"

Bane clenched his fists. "Careful, Wentworth."

Jasper dropped his hand and turned to the crowd, arms spread. "Ladies and gentlemen! Tonight, as you know, there is a scheduled demonstration of this fine fencing academy. What better way to display its accomplishments than with Bane's top students? Who would like to see me duel Miss Foster?"

The guests murmured of the impropriety, all scowling in disapproval.

"Wentworth, you are making a scene." Bane gripped him by the arm. "If you wish to duel someone, attempt to best me." He pulled off his coat and handed it to the footman, rolling up his sleeves. "Ladies and gentlemen, it seems the exposition is going to be happening prematurely. Please, gather at a safe distance to watch me best Mr. Wentworth."

With Bane's back turned, Wentworth leaned over and ran his finger along Edyth's bare shoulder. "Coward."

She jerked away from his grasp, seething, and crossed the room. She bypassed the blunted foils and yanked two rapiers free from their holds on the wall and tossed one to Jasper. His clumsy fingers nearly missed the handle.

Bane was at her elbow at once. "Edyth? What on earth do you think you're doing?"

Ignoring him, her brows drew together as she lifted her two-edged blade to the ready with one hand and with the other gripped her voluminous skirts behind her, showing a fair amount of petticoat and her ankles in the process.

Jasper's attention shifted to the still, crowded room around them, and he gave what sounded like a forced chuckle. "You didn't think I'd really fight you, especially not without a foil and mask or your plastron or gauntlet, did you?"

"I don't need them," she replied, her sharp blade slicing the air inches from his chest. "But you might. I suggest you put up your blade. En garde."

"I said I wouldn't—"

"Allez!" She lunged at him, and Jasper instinctively brought the blade up to block her, their steel crashing against one another.

"Don't be a fool. You will draw blood if you are not careful," he growled.

"That's the point." With a twist, she drove her blade down against his and, with a whipping motion, disarmed him. He lifted his hands in surrender, and despite her hunger for retribution, Edyth relented. She lowered her blade and stepped away from him. The thundering applause woke her from the haze of her temper. *Oh Lord, please let me not have ruined everything for Bane. Stupid, stupid temper.*

She drew in a deep breath and slowly turned and found that the women didn't appear horrified as she thought they would be; rather they seemed. . .impressed with her victory? The women crowded around, praising her that a lady could stand up for herself, even in a ball gown, and best a gentleman. And judging from the look on Bane's face, he was as shocked as she over the reaction.

"I wouldn't have believed it if I hadn't seen it. My husband always makes mention of a lady at the club who bests the men." Mrs. Marshall fanned her beaming face. "It was thrilling. Positively thrilling. I only wish I could have taken lessons as a girl. I always had a fascination for the sport."

"Mr. Banebridge is a wonderful instructor. I owe my skill with a blade to him." Edyth thought of the hours he had spent perfecting her use of the sword even though, as a female fencer, she had little hope of competing and bringing further glory to the club. Bane had given her as much attention as his best male student, Marvin Slater. She sent Bane a smile before adding, "If you are interested, you should consider joining his fencing class. And, if you are too shy to begin class in the main hall, Mr. Banebridge now offers private lessons in a smaller women's fencing area. A 'steel' of a deal, if you will." She laughed at her own joke along with the ladies, who tittered behind their silk fans. She looked over her shoulder at Bane, hoping she did not ruin his party, but from the grin on his face, she knew it was a resounding success. Perhaps dressing the part of a socialite had its advantages after all.

Bane waved Mr. Slater onto the piste, giving his own demonstration and earning more praise at his execution.

She felt a tug on her wrist, turning her, and scowled at the sight of Jasper. "Why haven't you departed yet? This is a party for respectable patrons."

"I wanted to warn you before I did."

She bristled at his threat and crossed her arms. "I already bested you, so I have proven I can take care of myself. Whatever you have to say—"

He grunted. "Blast you, woman. Your arrogance will be the end of you. Just listen to me for one second, will you, and let me leave."

She fought the urge to wave Bane over, not liking Jasper's tone. "Go on."

"The doctors weren't there for your aunt."

"Excuse me?" She had told no one about the lunatic asylum doctors at her house. How could he know about them?

"My father is one of the doctors from Blackwell's Island, and as you know, I am your uncle's lawyer. From what I have gathered from your aunt's legal requests of late, they were there to evaluate *you*."

She let out a little laugh. "You are the mad one if you think I would take your word and believe such an outlandish idea. Cease being such a poor loser and leave."

Jasper stepped back, his nostrils flaring. "Don't say I didn't try. Enjoy the island."

She rolled her eyes as he stormed away, and returned her attention to Bane's exposition.

At the end of the night, she still felt rather overheated from the excitement, so she waved away the carriage in favor of walking home in the crisp evening air with Bane at her side. She chatted away, almost afraid of what he would say. Edyth knew it was only a matter of time before he addressed the duel. She felt like a young, mischievous girl again, awaiting her father's stern lecture. At her street corner, he grasped her hand and pulled her toward him.

"That was rather daring of you, Miss Foster."

She pressed her palms to her stomach and groaned, truly remorseful for almost destroying the perfect evening. "I am so sorry. One day I shall conquer my temper. I really have been working on it, but Jasper was so vile. I've never been able to back away from a fight, I'm afraid. . .as you very well know. 'Tis my greatest flaw."

"True, but if you hadn't challenged him, I would have. However"—he grinned—"it turned out splendidly. *Four* wives signed up for classes and promised to spread the word amongst their circles and bring their daughters. Thanks to you, I will have almost a dozen new female students, and I can hire another instructor with the income they will bring."

"Bane, that's wonderful!" Edyth threw her arms around his neck before realizing how completely inappropriate her action was. She pushed her hands against his solid chest, but his hands found her waist and held her to him.

"You are wonderful." He leaned his forehead down to touch hers, closing his eyes as he drew in a deep breath that stole her own.

"What does this mean for us? Our seeing one another?" she whispered.

His brilliant jade eyes met hers. "We've been seeing each other for years, Edyth."

"Yes, but you've only been noticing me for a few days. Doesn't it seem rather odd to be holding me so close?"

He stroked a finger under her chin, lifting her face. "I should have been holding you long ago, but I was too distracted by the business."

"And my outlandish clothes," she added, hoping to break the tension but at the same time wishing to hold on to this moment forever.

"I see you now, but Edyth, it is not your clothes that I like." He smiled at her. "Don't get me wrong, you are stunning in them, but I think your gowns caught my attention long enough to wake me to the fact that you are more than a friend, and if some man tried to take my dearest friend away from me—" His voice deepened to a growl.

"What man would try to take me away from a fencing master?" Dare she reach out and tuck that loose strand of golden hair behind his ear? Her fingers twitched, but she held herself back.

He kneaded a thumb over her palm again and again. "Would you think it strange if I didn't want a long courtship? That is, if you'll allow me to call?"

"Do you think I'd let you hold me so if I'd say no to your calling?" she whispered over the pounding in her ears.

He grinned. "Then, Miss Foster, as long as you know my hopes are for a spring wedding, we shall have our first official outing tomorrow."

"Bane!" She giggled as he pulled her up into his arms and twirled her around on the sidewalk, catching smiles from passersby.

Slowly lowering her to the earth, Bane gripped her hand in his and pressed a firm kiss on the back of it, leaving her a bit dazed.

"Are you certain?"

"I don't see why we need to wait when we've known each other so long and so well. I will ask you when you least expect it, so be looking over your shoulder. I'll be coming to sweep you off your feet."

"You will?" Had Bane really just professed his intent? She rested her gaze on his lips, aching for him to tell her that he loved her and then kiss her senseless.

At the passing of a carriage that stopped at her door, she reluctantly drew back and saw the pair of doctors that had been there before pounding on the door. "Bane, I think those are the men from Blackwell's Island."

"What?" He blinked, clearly not having seen the carriage.

"Never mind. I better go inside," she said, squeezing his hands.

He pulled her back toward him. "Not without this," he whispered, lowering his head and pressing a tender kiss to her lips for a breath then two before pulling away, but her hands caught the back of his neck, silently asking him for another and he obliged, leaving her breathless as she blinked against the stars in her eyes.

Chapter Six

The world doesn't understand me and I don't understand
the world, that's why I've withdrawn from it.
~ Paul Cézanne

Edyth closed the front door behind her, leaning her head back and sighing. She lifted her gloved fingers to her lips, feeling the pressure of his mouth yet. She inhaled the scent of leather from his fencing attire on her sleeve from their embrace. She gave a little spin and pulled off her gloves one finger at a time. *Bane cares for me.* She could hardly believe it. She had dreamed of this moment for so long, she could hardly believe it was finally happening. Raoul Banebridge was intending on courting her.

"Good. You're home. Come with me." Her uncle's booming voice startled her.

She nearly dropped her gloves, her skin burning from being caught holding her sweet memories of Bane. His kisses had driven all thoughts of the two doctors out of her head. "Uncle, I saw the doctors return. Surely you aren't committing Mrs. Foster tonight? Shouldn't you at least wait until Lavinia returns from her trip? She would never forgive you if—"

"What's this I hear of your accosting Doctor Wentworth's son?" Her uncle motioned to her from the doorway of the parlor, crossing his arms as he glared at her.

Her stomach dropped. "Jasper Wentworth really is a doctor's son? He's not just a distant relative?" *And how did Doctor Wentworth find out so soon? Did he go running to his father the moment he departed?*

"Isn't that *just* what I said? It is most vexing having to repeat everything for you, Edyth. *Listen* so I do not have to say

61

everything twice, won't you?"

She jerked back from his strident tone, a sliver of fear coiling around her heart.

"What are you waiting for?" Uncle Boris motioned her inside the dark parlor where the doctors stood in front of the fire warming their hands.

Where were the servants to light the gaslights? Not wanting to prove her uncle right that she would question *everything* that he asked of her, she brushed past him and took a seat in a gilded Queen Anne chair beside the fireplace, keeping her feet tucked primly under her dress. She sighed. All she wanted was her bed, a cup of chamomile tea, to relive her kiss with Bane, and to think on how her dreams were coming true. Instead, she addressed the doctors. "Good evening, sirs. I trust my maids have seen to offering you a hot beverage?" Why was her voice wavering so? *Blast that Jasper for getting his lies into my head.*

All ignored her as her uncle removed a stack of papers from his coat.

"So, I suppose you are wondering why the doctors are present," he finally said.

"If they are not here for Mrs. Foster, as you claimed earlier, then, yes." Her gaze fell onto the papers, and she recognized them as the same ones he had been holding the other day. "But, uh, I must say that I strongly disagree with your decision to abandon your wife to the island."

He dropped the papers without ceremony on the side table with a thud and tapped the top sheet. "I recently uncovered a clause in the family will."

Edyth sat up straight. "A clause? What do you mean?" Would she be free from her uncle and his bitterness and his new wife's anger sooner than four months? *Or was it. . .the other thing that Jasper had insisted was true?*

Uncle Boris adjusted his monocle, the black string dangling past his fleshy jowls, and turned the pages, pausing at a ribbon marker. He lifted the page, his focus on her. "From what I understand, if you die unmarried and childless, or are declared mad and committed to an asylum, the fortune reverts to me and my heir."

"Why on earth would my father insert such a clause?" She snorted. *Ludicrous.*

He shrugged. Something glinted in his eyes, and it wasn't the monocle catching in the firelight. "I'm certain he had his reasons."

She tilted her head. She was her father's *only* heir. "Well, I am not fatally ill, and even though I am not married now, it doesn't mean that I won't marry later and have a child. I am young still, Uncle." The news of Bane's almost proposal crept to the tip of her tongue, but she wanted to keep that to herself for a little longer.

He slowly set aside the papers. "A fact which only leaves me with the second option." He crossed his arms and stared at her, as if waiting for her to understand what he was insinuating.

He can't mean— She rose from her chair, limbs quaking. "The doctors. . .they aren't here for Mrs. Foster, are they? You are trying to have *me*"—she fairly spat the last word—"*committed?*"

"We have been studying you, and our findings are quite disturbing." A nasally voice came from the shorter of the doctors.

She crossed her arms to keep her trembling from being visible. "Please elaborate, Doctor Wentworth."

The man with the spectacles and pointed beard stepped forward. She could now easily see how he was an older, stouter version of Jasper. "For one, your erratic behavior tonight. I have a firsthand account of the scene from one of the guests. Imagine a woman fencing my son in a duel of honor, intent on besting him."

The coward did go running to his daddy after all. "So, you admit it was a duel for *honor*, Doctor Wentworth? Did he happen to tell you that he accosted me most grievously? I would not stand by and allow that to happen to a friend, so why would I allow him to speak so to me? Your son acted in an ungentlemanly manner. And as for the duel, I bested him tonight as I do every week." She tilted her chin up. "It was nothing unusual. If he did not wish to embarrass himself, he shouldn't have goaded me."

"But it is a man's place to defend your honor," Doctor Wentworth replied with a dismissive wave. He looked to the other two men. "Based on tonight's events and the information we have gathered in the past few days from our man, I recommend immediate placement of Miss Foster in the Women's Lunatic Asylum on Blackwell's Island."

Someone has been following me? She curled her lip at the sickening violation and turned to the short doctor. "Sir, you have to agree this is unfounded." She returned her attention to her uncle. "And you. Why on earth would you wish to have me committed?"

He nodded to the doctors. "Thank you for coming out tonight. I will send for you should I have need, but your reports are just the thing for us to bypass the usual admission trials and have her quietly committed to avoid scandal."

Edyth flinched at the words, and all sense of calm fled her. She clenched her fists at her sides. "Quietly committed?" she yelled. Ignoring the doctors' abrupt departure, she skewered her uncle with her anger. "What have I ever done to you other than support you and your new family with my fortune? Have I been unkind to you, Mrs. Foster, or Lavinia? When Mrs. Foster wanted to redecorate her rooms, I agreed for you to allot her the funds needed, even though it was unnecessary considering you all are moving out come summer to your own place on Fifth Avenue that I will have furnished for you."

"And your kindness alone is the *only* reason I am offering you one chance to escape your fate. From what I've heard of the asylum on Blackwell's Island, it is not going to be to your liking. So, risking the wrath of my new bride, I am giving you a choice. Either you sign your fortune over to me here and now and you shall be free to live your life on a small stipend, or..." He sat down in the armchair beside the small side table with the papers atop, "I will have you committed to Blackwell's Island. The choice is yours."

She clenched her jaw. "You cannot be serious."

He extended a pen to her and tapped the papers with his finger in a steady rhythm. "You have sixty seconds."

"How dare you threaten me. No one will believe you!" she shouted as he kept up the incessant tapping. "Lavinia herself will testify on my behalf."

"Fifty seconds left. Are you certain you wish to spend them arguing?" He sent her a smile underlined with a hatred that alarmed her. "As you recall, I sent Lavinia to the Manhattan Beach Hotel this morning for a short stay. All of your other ostensible friends are from a *fencing club*." He scoffed. "Which would *not* help your plea of sanity."

"My lawyer—"

"No lawyer will be able to protect you against the word of the three doctors I have had studying you since Lavinia's welcoming party. Granted, one of the doctors was distracted by Lavinia, but if he wishes to continue seeing my stepdaughter, he will keep quiet when he discovers you at the asylum and agree with the other two doctors who thought you quite eccentric. They have seen you riding your velocipede in your ridiculous costume for all the city to see, and they've heard from your own mouth of your fencing lessons. And, of course, your bout with Jasper tonight did nothing to aid your case." He gave a chortle. "Imagine my delight when Doctor Wentworth informed me that you threatened and dueled his son in front of all at tonight's party. It's as if you *wanted* to help me commit you."

She lowered her voice and stepped toward her uncle. "I did not threaten him. I acted in defense of my honor, as you very well know."

"Which you should have left to a man, as Doctor Wentworth stated. In any event, the doctors have taken your eccentricities as signs of insanity, for what woman would ever want to cycle when she could ride in a fine carriage? What woman would want to fence when she could embroider or have tea parties or have whatever she wants because she is one of the wealthiest women in New York?"

She crossed her arms to keep her voice steady. "And my art? Did they take my painting as signs of a crazed woman as well? I am well respected in the artist community."

"Once I showed them the hundreds of paintings you store in your closet, they were never more certain."

Perspiration formed at her temples. "You showed them those? You know those paintings are private."

"Tell me, why on earth do you find the need to paint hands? Always three hands?" He sent her a smirk that revealed his triumph.

She swallowed and gave a slight shrug. "I don't know. I feel I must until I know why."

"You don't know." He snorted, shaking his head. "Your work displays the very definition of insanity. Only someone who is insane would keep painting the same thing over and over without a reason."

"I do still life paintings as well. Did you show them those?"

"Of course not. They have seen your particularities, and those will be your downfall. Time is up, my dear. You either sign over your fortune, or you will be committed to Blackwell's Island. The choice is yours."

"My father would never have included such a clause, and my lawyer will be testing the validity of your claim, which, I suspect, you added after my father died."

"Please do, for when your lawyer discovers that your maternal grandmother was as mad as they come, your fate will be sealed."

She stumbled, gripping the back of the settee. "Grandmother Blakely. . .she died when Mother was a child."

"She died in a cell on Blackwell's Island."

Her breath left her and she leaned against the wall, her head in her hands, trying to still her rising panic and remind herself that this was her uncle. Her father's only living flesh and blood besides her. Surely he would not do such vile things to her. But one look at his wild eyes, and she feared he was serious. Her gaze fell on the pen, her fingers twitching. But, knowing she had access to the best lawyer in the city, she turned her back on him and ran, slamming the parlor door behind her, and bolted for her bedroom. *I am not mad. He is lying. He is lying!*

Locking her door, Edyth threw aside her gloves, seething at his threat. She looked at the clock on her mantel. Midnight. She would have to wait until morning to send for her lawyer. *What is his name?* She dug through the papers in her writing desk and found sketch after sketch but no documents with his name.

Snapping her fingers, she went to her armoire and retrieved an old hatbox that had once belonged to her mother, and sinking to the floor, she sat back on her heels and riffled through it until she found the paper that her mother once gave her for reference should something ever happen to them or her in their absence. With trembling hands, she lifted it out and read the faded, fine handwriting until she found a footnote with *Mr. Pittman, Attorney-at-Law* scribbled as if he were an afterthought.

Satisfied, she took a seat at her desk to compose her thoughts, but her gaze flitted back to her french doors. Rising, she removed the key and deposited it into her chemise should she have need of it at a moment's notice. Taking an armchair, she propped it under the handle and bit her lip. *Should I just leave and seek out Bane despite the late hour?* She shook her head at that thought. She didn't want Bane to think that she created drama everywhere she went, even at home, not when they had just begun courting. Her uncle was surely only bluffing to get her to sign away her inheritance. Why become hysterical over a threat he would never act upon? She ran her fingers through her hair and grunted. "But he has doctors ready to testify, and papers," she murmured to herself. Crossing the room, she removed her rapier from the box under her bed and held it up to the firelight, the sharpened steel deadly. She sighed, feeling a bit safer with a blade at hand should her uncle challenge her right to seek out her lawyer come morning.

She propped the blade beside the fireplace and returned to her desk, intent on writing a solid letter for her lawyer, but every time she wrote the words *Blackwell's Island*, her temper would threaten to overtake her. She crumpled paper after paper and tossed each into the rubbish bin. Finally she wrote the initials *B.I.*, *B.I.* over and over, hoping to make sense of what she would write to her lawyer. But the words would not come.

Unable to concentrate, she reached for her paints and once again painted what she always painted when she could not bear to be left alone with her thoughts any longer, a trio of hands, reaching for one another. Tonight's version was full of dark grays and cold blues, capturing the sensation of being underwater and sinking into the murky depths. She painted her fear as her vision blurred and her body grew weak, but the irresistible urge to paint kept her going as it always did until the vision of the hands faded to a dull ache. At the clock sounding three, she sank, still in her evening gown, onto the settee for a moment's rest.

※

"Will you never cease your tossing, Brother?" Bertram called from his bed across the dark room.

"I can't sleep."

"Thinking of a pair of fine eyes, are you?" His rumbling chuckle reached Bane.

Bane rolled to his side, propping his head up with the palm of his hand. "Is it that obvious?"

Bertram laughed. "Raoul. This is the first time I've ever seen you so taken with a girl. But what I want to know is, why didn't you notice her before now?"

Bane dropped his head to the pillow and sighed. "Stupidity? My sights were so fixed on developing the business, I failed to see what was right before me."

"Or perhaps you had to wait for her to dress brightly enough to capture your attention so you could see beyond her layers of eccentricity and find that she is your perfect match?"

He sighed again. "As superficial as I may sound by admitting it, yes. I believe her styles in the past kept me from noticing her as more than a friend." He thought back on the evening's events and couldn't keep his grin from spreading at the thought of Edyth swirling around with him on the dance floor in her crimson gown, her eyes sparkling in the candlelight and their passionate kisses afterward. He couldn't wait for their ride in the morning. And even though they had kissed, he wanted her to be certain of his feelings, of his love. He had only to wait until morning to know if she felt the same and if she would accept his offer of marriage. . .but morning felt like years from now.

"Raoul?" his brother whispered. "Are you asleep?"

Bane rolled to his side again. "No, and I won't be for a while. Want to spar with me? Maybe it will help encourage my body to sleep if I can put my nerves to use."

His brother sighed. "I will agree to get out of my comfortable bed for one reason. The only reason why I keep waking from a fitful sleep. Leftovers."

Bane laughed. "Well then, you best come spar with me, because I have a maid cleaning first thing in the morning, and I told her to take whatever is left."

Bertram scrambled out from beneath the bedclothes, mumbling. "You should have mentioned this before bed. No wonder I couldn't sleep. Those poor leftovers have been calling to me."

Dressed in their loose fencing trousers and with their shirts untucked, they tromped down the stairs in their bare feet to the deserted great hall. While there wasn't an abundance of food, for the two brothers, it was a feast. Bane grabbed two tarts from a silver tray and popped one after the other into his mouth, not caring that the sugar could keep him up.

He grabbed a foil sword from the wall and swished it in the air, motioning for his brother to take one as well and join him on the roped-off piste. Holding their treats in one hand and using the other to casually spar, the brothers laughed and ate until they acquired side stitches. Afterward the two lay on their backs on the cool floor, panting, and between his full belly and the exertion of fencing, Bane felt his eyelids growing heavy.

"Raoul? Why did you decide to be an instructor when you could have continued being a champion and obtain a legendary status?"

Bane answered sleepily. "I knew I could win, and that took the fire from the competition. And in the back of my mind, I knew with you and all our brothers having a piece of the family fortune, I needed to think of my future, much like your motivation for studying to become a doctor while you work here. There simply isn't enough money for all the Banebridge sons to live like gentlemen. I have awhile to go yet to make my own fortune, but this place is almost paid off, and when it finally is next year, I'll be able to save a tidy sum."

"A tidy enough sum to take care of a wife?" Bertram ventured.

"Should I be so fortunate for her to accept my suit, yes."

"Too bad you didn't notice her sooner. The girl has carried a torch for you for years and gladly would've paid off your loans."

"Edyth has liked me for *years*?" Bane couldn't keep his grin from splitting his face. He would enjoy teasing her over that bit of knowledge.

Bertram chuckled. "Seems like I got the good looks and the smarts of the family. You really are stupid, aren't you?"

"I'd rather call it focused. But I guess that's why I wasn't supposed to notice her until now. I needed to prove to myself and society that I don't need her for her fortune. I only ever need her at my side."

"Spoken like a true lovesick pup. Good night." Bertram rolled over to his side, and his snores soon echoed off the empty walls, leaving Bane to his thoughts, his last one being of Edyth's present, still wrapped, sitting on his desk.

Chapter Seven

Drawing, and music occupied my every moment.
Cares I knew not, and cared naught about them.
~ John James Audubon

The sound of wood smashing jarred Edyth to her core. Limbs shaking and her head aching, she blinked in the light flooding her room, disoriented as her uncle charged inside followed by two burly men in greatcoats that dripped onto her Persian rug, their eyes fastened on her. Blood surging, she bolted backward from the settee toward the corner of the room. "What on earth do you think you're doing? Remove yourself from my bedchamber at once."

"Ignore anything she says," Uncle Boris instructed the henchmen, who moved toward her, their dirt-creased hands outstretched.

"Stop!" She stumbled backward and caught sight of her rapier leaning against the corner of the fireplace. She scrambled for it, tripping over the wretched skirts of her ball gown, the tips of her fingers brushing the pommel.

One of the men wrenched her skirts backward, lifting her off her feet. Edyth screamed, kicking and clawing at her assailant. "Release me at once, or so help me, I'll have you thrown in jail for the remainder of your miserable days," she shrieked. "Police, help! Police!"

"Keep a firm hold on her, Meyer." Her uncle waved away her distress, as if she were merely complaining of a pinching corset. "Do not worry, gentlemen. She is harmless, though out of her wits. The staff have all been informed and will not be coming to her aid. Holden, make yourself useful and secure her wrists."

She kicked ferociously against the men, releasing a continuous stream of screaming and scratching at them, aching to get her hands on her rapier. If she had reached it, these men wouldn't have touched her. Tears filled her eyes at being handled so roughly. For all of her years, no one had dared lay a finger on her. Her wealth had protected her. But these men didn't care about her wealth. To them, she was simply a madwoman. The man her uncle called Meyer set her down, pausing only long enough for the other man, Holden, to secure her wrists in front of her with a length of rope he pulled from his coat pocket.

"She won't get loose. Let's go." Holden's thick southern accent cut the night.

She scraped her heels against the floor as the men dragged her out into the hall. She swung her leg up with all her might, intending to kick them, but her foot tangled in her voluminous skirts. Why had she worn such a ridiculous gown? Why had she fallen asleep instead of running for help the instant Uncle Boris made his threat? She hadn't thought he was serious enough to act at once. She thought he would at least ask her to sign the document again before—

"Why bother struggling, Edyth?" Her uncle followed them into the hall, snacking on a bag of roasted nuts from his pocket as if he were at the circus.

She speared him with her gaze and shouted, "Traitor!"

He did not flinch, nor motion for the men to halt. They pulled her toward the main staircase with ease, and she shrieked again and again, calling for the servants, anyone, to rescue her. "Help me. Why is no one helping me?" She fairly sobbed in frustration, her breath coming in heaves when she spied a maid cowering in a doorway. "Katie, you must send for Bane. Get help."

"She will not be helping you, not with the doctors on our side." Uncle glared at Katie. "Get out of here. I told you that you were not to leave your quarters. If you breathe a word of this, I'll make certain you never work anywhere respectable again."

"I summoned her, dear." Mrs. Foster stood in the threshold, her cold, hard eyes meeting Edyth's as she kept one hand poised on the doorframe and the other resting on her abdomen. "You should have taken your uncle's generous offer, girl. Look where your greed has gotten you." The corners of her lips twitched upward. "Poor, dear, mad girl." She waved them along. "Take her and be quick about it. I need my rest."

Edyth would have responded, but her rising panic threatened to overwhelm her. She flailed her legs, kicking at the walls and glass cabinets, knocking over expensive vases that her relatives had collected with *her* fortune. Edyth didn't pay mind to the mess she left in her wake. All she cared about was alerting the servants and having them defend her. But besides Katie, they were nowhere to be seen as the men dragged her down the stairs, her knees slamming into each step.

"You cannot do this. Help me! Someone help me." Her throat grew thick with fear. She looked over her shoulder, causing the men to tug her with more force. "Uncle, I am your own flesh and blood. I beg of you. Think of my father, your *brother*. What would he say if he saw you treating me like this? Where is your compassion?"

At this, his brows lowered to a point, and he rested a hand on her shoulder, stopping them as her sobs hitched in her chest. "Since my brother refused to share our inheritance, more than a measly amount per year, I would say he should expect such a thing from me." He reached out, plucked a rose from her hair, and crumpled it in his fist, allowing the petals to flutter to the floor. "He was selfish to the core, and I can't take the chance on you not following in his footsteps once you see exactly how much wealth you are set to inherit." He grinned. "Or were."

"But he gave me over into your care. You must have loved one another. I thought he did so because you were close—"

"You were foisted upon me because I was the only family you had left, and he never thought he would pass before you were raised. Because of you, I had to give up my bachelorhood and become a father to a girl I never wanted." He sneered. "My only regret is that I did not find the clause sooner. I assumed my darling brother left everything to his little girl without a condition besides your age." He laughed without mirth. "But I suppose he was worried that since your mother was beginning to display eccentricities that you might finally be the one to go mad."

Her stomach twisted. She thought back on her mother's peculiarities such as never wearing shoes in the upstairs chambers or her aversion to cut flowers left too long in a vase, their dying scent bothering her. "You are lying."

He shrugged. "If I am, you will never know, now will you? I am only thankful that Mrs. Foster made me take a second look at the will. Now, enough talk. I'm tired and wish to return to bed." He waved his hand to the men. "Take her to Blackwell's Island on the first ferry out."

And with that, Edyth released a scream that would wake the block, only to have a rag shoved in her mouth followed by a gag to secure the rag and a black sack drawn over her head. One of the brutes threw her over his shoulder as she kicked, screaming through the cloth until she felt one of them wrap his hand around the back of her throat and press down hard with two fingers.

"Don't make me knock you out, miss," the man growled. "But I will. You aren't the first woman I've taken to the island. Your uncle hired me for a reason. I warn you *not* to test me, else I shall use my experience against you."

She flinched as they gripped her wrists and gave the rope a sharp tug before she was tossed onto the floor of what she assumed was her uncle's carriage. A boot was pressed firmly into her back as a reminder not to stir or scream lest she be kicked in the ribs. She gingerly touched where the brigand had squeezed her neck, wincing at the bruises that were surely already appearing. The sound of corks popping caught her ear and the men laughed, clinking glasses together before one belched and the scent of whiskey filled the small compartment.

In what seemed an eternity, they finally rolled to a stop. Seizing her arms, the two men dragged Edyth out of the carriage, keeping both of her arms in iron vises for grips. The scent of the river greeted her, along with a lone bell ringing in the silence. She squinted in the darkness, making out precious little from the lantern's light seeping through the thin sack just before it was ripped from her head and the gag was removed. She gulped in the fresh air, but before she could even think about crying for help, a massive hand clamped onto her shoulder, pinching down and making her feel faint for the pain.

"I'm only removing it so as not to draw attention, but if you utter anything over a whisper, I'll return the gag and tie it even tighter. So much so you'll fear you'll never draw another breath," Holden hissed in her ear.

She hated herself for shaking. She sized them up, wishing she were taller. She could never hope to best them without a weapon. She looked about for something she could use. *Perhaps I could swim for it...if I could only throw myself into the water and swim deep enough for them to think I drowned.* She was a strong swimmer, but in the East River...she knew it would be risky.

"I got the ferry tickets. The first leaves in fifteen minutes. With all these doctors' signatures, we can head straight to Blackwell's Island without stopping at the other stations first. Saves us a good bit of time. We may be able to get in another job before the day is out."

"I need a moment of privacy," Edyth announced and lifted her chin and glared at them, daring them to say no.

They looked to one another before Meyer shrugged and nodded. "Fine. Take her to the outhouse, but hurry."

Holden gripped her by the arm, squeezing a whimper out of her as he jerked her down the dock. "If you try anything, I'll see to it that you get worse than a few bruises once on board. Your uncle won't begrudge me once he hears you attempted to escape and that a beating was the only way I could subdue you."

She wrinkled her nose at the burning scent of his breath. *Lord, give me an escape.*

He threw open the door of a small shack and pointed to a primitive toilet in the corner, a board with a hole cut out of it. "You have three minutes. Any longer and I'll come in here no matter if you're ready or not." He sent her a toothy grin that sent shivers down to her toes as he loosed her bonds.

Alone at last, she scrambled to the corner of the room where the only window was covered by a filthy, ragged curtain. She tossed it aside and nearly cried when she saw that the window was haphazardly boarded up. She jerked on the moldy boards, but they didn't even budge. Grunting in consternation, she searched the nauseating outhouse for anything she could use as a weapon, but the only item in the room was an old catalog hanging from a string attached to a nail in the wall, its torn pages lying motionless. She gave the nail a jerk, but it was embedded far deeper than it appeared.

"I'm coming in now." A voice boomed, and Edyth scurried to the door and let herself out of the outhouse into the breeze smelling of fish.

"Come on." Holden pulled her toward the ferry.

Passing a group of sailors lumbering down the dock, Edyth elbowed the man gripping her arm and threw herself into the men that she normally would have avoided at all costs. "You have to help me! These men are taking me against my will." Her frantic gaze flew from man to man in the group, some grinning, some bored, and a few slack-jawed.

Holden made a swipe for her, but she ducked his fist and ran into the chest of one of the sailors, a young lad with kind eyes who grasped her elbow, steadying her. "Did they kidnap you, miss?"

"Yes." She grasped the front of his shirt in both her fists, the desperation to be heard and understood causing her to disregard all propriety. "If you help me escape them, I will reward you hand-somely. You see how I am dressed. I can follow through with my promise."

"That one's as mad as they come. We're taking her to Blackwell's Island." Meyer spat a wad of tobacco juice at her slippers.

Sadness filled the young man's expression as he shook his head, his hold loosening on her. "I'm so sorry, miss. I wish I could help you, but if you are heading to the island, there is naught I can do but pray for you."

"But I'm not mad. I'm not," Edyth fairly whimpered as he stepped away from her and followed the rest of his mates. "You have to believe me." *Someone has to believe me.* She sank to her knees, her palms hanging open at her sides.

"I warned you." Holden gripped her by the arm, his fingers dig-ging until she cried out. He stuffed the filthy rag between her teeth, his calloused fingers brushing her tongue and leaving behind a taste that made her want to retch as he secured the gag in place and haphazardly wrapped the rope around her wrists. He dragged her tripping down the plank into a waiting ferry with what appeared to be a sleepy crew and captain and joined his fellow henchman. "Need to have us a good long smoke after we deposit this banshee, eh, Meyer?"

Grasping her elbows, the two steered her into a cabin that looked like it had been accumulating grime for years with a smell to match. Shoved inside, she was left to find a seat on one of the nar-row benches lining the walls while the two men stood just outside the doorway. She clawed at the gag, desperate for air, and spat to free her mouth of the vile residue left from the man's grubby fingers. Eyes glazed over, Edyth ignored the benches and stumbled toward a small cot on the far wall. But one glance at it, and she knew it would smell even worse than it appeared. She tucked her nose into her shoulder, inhaling the lingering scent of her favorite perfume as tears escaped her lashes and desperation threatened to consume her.

"Lord help me." Her prayer slipped from her lips.

Her tears fell unrestrained, and she bit at the knot at her wrists, working away at the already loose rope. She checked to ensure the two guards had not noticed, but they were busy flirting with two substantial female attendants dressed in gray uniforms who had boarded behind them. Their bawdy laughter over what was ahead of Edyth at the asylum flowed into the room. If these two women were a sample of the island's staff—

The boat swayed as it moved out from the dock, the churning waters turning her stomach. She buried her face in her hands and wept over the loss of her uncle's love that she had never possessed and the loss of Bane and the love they could have had. "Lord, if You are listening, save me. Save me." But with every rock of the waves against the ferry, her heart fell further. "Why aren't You saving me?" she whispered. *I don't understand.*

"Ain't no one going to save you now." The thick-boned woman that she had heard the others call Nurse Sweeney came in the room and crouched beside her. She spat a wad of tobacco onto the wall, which explained the dark stains dripping down to the floorboards. "Poor dear." She murmured the words sarcastically and lifted a finger to trace a tear down Edyth's cheek before drawing back her hand and slapping her.

Edyth pressed her hands against her stinging cheek and rose to her feet, finding her voice at last. "How dare you. You try that again and you will—"

The woman turned on her heel and left the cabin, laughing. "I told you I'd do it, gents. Pay up now before you go up top to smoke."

Meyer and Holden grunted and handed over a few bills to the woman, who immediately counted them before stuffing them into her bodice.

She struck me for a bet? Edyth bristled and gave the ropes a final tug with her teeth, allowing them to fall away. She studied the room for anything that could be used as a weapon. She made her way to the cot and, holding her breath, drew up the grimy mattress and tugged on each of the slats, hoping for a loose one. At the low creak of a nail, she glanced back over her shoulder, but the couples were still flirting, the other, shorter nurse running her hand up and down Holden's sleeve. With a jerk, Edyth freed one of the slats and waited for the men to take their smoke on deck, leaving the women alone to guard her. She flipped the board so the nails would not seriously injure them, and lifting the wood above her head, she charged out the cabin door, slamming the board down on the head of the woman who had struck her. Before the other could cry out, Edyth swung the board around and hit the second square in the jaw. Dropping the board to grab up her skirts, she bolted for the stairs, the glimmer of dawn's light greeting her along with a burst of glorious fresh air and freedom. She threw herself at the rails, intending to plunge into the East River and swim for shore when she felt sturdy hands enclose her waist, yanking her away.

She shrieked through her teeth and clawed, desperate for a chance to escape. "No! Release me. You cannot take me!"

"You really are mad. In that heavy dress, you'd sink like a stone," Meyer mumbled around the stem of his pipe.

She jerked her arm back, but he held firm as the ferry docked. He and Holden led her up the plank to shore where a dilapidated ambulance wagon stood waiting. She dug her heels into the muddy earth and cried out, "Someone help me! I'm being taken against my will."

Her companions seemed to take pleasure in her pleas, and the people about the makeshift town turned wide eyes to her and viewed her with interest, but not a soul possessed sympathy enough to come to her aid. "If anyone has a heart, find Raoul Banebridge of New York City's Banebridge Fencing Club and tell him what has happened. I beg of you—"

Meyer clamped a hand over her mouth and nose, gripping her so tightly her head began to swim for lack of air.

"Shut up, or I'll be forced to shut you up, miss." The man released his hold on her, and Holden tossed her into the back of the closed wagon, locked the door, and climbed into the seat beside the driver. Their laughter sounded demonic as Edyth gasped for air, the spots in her vision slowly abating.

The two nurses stepped up beside the wagon, scowling at her through the small open windows. Nurse Sweeney held a rag to her head, blood seeping from the gash left from Edyth's board. "You are going to pay for hitting Nurse Madison and me," the woman said through her teeth. "You will find that we only ferry mad girls two days a week, and the rest of our working time is spent in the asylum. You can bet we are going to have some diversion with you come our shift in your hall."

Edyth met their glares. "I should have wielded the side with the rusted nails."

"Yes, you should have when you had the chance." Nurse Madison cracked her overlarge knuckles as they moved on to a second, smaller wagon.

The ambulance wagon bumped down the dirt road, flying past picturesque lawns as Edyth dug her nails into the rough wood of the window frame, her eyes fastened on the trees painted with the fiery brush of fall passing by. She was truly afraid that this was the last time she would ever see such vibrant colors again. She did not imagine that the doctors allowed the inmates of the asylum to wander freely about the island. The wagon turned with the road alongside several long stone structures, and the stench nearly overwhelmed her.

The wagon rolled to a stop in front of a massive gray stone rotunda connecting the asylum's two wings that stood three stories high. Looking up, she spied a ghostly face pressed against the bars of the third floor.

With a cry, Edyth attempted to plead her case once again. But her pleas fell on unaffected ears, and she was thrown over Meyer's shoulder and carried up a flight of narrow stone steps that led into the great rotunda. She managed to twist her neck enough to see a plaque mounted beside the door that read Blackwell's Island Women's Lunatic Asylum. "Please, God, no," she whispered. "No."

"Look. You seem like a nice girl, but the more fuss you make, the harder they'll be on you now that you're here," Meyer whispered in a tone that almost sounded like pity.

She stopped kicking since it wasn't doing her any good, deciding on a different tactic. She would be docile until they grew lax, and then she could bolt.

"I'm going to set you down now, but don't you go and fight us, or I'll have to knock you out. Holden is looking for an excuse to hit you. So you better keep still or he might try more than knocking you out." Meyer set her firmly on her two feet, keeping a guiding hand on her elbow as they entered the massive rotunda.

The large spiraling staircase with a chandelier at the center and stunning arched ceilings held the promise that perhaps the nurses and her uncle had exaggerated the condition of the asylum. If it was so elegant and well kept, surely its doctors couldn't be quite so horrible and she would find a sympathetic ear somewhere and a means of escape.

"Would you like to bring her to the vestibule to wait for the doctors for her final admittance examination?" asked a woman standing behind a tall reception desk, her spectacles perched on the edge of her nose while she took in Edyth's torn ball gown that bespoke of her wealth.

Holden shook his head. "This one's a special case. Her uncle had doctors evaluate her in the city before bringing her to the island. He wanted her put away without the news being alerted. Guess their family is high society."

"My uncle only wishes for discretion because he is trying to seize my fortune," Edyth protested. The guard squeezed her arm, but she jerked away from his grasp and gripped the counter in one last desperate attempt. "Send for different doctors. Let them evaluate me, and I can *prove* that I am as sane as you are."

"I doubt that," the woman murmured, her lips pinching as she waved at Meyer to restrain Edyth again before she continued. "Do you have the papers, Mister—?"

"Holden, and yes, miss, I do." He slid the folded documents across the desk. "Mr. Foster promised a hefty bonus if there's no trouble." He withdrew a roll of bills from his pocket, which the woman's hungry gaze roved over. She snatched the roll, counting the bills before unfastening the top three buttons of her bodice, drawing Holden's disgusting leer. She slipped the bills inside and secured the buttons once more. She rang a bell and motioned the responding female attendant over, causing Edyth to cringe at the sight of the nurse from the ferry. "Nurse Madison, take this patient to an isolation room and let her work out her passion. She will be more docile tomorrow morning when she is hungry and tired enough to meet the matron and allow the staff to bathe her and get her into her uniform."

"Gladly." The nurse gripped Edyth by the hair at the back of her neck, wrenching her away from the desk.

Edyth held back a cry of pain. "Please, someone send for Doctor Hawkins. He will vouch for my sanity."

The nurse's grip faltered, but only for a moment. "Only a madwoman would attack us with a board." She jerked her down the hall. "Doctor Hawkins will see you when he is good and ready and not a moment before. You best get used to your new life, *duchess*."

"Doctor Hawkins!" Edyth screeched. "Roger Hawkins. Help! It's Edyth Fos—"

The woman's wide hand pinched Edyth's nose and jaw closed, drawing the fight from her veins as her lungs screamed for air. "Shut your trap."

Edyth clawed at the woman's hand until her arms grew weak. Just when she felt herself slipping away, the nurse released her hold and nodded to a male attendant standing beside a door. The man unlocked it, and Edyth felt herself being dragged into the hall, the moaning of patients at their cell doors striking fear into her core. The dark, arched doorways of cells pressed in on her from every side, and at the end of the hall, the nurse flung open the door to a vacant room with two disgusting cots, but only one with bedclothes.

"Maybe a day without food and a night in the dark will help you calm down and remind you that you are no longer an heiress. As far as the world is concerned, Edyth Foster is dead."

Chapter Eight

Paintings have a life of their own that
derives from the painter's soul.
~ Vincent van Gogh

Edyth did not show up for their early morning ride, and Bane began to grow apprehensive that he must have said something the night before to frighten her. The thought plagued him all through his morning ride. Knowing he wouldn't be able to concentrate on his fencing class if he did not first stop by her house to inquire after her, Bane directed his charge toward her gray stone mansion on Fifth Avenue.

Handing the reins to the groomsman who trotted up to greet him, Bane swiped off his hat and lifted and dropped the bronze knocker against the door. When no one answered his knock, he peered through the transoms on either side of the mahogany door, attempting to spot anyone or a light inside when the flash of an emerald skirt caught his attention. He knocked on the door again, the impression that he was being avoided growing. Bane gnawed on the inside of his cheek, concerned that perhaps his momentary foolishness with Lavinia had come back to haunt him. *Maybe Edyth has decided that she doesn't wish for Lavinia's sloppy seconds or that I should have known that I was meant for Edyth all along, but how could I when the thought never crossed my mind?*

The door jerked open three inches. "Mr. Banebridge, my apologies, but it seems Edyth has contracted an illness and won't be joining you this morning for lessons."

Bane's brows rose at the sight of her uncle behind the door. "An illness? Is it contagious? Is that why the servants aren't answering the door?"

Mr. Foster shook his head. "No. I was simply near the door because I am expecting Doctor Wentworth. He should be arriving soon, so if you'll excuse me, I need to return to my breakfast or I'll be too hungry to focus on the doctor's diagnosis."

"Doctor Wentworth? Jasper's father?"

"He's newly appointed as our family doctor. Something about wishing to quit his current place of employment."

Mr. Foster moved to close the door, but Bane shoved the toe of his riding boot over the threshold at the last moment, wincing at the weight of the door against his foot. "Is that why she didn't join me today or send word of a cancellation?"

"Of course. As I just explained, Edyth is ill. I doubt she will be riding or fencing anytime soon."

At this, Bane's heart seized. "Do you know what she has? Surely she is not in danger?"

Mr. Foster shrugged rather callously. "The doctor mentioned something about a fever, but I was more concerned about my wife contracting the illness from Edyth than attending to my niece's absurd requests." He shook his head, annoyance clouding his tone. "Really, the girl is ill, not dying. Good day, Mr. Banebridge."

"I *need* to see her, sir, if only for a moment." Bane cleared his throat from the awkwardness of his insistence, but better to bear embarrassment than burn with this unknowing for one moment more.

"That is not possible. You would be risking yourself, not to mention the possibility of becoming the harbinger of illness to your club, and we both know that you and my niece would not wish to have that on your conscience." Mr. Foster wouldn't meet his gaze and moved to close the door again. He motioned for Bane to remove his boot from the threshold.

Bane frowned. Edyth had been perfectly well last night and had exhibited no signs of illness. He knew for a fact that she had not been around anyone ill, since she had spent most of the past three days either inside painting or out with him. And as he was not feeling ill after sharing a kiss with her, he was certain something was not right. "My adamancy is inexcusable, but I'll only be a minute. It is of the utmost importance. I promise to speak my piece and take my leave at once."

"The answer is still no. Now, I would suggest that since you were recently in contact with her, to see my doctor at once. I'll have him over to you as soon as he is finished here, so be certain that you are at your apartments to receive him," he instructed in a rush, obviously ready to close the gap.

Bane surveyed Edyth's uncle, not trusting him one bit. He could force his way inside without much effort, but thinking it might be best to heed the man for now, he gave Mr. Foster a short nod and stepped back. On the sidewalk, he craned his neck to see into Edyth's second-floor window, desperate to catch sight of her. Her still curtains revealed nothing, and looking down the row of windows, Bane did not spy movement in any of them, which made him wonder where all the servants were.

He returned to the waiting groomsman and took the reins. "Thank you, uh, Newton, isn't it?"

"Aye, that's me, sir. Is there something else you'll be needing?" Newton straightened his livery jacket and stood at attention.

Bane stroked his steed's mane. "Have you seen the servants outside the house today? I only ask because Mr. Foster answered the door. In all the years I've come calling, not once has he done so."

"That sounds strange to me as well." The young man removed his hat and scratched the top of his wild hair. "I haven't seen any servants milling about since yesterday evening. I think Mr. Foster gave most of them, except the cook and one maid, the evening and today off to visit family."

"Why not you?"

He chuckled. "I was part of the staff he ruled as essential, so I stayed on duty while the others left."

Bane drummed his fingers on the leather saddle. "Did Mr. Foster offer any explanation for his sudden bout of generosity?"

"No one dared ask. When your employer gives you unexpected time off, you don't question him."

Contemplating this bit of news, Bane slipped his hand from the saddle and stepped back, all thoughts of departing ebbing as his blood pulsed with suspicion. "And what of the family? Have they received any visitors? Have you noticed anything out of the ordinary?"

If Newton thought Bane's questions were a bit peculiar, his expression did not betray him as he answered, "Miss Birch departed for an unexpected trip with a friend, but I don't know her, so I can't rightly say if it is out of the ordinary for her to be spontaneous." He pulled at his white neckcloth, shifting in place. "I didn't wish to mention it, lest you think me odd, but uh, I have a lot of nightmares, so don't think me heartless when I tell you what I think I heard."

"Of course not. You can tell me." He pulled a sugar cube from his riding coat pocket and fed it to his horse to keep his mind steady, wiping his gloved hand against the back of his coat.

"Well, it was probably only my vivid dreams, but it sounded like there was some kind of commotion late last night, like a girl screaming or something. I looked out my window above the stables, but when I didn't hear nothin' else, I went back to sleep, not thinking much of it." He shoved his hands into his pockets and kicked a loose pebble into the shadows of the house, the stone skittering down the cobblestone driveway. "When I mentioned it to Mr. Foster on the ride to the doctor's this morning, he told me to quit my jabberin' and keep it to myself, else he would fire me." He threw a hand in the air and grunted, stepping toward Bane. "You can't tell him I forgot that and told you, sir. I need this job. My mama always told me my gift of gab would get me into trouble."

"I will keep it to myself, never fear. But you said that Mr. Foster was out this morning fetching the doctor? Why didn't he just send you in his stead?"

"He didn't fetch him. Just went inside for a moment and came back a lot calmer than when he first arrived."

If Edyth was indeed ill, why hadn't the doctor come to the house then and there? What could they have been talking about? "How strange."

Newton shrugged. "I don't question the ways of rich folk. I only do as I'm told. Their whims are foreign to me."

Still unsatisfied with Mr. Foster's answer but unsure as to why he would tell an outright lie, Bane asked again, "You heard screaming? You are sure?"

"No. As I said, I have nightmares, but I may have also seen a rough-looking fellow getting into a closed carriage before it drove off. It might have been part of my dream though, because it seems odd to have visitors at three in the morning. But then, Miss Edyth doesn't really conform to society's rules, so why would she bother with normal visiting hours?"

His head spinning from the lad's disconcerting tale, Bane balanced his hat on the saddle and dug into his pocket and produced a coin, tossing it to the groom. "You've been most helpful. If you wouldn't mind, could you tie my horse in the stable?" *And out of view of the house?* "I may go and see if I can speak with the cook and the maid."

Newton pocketed the coin and, replacing his hat, tipped it to him. "Certainly, sir."

Waiting until the young man was out of sight, Bane took a quick gander of the place before letting himself in through the service entrance. As young Newton had promised, the kitchen only boasted one cook and a scullery maid, both of whom were far too busy to notice him slipping past and up the servants' staircase. Climbing the winding stair, he halted at the second floor and cracked open the door, listening and watching for anyone.

Hearing nothing, he drew a deep breath and darted down

the red-carpeted hall, making for Edyth's rooms. She had once pointed them out on his first visit during a tour of the house nearly a decade ago.

Pausing outside the french doors, he gave a light knock, surprised when the door swung open on its own accord to the peach-colored bedroom. Bane ran his finger over the latch to confirm that the lock had been broken, finding the wood splintered. His breath shallowed as he surveyed the mess in front of him—a shattered vase, an overturned chair, her rapier lying on its side by the ash-filled fireplace, and wilted rose petals strewn on the fine Persian rug. He bent and scooped one up. *Why would Edyth throw her roses on the floor? And why would no one pick them up? She hates dead flowers.* Something on the rug glinted in the sunlight filtering through a crack in the thick curtains that no one had bothered to open despite the late morning hour. The object winked at him again, catching his curiosity. Crouching low, he found her stickpin. He rubbed his thumb over the ruby, his thoughts wild. She never would have dishonored his gift in such a manner. He pocketed it and perused the room anew. "Dear God in heaven, what happened here?"

Bane spied her easel angled toward the fire as if she had been using it to see her work. Her paints were on a small table, her brushes still coated in gray paint. He scowled. It was not like Edyth to waste perfectly good brushes. He crossed the room to the painting and spied three hands reaching for one another. *Odd.* He made his way to her writing desk, littered with notes and crumpled paper. Scooping one up from the table, he made out a scrawl written a dozen times over. *B.I.* He didn't know anyone who had those initials. *Could they be a gentleman's? Did she leave with him?* He shook his head. Edyth would have told him about anyone interested in her. Perhaps B.I. was a destination, and that was why her room was in such disarray. . .because she was in a hurry? He hadn't been in her rooms since her girlhood, but Edyth didn't strike him as a lady to throw a tantrum and make a mess. Hearing voices, he darted to the left corner of the room, hiding behind the curtains.

"Have her room cleaned up, Katie. I don't want Lavinia to see any of this when she returns. And be certain to pack up Miss Edyth's things in her traveling trunks. She is gone now, so it is best her room reflect that fact."

"Where shall I send the trunks, Mr. Foster?" came the maid Katie's reply.

"I will tend to that. You just see that everything of hers in this room is packed away, and notify me when you are done. My wife is determined that this room be transformed into a nursery given its ceiling fresco and picturesque view."

Bane tilted his chin up to find a charming scene of cherubs framed with opulent molding before returning his gaze to Mr. Foster. Edyth was gone, that was for certain, but where was Mr. Foster hiding her? He held himself perfectly still behind the curtain as the maid threw open the pair of curtains to the right of the bed and another near a dressing screen, mercifully leaving the windows beside the settee, where he was hiding, untouched. She cleaned up the room, humming to herself. He peered through a space in the curtain and watched while Katie swept the papers from the table into her wastebasket. He grimaced, wishing he could have saved the papers to search for clues as to where Edyth had disappeared. For now, he would start with the initials and make a list of potential names.

"Are you almost finished?" came a shrill voice from the doorway.

The maid dipped into a curtsy. "Yes, Mrs. Foster. I only need to clear away Miss Edyth's paints and pack her jewels."

Mrs. Foster waltzed past the maid, brushing the carved mantel and wiping her fingertips together with a satisfied nod before rustling to Edyth's vanity. She flung open a case that was so decorative that it surprised Bane. He had not taken Edyth for someone who would care for such a feminine thing. He had much to learn about her. Once he found her.

Mrs. Foster riffled through Edyth's jewels, removing strands of diamonds, earrings dripping in emeralds, and a ruby ring of astonishing size, none of which Bane had seen before, and dropped them into a beaded reticule retrieved from Edyth's top drawer. "Leave the rest in my armoire in case Lavinia or I have use for them."

"Yes, ma'am." Katie curtsied again, accidentally dropping her cleaning bucket.

A kitten that apparently had been hiding in an adjoining room shot across the floor, startling Mrs. Foster and causing her to catch her toe on the easel. With a grunt of annoyance, she seized the painting, jerked open the closet door, and pitched it inside, leaving the door ajar. "Have this all thrown out into the rubbish by the end of the day. And as for that cat, I want it and all the others out in the street today."

After Mrs. Foster left, Katie disposed of the paints, retrieved the wastebasket and her cleaning bucket, muttering about having to mop now, and disappeared out the door, leaving it open for her impending return.

Not daring to wait another second, Bane darted to the closet and discovered row upon row of canvases in a variety of sizes stacked up against one another, all displaying a trio of hands painted in different scenes, but all grasping toward one another and never quite touching. He ran his fingers through his hair and exhaled. "Edyth, my girl, what is all this you are keeping hidden from the world?"

He found her leather sketchbook carelessly tossed inside, and he snatched it up, his heart hammering. Edyth would never have voluntarily left it behind. He pocketed it, unwilling to allow anyone to pick through her private musings. A soft mewing at his feet stopped him from hurrying out of the room. *The cats.* He grunted. He wasn't overly fond of the creatures, but knowing Edyth would be heartbroken if her rescued kittens were returned to the streets, he knelt down.

"You must be Michelangelo," he whispered. Bane scooped the

kitten up and put him in his jacket pocket. However, the little one did not seem to wish to be carted around so and let out a growling hiss. "Shh! Fine then. You win," he mumbled. He pulled the kitten out and held it to his chest before racing out into the hall and down to the last guest room that Edyth said she'd turned into a sanctuary for her animals. Throwing open the door, he found two cats lounging on a settee and one perched on the windowsill, all looking rather bored with his appearance. He spied a large basket in the corner of the room and quickly set the kitten inside, then slowly approached the cats.

The one on the windowsill darted from his grasp, while the two on the settee remained docile and even purred at his touch. With a whispered apology, he plopped the pair of cats in the basket and draped a blanket over it while he chased after the calico that Edyth had affectionately named Leo. All cats secured and his coat sleeve ripped, Bane bolted down the hall, toting a mewing, growling wicker basket.

Chapter Nine

Life etches itself onto our faces as we grow older,
showing our violence, excesses or kindnesses.
~ Rembrandt

This is a dream. A nightmare. I'll wake up. Edyth rocked back and forth in her bed, if one could even call the dilapidated cot a bed, desperate for warmth and a drop of water for her parched throat. After a long day locked away in her cell followed by a freezing night, her body ached for a bit of comfort. Her silk stockings and satin gown did little to dampen the cold, but she was thankful for the layers of petticoats to keep her legs warm at least. She pulled away the top part of her corset in an attempt to draw a full breath, longing to be released from the tight stays. But she hadn't dared to sleep in her chemise and drawers last night, for she didn't know who might come barging into her room next. Someone checked on her hourly, and she did not care to risk the degradation of exposure for the sake of freeing her waist.

The asylum had supplied her with a single scratchy blanket, but every time she pulled it up to her shoulders, her thin slippers would be exposed to the brisk night air, so her only choice was to curl up into a miserable ball in her satin gown and pray for morning and the sun to rise. But each time she managed to fall into a fitful sleep, a pair of uniformed nurses would come down the hall, their chatelaines rattling as they unlocked each door to check on their patients, the locks grinding each time. She eventually lost count of how many doors she heard open and close.

Edyth was merely one of many patients, but the female attendants found a special way to plague her with their pointed questions each time they entered her room, curious about the newcomer. From overhearing bits of the nurses' conversations throughout the night, Edyth gathered that most of the patients had been living there for years and that new inmates were always a welcome reprieve for the nurses. They took great enjoyment in the sport of tormenting their charges with their pinches, slapping, and shoves. Edyth rubbed at the bruises sprinkling her arm, her cheek still smarting from that devil of a nurse from the ferry. She was beginning to understand the awful truth of how unlike they were from the nurses who attended to her in the comfort of her own home on Fifth Avenue whenever she was ill.

Edyth had not heard much about the asylum. She'd known about it, of course, but she'd only been to charity events that raised money for all the buildings on Blackwell's Island as a whole. Before that first initial conversation with the doctors at Lavinia's party, Edyth hadn't paid attention to what was said beyond that the asylum was a very nice place filled with happy inmates cared for by the best of doctors while enjoying the beautiful grounds and weekly musicals. *Lies. All lies besides the beauty of the island.*

At the thought of the lawns, she rose with the blanket draped over her nearly bare shoulders, teeth chattering, and peered out the window that was barred on the outside. Pressing herself to the glass, Edyth warmed herself in the broken rays of sunrise that managed to steal through her barred windows. She didn't have a view of the sprawling green, only the roof of what she supposed was the kitchen, judging from the trays of food being brought to and from the asylum like clockwork yesterday.

Dear Lord, why did You allow me to be captured? Why didn't You send me aid right away? She tentatively lifted her gaze to the gathering clouds. *I beg You to somehow get word to Bane that I am here, and I promise I will do better. I won't be so arrogant with the freedom my wealth lends me. Only, please, don't let me perish in here, not when Bane and I—* She swallowed against the pain of what might have been.

Bane. Her body ached with the thought of him waiting for her yesterday morning and wondering all day why she had not shown and why she didn't even bother to attend class. *He must be worried to distraction.* She rested her head against the cold glass window-pane and sighed. Why did she have to play coy and make him wait for her answer on his musings of marriage? She groaned. *Surely he doesn't think I am running from him?* The thought made her stomach turn. And if Bane didn't look for her, who would? And if she didn't escape this nightmare, she would never be able to tell him—

The keys rattled at the door and she stiffened with her blanket slipping from her grip and revealing the torn crimson sleeves hanging limply from her gown. The door swung open with a groan, and a severe-looking woman in a black gown trimmed with lace stood in her doorway. Nurse Madison stood beside her, with a satisfying dark bruise along her jawline, holding a gray piece of fabric folded into a neat square.

"The luxury of having a cell to yourself is at an end. You are to be transferred to a different chamber that you will share, but for now, it's time you join the others in the dining hall." The woman in black motioned to the nurse's bundle. "Properly clothed, of course."

Nurse Madison shook out the material, and Edyth's jaw dropped at the thin dress held out to her. She brushed her fingertips on the sleeve of the dress, giving the nurse a stare that she hoped conveyed her displeasure. This had less substance than her chemise. *This is properly clothed?* "If you are going to insist on not heating the institution, the least you can do is provide warmer clothes and more blankets. You cannot expect people to live in these inhumane conditions."

Nurse Madison curtsied, holding out her skirt. "As you wish, my lady."

Taken aback at the nurse's response, Edyth drew herself up and gave her a gracious nod. "Well, thank you—"

The other lady threw back her head and emitted a cackling, guttural laugh. "The woman actually thought you were serious!"

Nurse Madison gave her a devilish grin. "Told you she was fun, Matron. Girl, get in the gown and be grateful that you have anything more to wear than your chemise. We don't cater to nobody, no matter who they claim to be."

"Claim? But surely you know who I am? My papers—"

"Yes, your papers, which is why I am here." The matron clasped her hands around a thin portfolio, her lips pursed. The wrinkles about her mouth revealed the action to be a habitual one. She ran a hand over her severe bun, the gray hairs in perfect placement. "Mr. Foster informed us of your obsession with your cousin, which has led to the mania you suffer from at present," she stated.

"My cousin? What are you on about?" She pressed her hand to her chest and spoke slowly so they would understand her. "I am Edyth Foster."

The matron stepped forward, narrowing her eyes. "This is your first and only warning. Do not interrupt me. You are to obey me and the rules, or you will be returned to solitary where you can spend your days staring at the wall, contemplating your choices. If you strike one of the nurses or one of your fellow inmates, you will be sent to the violent ward in the Lodge, which will not be pleasant. Repeat the offense of striking or continually speaking out of turn, and you will be recommended for undergoing a treatment. Obey and live in peace. Disobey and, well, we have ways of making you comply. Is that clear?"

A dozen questions sprang to mind, but she was unsure of this woman, and remembering her conversation with Doctor Wentworth, she knew to be afraid. Her body ached for food, so Edyth swallowed her queries, eager to hopefully finish here so she could break her fast.

"Good. Now, I have others to see to this morning. Nurse Madison, please continue."

The nurse clicked her tongue to Edyth as the matron stepped from the room. "You will soon find that if one inmate claims to be the queen of England, ten more will declare themselves an heiress."

"But you see, I actually *am* an heiress." She seized the woman's arm. "If you will only send a message to Raoul Banebridge of the Banebridge Fencing Club, he will reward you handsomely."

The nurse paused in her mocking, tilting her head. "*He* will reward me?"

"Yes." Her parched throat nearly cracked with hope, barely keeping herself from stepping forward. "Yes, if you tell Mr. Banebridge where I am, he will pay you."

Nurse Madison thrust the gown into Edyth's arms. "I'll be sure to do that, duchess."

Edyth's spirit collapsed. "You aren't going to send the message, are you?"

The nurse gave a cackling laugh and slapped her thigh. "You think? This is too easy. Nurse Sweeney and I have a long memory and plenty of time to make your life a living hell after your little show of rebellion on the ferry, lovey. Now, get dressed before I strip you to your chemise myself."

Edyth's skin burned at the open door and the nurse standing over her, eyeing her as she peeled off her soiled gown. Laying it atop her cot, she stroked the bodice, somehow sensing it would be the last she would see of something beautiful, soiled as it was. She loosed her corset and tossed it on top of the gown, drawing a full, ragged breath for the first time since before the ball. She tugged on the thin dress, the fabric scratching her skin, grimacing at the tight fit about the sleeves and waist. She looked down and found that the skirt didn't even reach the top of her ankles. "Do you have anything a few inches longer? This dress appears to have been made for a girl, not a woman. You cannot expect me to wear something so immodest."

"Aw, does the poor duchess want something a little more to her liking?" Nurse Madison thrust her bottom lip out in a mock pout. "Well, you'll lose whatever little padding you do possess soon enough." She nodded pointedly to Edyth's bodice. "No one here keeps much weight on them after a few weeks."

Ignoring her, Edyth wriggled a scarlet-clad foot. "Do you have any shoes for me? These were not made to last for more than one party."

The nurse sniffed. "Our shipment from the charity has been delayed until next week. You'll have to make do with your royal shoes until then, but you'd better watch your back." She motioned Edyth out of the cell before she could inquire why she needed to watch her back over a pair of dancing slippers. "Come on. Breakfast won't be kept warm for anyone."

"But I need to dress my hair," Edyth said before catching herself.

"Your hair will be brushed after breakfast, *my lady*." The nurse spat the title, her fingers clawing the air, motioning Edyth through the door. "Hurry it up. I have much to do this morning."

Moving down the hall, Edyth held her head high despite the grime covering her face, her broken nails, and hair all askew. She paused on the threshold of the dining hall that was a bit smaller than her elegant dining room at home and stared at the row upon row of crude, narrow wood tables and long benches, each setting boasting of two small bowls with a slice of bread tossed on the table beside them, but no flatware in sight.

The patients were already crowding into their seats, a few speaking inanely while rocking back and forth. A woman seated on the far end was fixated on pulling out each eyelash, but from the looks of it, the poor dear didn't have any left to pluck. Her companion continuously rubbed her face with the back of her wrists and hands, her mouth agape and her focus fixed on the ceiling. Edyth looked up and saw naught but a metal pipe.

The nurse pushed her inside, causing her to trip over her feet. The other patients turned as one, their long hair hanging in wild tangles, staring at her as if she were an exhibit, many pointing to her shoes with a look of interest that alarmed her. Edyth regarded the room and paused at the sight of a petite young woman with pretty brown hair and striking, wide staring eyes who was keeping a vacant seat between her and a waifish girl. Judging from the petite woman's cleanliness and the rosy hue in her cheeks, Edyth thought she must be a new arrival to the asylum. Insane or not, this girl would be her best chance of finding out what was going on outside the island. *Maybe she read the papers before she was taken. . .maybe an American heiress was mentioned leaving the city for parts unknown.*

It wouldn't be out of the ordinary for the society column to comment on her. After her disastrous debut season, she had decided to step out of the light of the papers by swearing off attending further parties put on by society matrons, but being one of the wealthiest women in the States, she was still followed by the press. And she was fairly certain her little bout with Jasper Wentworth had made quite the stir among the ladies in attendance at the fencing club's celebration, a few of which were part of the coveted Four Hundred set, a title she had spurned after her humiliation at the hands of Miss Finley and her mother. For once in her life, she hoped the papers had been following her again and at least noted her abrupt absence. *But is two days of not stepping outside enough to garner their interest?* She grunted, for once annoyed at her tendency to stay holed up painting for days on end. *I doubt even the servants are aware of what happened. . .Uncle probably lied to them as well and paid Katie a ridiculous sum to keep silent.*

Edyth slipped into the available seat and peered into the bowls to find one contained tea and the other some sludge that appeared to be oatmeal. She looked about to see where she might find utensils, but as everyone around her was using their fingers, she sucked in her breath and dipped her fingers into the stone-cold concoction. The slimy oats slid from her grasp and returned to the bowl with a plop. *Mm, delicious.*

Her stomach protested, but since she hadn't eaten since the party, she drew in a deep breath and scooped up the fare with her middle three fingers and shoved the oats into her mouth, fairly gagging from the lack of flavor and the texture. She lifted her bowl of tea to wash it down. While it was weak and bore little flavor, at least it was warm and helped abate the taste and wet her parched throat. The liquid stung at the back of her throat and she took a second draft, the tense, inflamed muscles of her throat relaxing a tad. Her body awakened with the food, and she reached for her bread, the blackened crusts proving to be more like a biscotti in consistency but not nearly as enticing, with its hardened dough in the middle that rendered that portion inedible. She bit down on a corner of the bread, wincing as it scratched her gums. She held a finger to her top gum and moaned.

"You have to dip it into your tea," came a birdlike voice beside her.

"Oh?"

The girl nodded, rested a Bible on the table, and opened it to a passage. "You best eat, or you'll get sick. But if you don't want it. . ." Her words and stare lingered on Edyth's portion.

Edyth took one soaked bite and nearly tossed the contents of her stomach. Shuddering, she slid the bread to the girl and watched it vanish in four tea-soaked bites.

"Thank you, Miss—?"

"Please call me Edyth." Any formality under the circumstances seemed preposterous. "They let you read here?"

She dipped her head and smiled. "Poppy Reed. It is a pleasure to meet you. And no. It's against the rules, but they let me because of my parents."

So, parentage can protect you here after all. Good. Maybe she could find a way out of here. "Tell me, Poppy, why are you here?" *You seem as sane as I.*

The girl looked up at her and blinked her long brown lashes. "People say I'm addled."

"Are you?" She rubbed her thumb into her palm against the hunger pains. Bracing herself, she dipped her fingers into the mush and shoved another bite into her mouth, managing to swallow even as her stomach turned against the vile fare.

Poppy shrugged, wrapping both hands around her bowl of tea. "The doctors say I am, so who am I to argue?"

Her nerves bristled. *How many poor girls have they falsely imprisoned?* At the stirring of a nurse doing an inspection as she walked down each long table, Edyth leaned back and watched as the woman jerked an old, battered comb through an elderly inmate's matted white locks, pulling out a chunk of hair and setting the woman to whimpering at what would have made Edyth use a few choice words she had picked up from her years at the fencing club.

She shivered and asked, "Do they do this every morning?"

"They comb our hair the morning after bath night," Poppy replied, and stared at Edyth's oatmeal.

Bath night. She swallowed, thankful that she had at least been spared that humiliation last night. But she couldn't avoid it forever. Edyth forced herself to take one more bite before sliding the oatmeal over to Poppy as well.

The girl finished the contents of the bowl, returned it to Edyth, and looked over her shoulder. "What's that, Papa? Oh yes, I agree."

The hair at the nape of her neck rose. Edyth looked sideways at Poppy and asked slowly, "You see your father?"

"Don't you?" Her eyes grew wide. "He is wearing his best suit today and is looking ever so dapper for Grandmother's birthday. I wanted to go shopping for her gift, but the nurses wouldn't allow me to speak with the matron to even ask for permission."

"Uh. . ." She searched for anything to say that would not vex the girl, but as Poppy became distracted in an animated conversation with her father, Edyth mercifully returned to finishing her weak tea, gathering her courage to speak with the new inmate on the other side of her. Part of her feared that if she found the new girl to be mad as well, she would begin to question the validity of her own claim to sanity.

"She had a fever and lost her parents to it. You best say you see them, else she will grow hysterical." The whisper came from the petite woman at Edyth's other side. "That's what I heard from the lady beside me."

"Y—yes, hello to you, Mr. Reed." She nodded to the air behind Poppy, who went back to munching on her crusts left over from her own bread while the nurse finished another poor soul's combing.

Edyth waited for the nurse to grow distracted with another patient's hair before whispering, "So, why did they send you here? Have you been here long?"

The woman turned her wide eyes to Edyth and answered, "They think I'm mad. But no one will believe me that I just can't remember where I am from. My name is Nellie. Nellie Brown," she said with a faint accent that Edyth could not place. "I only arrived last night."

"Nice to meet you, Nellie." She cracked a smile, finally realizing how many times the inmates must proclaim themselves sane. But Edyth decided to give Nellie the benefit of the doubt nonetheless. After all, wasn't that what she longed for herself?

"Are you mad, Miss. . . ?" Nellie asked.

"My apologies. I'm Edyth Foster." Edyth finished off her now cold tea to keep from bursting into tears at the question. A day and a night alone in the freezing cell had pushed her to the brink of hysterics. She could not afford to give in to her tears here where the staff would respond with anything but kindness. She shook her head. "No. I am not mad. My uncle wanted my fortune and this is the only way he could get it. . .by locking me away from my future." *And along with it, any love I could have with Bane.* "Perhaps you've read something about my being committed in the papers?" She knew it was foolhardy to think that the papers would have printed any news of her absence so soon, but she was desperate to latch on to any bit of hope that perhaps someone had spotted her being taken or that Bane had alerted the newspapers. Once again, she could kick herself for being such a recluse from parties in recent years. No one would miss her, except Bane.

Nellie's eyes widened even more. "Papers? No, I'm sorry I haven't. Why?"

Edyth dropped her gaze to her lap and drew in a breath, steadying herself. "I used to be someone of standing." *Used to be.*

"But didn't you see any doctors? Didn't you tell them what was happening? No one on the different stops here believed that you were being falsely committed?"

Edyth rubbed a finger over a stain on her skirt left from the previous owner. She wondered where the girl was now, but she stopped herself from finishing that thought as the logical answer would not be the desired one. "The only doctors I saw were the biased ones who came to my house, whom I'm certain were paid generously by my uncle, using my own funds, for their diagnosis of insanity."

Nellie twisted her hands on her lap. "I saw many doctors and made many stops along the way here. But all said I was mad as the hatter from that Carroll novel."

Edyth scrunched her mouth, trying to remember the name of the odd novel she had heard about in passing. "*Alice in Wonderland*?"

"Yes, that's the one. I fear that this is a rabbit hole we shall never escape from, don't you?" Nellie glanced over her shoulder, the nurse's approach eminent.

This woman sounds no more mad than I am. Edyth pressed her palm to her stomach to halt the violent churning of the contents. "Do you have any ideas for attempting an escape? I was taken at night, so I was quite disoriented when I arrived at first light, and then I was taken straightaway to a cell by myself for a day and a night."

"I'm sorry to find you in the same predicament as so many others here. It is a hard thing to be sane in this pit that seems to be designed to make us mad." Nellie nodded toward the young Poppy laughing at something the ghost of her father said to her, before giving Edyth a slow shake of her head, sorrow lining her features. "I have no such ideas. . .I have only been here a morning, yet I can already tell that Blackwell's Island is like a human rat trap."

The nurses worked on the patient next to Nellie, ripping the comb through her tangles, exposing inflamed, angry scabs on her scalp, and finished her hair with a long braid down her back. To Edyth's horror, they moved on to Nellie without sanitizing the brush. She shivered. She had never paid much attention to her hair, but she knew Bane found it lovely. But after a week of living in the asylum, she was certain she would be missing whole chunks of her black locks. *Lord, be swift.*

Bane executed a perfect circular parry with a riposte, ending with the tip of his foil at Jasper Wentworth's shoulder, which sent his student into another long monologue. It didn't take any effort for Bane to ignore Jasper and his incessant boasting as they began the second bout.

The Fosters' doctor had indeed come to see Bane yesterday afternoon, and at first he was going to dismiss the doctor without seeing him, but thinking the man might inadvertently help him figure out where Edyth had disappeared to after her claimed illness, he took the appointment. And as he suspected, the doctor's lack of information on the supposed illness confirmed his suspicions that Mr. Foster had sent his niece somewhere, paid the doctor for a false diagnosis, and was using it to his advantage. But *why* was still the festering question.

He twisted his blade upward, disarming Jasper, who laughed and accepted his weapon as they readied themselves for their third bout. He began to drown out Jasper again, but when the Foster name came up, Bane dropped the tip of his foil to the ground, nearly sacrificing his stance. He recovered at the last moment, blocking Jasper's strike, and asked, "What about the Foster family?" He shuffled his feet and thrust his blade in such a way that

Jasper could easily evade its touch.

A gleam sparked in Jasper's eyes as if he knew he held Bane's interest at last. "I probably shouldn't mention any more because of client confidentiality, but I suppose this once it wouldn't hurt. . .if you understand that this is a gentlemen's agreement to keep silent? I would not wish to jeopardize my position as the Foster lawyer."

"Certainly." He paused in their duel and motioned Jasper over to the water stand and out of earshot from any of the other men practicing with Bertram.

Jasper poured a glass from the pitcher of water, and taking his fill, he released a long exhale, trying Bane's patience. But Bane held his emotions intact and waited for the man to finish off his second cup. He focused on the sounds of steel against steel, calming his nerves as it always did.

"Well, not too long ago, the new Mrs. Foster demanded to see the Foster family will. Mr. Foster has never really bothered to see it, or ask about it, so I never looked into it. But, apparently, the missus is the daughter of a lawyer and wanted to look for something." He chuckled. "I, of course, complied by giving her a copy, but I didn't think a woman could be astute enough to sort through the details on her own. However, I underestimated this one. She discovered a very small clause in a very large will, that should Miss Edyth Foster perish without a husband and heir, or should she be declared mad, the fortune would revert back to Boris Foster and his heirs."

Bane's stomach flipped at the odd stipulation. *They wouldn't harm her, would they?* He thought of the stream of dead rose petals in her room, the overturned objects, the broken vase, and her rapier on the floor, and his heart stuttered. The signs all pointed to a struggle, and he could not think of another thing that would explain away such destruction in her room. She had been taken.

Jasper let out a snort. "As you can imagine, after that little discovery, Mrs. Foster grew quite excited and sent me out of the room." He laughed and leaned his elbow against the mantel of the dormant fireplace. "I'm not exactly sure what that woman is planning, but if Edyth doesn't marry and have a child soon, I'm pretty certain they will attempt to commit her to the asylum." He grinned. "However, I am intending to offer my hand to her now that Bertha has seen fit to throw me over for a duke. Even though I was well compensated for my troubles, I do need to marry well to secure my future. Edyth will be desperate enough and, well, I could use a fortune. And as we saw from the party, she does look fine enough in a fashionable gown to tempt me down the aisle."

"Have you attempted such an offer?" Bane asked, only inquiring so he might discover if Jasper knew where Edyth was located.

He shrugged. "Haven't had much of a chance to, but I intend on asking the next time I see her. I have no doubt that she will accept when I present her with the facts. While Edyth and I might have our differences, I'd hate to see a pretty, wealthy girl wilt away in an asylum, and we both know she would rather marry a dandy like me than relinquish her freedom."

Bane ran his thumb over the plain pommel of his sword, measuring his words. "And if they have already taken action? Do you have any idea where they would send her if they had her diagnosed as mad?"

Jasper scratched his chin. "As my father practices at the nearest asylum, I would assume that the obvious choice would be on Blackwell's Island. The entire asylum is designated for women now." He gave a shudder and shook his head. "I went there once to visit my father while he was working, but I did not linger long. It is not a place for the faint of heart."

The scrawled lines on the paper flashed in his mind, and Bane knew the horrible truth. Edyth was trapped on Blackwell's Island.

Chapter Ten

*In rivers, the water that you touch is the last of what has passed
and the first of that which comes; so with present time.*
~ Leonardo da Vinci

After a long morning of cleaning the central rotunda's apartments for the physicians, offices, and parlors with the rest of the women from Hall Six, Edyth's back ached from scrubbing the hard floors, her knees throbbing with each step as she left the dining hall. The midday meal had consisted of not much more than breakfast, with its unsalted food that she barely choked down. Now, her only concern was keeping it down to maintain her strength.

She followed Nellie into the hallway where there was a growing commotion as the women were being herded to a side door. Her stomach fluttered at the thought of possibly stepping outside the building.

"What are you waiting for, girl? Time for the promenade. It's not every day you'll get the chance to stroll outside the fenced yard of the west wing, but we nurses need to see outside the fence every now and again lest we join you wretched souls in your madness." Nurse Madison shoved Edyth into the crowd of women.

"Get a hat and covering from the rack. You have a half hour." The matron shouted instructions, taking a seat in her wooden rocking chair beside the window as she threw back her coffee, the smell making Edyth dizzy.

Edyth pressed her hand to her waist and breathed a prayer of thanks. She hadn't dared to hope that they would be able to go for a stroll about the grounds outside the fenced-in area, much less this soon. This could be her chance. *Please, God, let it be so.*

There was a scramble as the women from Hall Six dove for

hats and cloaks, attempting to snatch those they deemed best. As Edyth didn't particularly care which hat she wore, she hung back to avoid being trampled, but at the end of the scramble, she was left with nothing but a tiny straw sailor hat that would do little to block the wind and a cloak that was more threads than fabric. But as the disgusting piece was brown, it would help her blend into her surroundings should she have a chance of escape and need to hide somewhere on the island.

The women queued up in a long line, and spotting Nellie again, Edyth wove her way to Nellie's side.

"Are you enjoying your stay? I quite liked the calisthenics that they boasted of in their promotions of the asylum," Nellie commented, her light tone sounding out of place.

Is she mad? Edyth snapped her head toward Nellie and nearly laughed at the inane smile at the corner of Nellie's mouth, revealing her teasing.

Nellie joined in her giggles. "If I do not make some mild attempt at humor, I will be driven mad by the alleged gentle treatment of their patients." She tied her cloak at her throat and pressed her lips together at Edyth's wrap as Poppy joined them.

Poppy shook her head, clicking her tongue in disapproval. "You need to be faster, Edyth. You can never tell how chilly it is outside until it's too late to find a good wrap, but usually the winds ripping across the island can chill you to the bone, and you will be hard-pressed to warm yourself upon your return." She unfastened her hat and handed it to Edyth. "I managed to secure the warmest wrap, so let's swap hats. Mine offers far more protection than that paltry thing."

Edyth swallowed back the sudden lump in her throat at this sweet girl's offering and that she would willingly sacrifice her own comfort to keep a stranger warm. With stiff fingers, she untied the tattered, stained ribbons that once may have been a vibrant green but were now a mottled brown. She handed the hat to Poppy, grateful for the ratty fur-trimmed bluish bonnet Poppy held out to her in return. It possessed the fierce aroma of a wet mutt, but it would be warm. "Thank you," she whispered.

Edyth fairly shook with the anticipation of being in the fresh air again and stepped through the threshold to the unfettered grounds at the south wing, drawing in a deep breath of the crisp, sweet air that she had always taken for granted. She looked about the open grounds and thought of the lone gate at the end of the asylum's road separating her from the ferry. If she could only get away from the group without being noticed, perhaps she could escape through the sparsely wooded area and swim for it.

Her fists clenched at the thought of what she would do when she finally confronted her uncle and aunt. . .if she could without fear of being returned to the island. While part of her longed to settle the score with the couple who had betrayed and abandoned her, she hated that inkling of hope that remained inside her heart that her uncle would forsake his wife's scheme and come to his senses and her rescue. She wanted to loathe him, much like she had the night of his betrayal. But now, all that remained was a deep sorrow, a sense of loss of her uncle's love that she had apparently never possessed. Her new aunt was another matter entirely. Edyth had no qualms of throwing that shrew from her home. The woman had poisoned her uncle towards Edyth, of that she was certain.

But what of his declaration of not wanting her, or his claim of her grandmother's passing? No, she could not ignore those allegations like she had ignored anything unpleasant in her past by keeping busy. She would have to deal with the pain or it would fester and grow into something else entirely. She reached out and snapped off a naked twig and ran her fingers over the soft bark, when someone reached out and slapped her hands, causing her to drop it.

She jerked back as Nurse Sweeney's eyes burned into her. "Fall in line. Do not touch anything. You are to do nothing but walk. If you try to do anything else, you will be sent back inside at once. When we are outside the fenced area, you are to keep your hands at your sides or clasped at all times, else you will ruin the promenade for the rest of us. The matron does not allow anyone to bend the rules, understand?"

Edyth gave a short nod and tucked her smarting hands under her arms to keep from striking the woman, watching her move on to another unfortunate soul. *How dare she hit me over nothing.*

Poppy shook her head and whispered, "I'm sorry. I should have warned you, but I didn't think. If we had taken our shorter walk in the west wing's fenced yard, it wouldn't have been a problem, but some days the nurses want to take the longer, scenic walk. They are almost just as much prisoners as we are."

"It is of little consequence. My hands don't hurt anymore," Edyth replied, her voice rough from suppressed anger.

"They've struck you before, I take it," Nellie said, her eyes widening under her fringe of bangs that would be pretty if curled but on the island were a frizzled mess.

Edyth didn't dare think what she looked like now without her special concoctions to tame her wild locks and lotions to soothe her reddened skin. Edyth lifted her eyes skyward, but at the sight of the blue darkening into the water-colored painted sky of dusk, her heart became lighter if only for a moment. "Yes."

Nellie exhaled with a grunt and shook her head. "I wish the doctors would protect us more, but merely the claim of being mad is enough for them to commit us and leave us to the mercy of the staff. It already feels as if I've been here for an eternity."

"I've been here for years," Poppy whispered, keeping her hands clasped in front of her skirts.

"Do you know of any weak points?" Edyth asked, taking Poppy's elbow before dropping it in fear of the nurse's heavy hand and threat.

"What?" Poppy blinked as if the thought had never occurred to her.

Dear girl. She probably has no one to run home to. "Are there any points where escape is possible? Perhaps the river? I might take the risk and swim."

The woman in front of them laughed softly and replied in a low voice, "If the river was a viable option, I would have taken it long before now, and so would have every poor soul who has ever seen the inside of the Gray Chamber, but the river is not called Hell's Gate for nothing. Many a ship has gone down in those dark waters, and anyone fool enough to attempt swimming to shore would drown. No. You best act without emotion, and hopefully you will be spared from ever finding out what they do inside that room." Without another word, the woman quickened her pace and joined another patient a few rows up.

Edyth grunted. "No matter what she says, I *know* I can do this. I am a very strong swimmer."

Poppy grasped her hand. "If you make a run for the river, it has to be when we near this next corner. There should be some foliage where you can hide yourself. From what the nurses say, this side of the island is not as populated, but be warned, there is a lighthouse on the northernmost point. If the guard there spots you, there will be no hope for escape."

Edyth bit her lip. Dare she trust a mad girl for information? She weighed it quickly, thinking that, yes, while Poppy talked to ghosts, everything else about her seemed sound. Besides, if she didn't try, Edyth did not know if or when another chance would come.

Nellie wrung her hands, whispering, "But won't it be dangerous? You could drown."

"More dangerous than her undergoing a treatment in the Gray Chamber if they catch her committing some small offense, such as snapping a second twig? They would see that as open defiance." Poppy shook her head. "That happened to me once in the beginning, and I have not made the mistake again."

Edyth pressed her sweaty palms together. "What is the Gray Chamber?"

Poppy's gaze shifted. "It is where they administer treatment that is not fit for dogs."

Edyth shivered, her decision made. "The nurses and staff have marked me for punishment, and I cannot give them the chance to act first." She looked ahead to the south side of the island and shook her head at the thought of the many buildings along the road to the ferry. "No. I cannot risk taking the roads. I'd be spotted for certain. I will swim for it."

"But the currents." Nellie twisted her fingers around her wrist as if she were fidgeting with a phantom bracelet of old before catching herself and dropping her hands to her sides.

"Hush." Edyth seized her hand. "I would not risk crossing the river if I were not such a strong swimmer, and besides, we can see the city from the shore. It is not too far. Trust me. I can do this, and you need not fear your conscience for allowing me to go. You know that I must try or loathe myself for the rest of my miserable days under this roof."

"But what is so important on the other side of the river to risk your life to have?" Poppy asked.

"The freedom to love a man who was meant to be my husband," Edyth answered simply.

Poppy slowly nodded. "I have never loved a boy, but if I had, I would try to reach him with every breath of my lungs. But I have no one except Papa, who is here with me."

Nellie clasped Edyth's hands. "If you are certain, then I will cover for you as long as possible. Best of luck."

"I will pray for your safety, dear Edyth." Poppy pressed a quick kiss onto Edyth's cheek.

Edyth squeezed her newfound friends' hands and switched places with Nellie so that she would be on the outside of the group.

They rounded the corner, where Edyth spied the bushes and waited until it was her turn to pass by. She dove for cover, rolling to her feet and holding her breath, waiting and staying crouched. *One, two, three,* she counted until the last of the women and nurses passed her. Heart pounding, she viewed the group as they slowly marched up the narrow steps and into the building. When the last woman had vanished, Edyth scanned the area surrounding her and, seeing no one, spied another patch of trees about twenty yards from the clump of bushes she was hiding behind. She searched the long windows lining the sides of the building where the matron could be watching from her chair.

Not daring to wait a minute longer for fear that the alarm bell would sound, she slipped her feet out of her useless crimson shoes. Gripping them in one hand, she sank her toes into the freezing earth and bolted for the tree line, her arms pumping at her sides. Reaching a tree, she pressed her back against the bark and listened. But no alarm sounded. Nothing sounded except the pounding of her pulse in her ears.

Drawing a deep breath, she sprinted through the sparse wood, branches slapping her cheeks and dried twigs biting into her soles as she sprinted for the shoreline. Pausing in the brush, she removed her hat and slipped off her thin gown and rolled them and her slippers into her cloak and tied the ends into a bundle. She would rather leave the filthy, lice-ridden items, but she would need them when she made it to the other side and to Bane. Her tears threatened to well at the thought of him, but she straightened her shoulders and cleared her mind. If she was going to make it across, she needed to be focused on the river and nothing else.

Edyth stepped forward in only her chemise and drawers as twilight darkened into night and the scent of impending rain drifted to her in the cool air. She waded into the reeds at the base of the bank, sucking in her breath as the icy waters stung her skin and the mud curled between her toes. Stepping deeper, her drawers billowed out atop the water until the bank dipped and she sank to her waist. Stifling her gasp, she kept her arms out of the freezing waters as long as she was able, but as the river continued to deepen, she was forced to swim. Holding the bundle out of the water as best as she could, she kicked her legs underwater and pulled with one arm to silently cross the river toward home.

The water about her swirled, and she felt the current's steady pull. It grew too strong to swim with only one arm, so she moved the foul bundle to her mouth, biting down while she used both her arms to stroke. *I can do this.* She willed her teeth not to chatter, for once that began, she would never tame her mind over the freezing water. *Stroke and pull. Stroke and pull.* She kept her mind on her form as if this were merely an exercise that she used to perform with her mother during those summers spent at their cottage in Newport. She hadn't been back since the accident. She was afraid her happy memories of those times with her mother and father would become tainted with the sorrow that shadowed her.

A bell jarred the night, and she started back to life with a muffled cry, knowing she didn't have time to waste. Releasing her bundle, she increased her pace along with the frantic peal of the bell as the lighthouse beam swept the island and waters once, twice, and then held on her.

Using her arms to stroke above her head and pulling the water underneath her body, she kept her head above the freezing water and saw that she was nearing the shoreline. Three minutes more and she would be there. *Dear God. Please.* Her breaths came in sharp pants as a stitch pierced her side. She could no longer feel her limbs, but she kept them moving, her mind stalwart.

Men's cries wafted across the water, and with them, the waves grew, knocking her under, sending her tumbling head over heels, and disorienting her. Her cheeks bursting, she twisted around, uncertain which way was up as time drew the air from her lungs. The water churned beside her, and she felt arms encircle her waist and draw her upward until she burst through the surface, gasping for air and blinking in the light beaming from the house and lantern light on the ferry.

The current must have pulled her back to the ferry's route. "No!" She screamed again and again, kicking the man holding her and pounding her fists into his back, but two days without proper nourishment and the freezing swim had taken their toll. "God. No." She wailed, begging the man to allow her to go home, bribing him, threatening him, and weeping.

"Why, calm down, little lady. Don't you know I am taking you home?" he cooed as hands drew them aboard. The action flickered an image in the recesses of her mind, but as fast as it had appeared, it vanished, leaving her shivering on the ferry's deck in a puddle.

The man's stare flitted to the side and she at once remembered her state of undress. She crossed her arms over her chest, quaking, afraid to even whisper the hope-laced word. "Home?"

"Yes, the asylum has been asking about you. You'll be home in two shakes of a lamb's tail."

She dove for the railing and was met with splintering pain.

Chapter Eleven

*Everything that is painted directly and on the spot
has always a strength, a power, a vivacity of touch.*
~ Eugène Boudin

Bane clenched and unclenched his fists as he paced the length of Edyth's reception room, waiting on Miss Birch to join him. He had sent messages to Blackwell's Island multiple times to no avail, and he knew the reason behind the silence had to be because of some stipulation set into place by Mr. Foster. He was fairly certain the only way he was going to gain entrance into the asylum was if he had a relation of Edyth's at his side. So, he had waited impatiently for Miss Birch to return home from whatever place she had been hiding.

Bane watched as the crystals of the chandelier above him swayed and clinked against themselves with each step of someone upstairs. He studied the coved ceilings and exhaled, determined not to appear panicked. He looked at the long portrait on the left wall of a woman who bore a strong resemblance to Edyth but wasn't the woman he remembered as her mother. He stepped toward it to read the gilded plaque on the bottom of the frame. LADY EDYTH HORTENSE BLAKELY. Edyth had inherited her grandmother's dark eyes. He ran his fingers through his hair, the hope of being distracted vanishing as concern for the woman he loved threatened to paralyze him yet again.

Miss Birch appeared in the door in a stylish filmy dinner gown of green. "Why, if it isn't Mr. Banebridge. What a pleasure it is to hear that you have been calling for me in my absence. I didn't know you were going to join us for dinner."

"Miss Birch." He gave her a sharp bow. "I have to admit that I have been rather frantic for your return."

She sent him a soft smile and folded her hands in front of her skirt. "So it would seem, and while I am flattered by your attention, I do not think it would be wise for us to form an attachment given—"

"That's not the reason why I am calling. Do you know where your cousin is residing? I think I know, but I want to hear from you. . .if you do."

"That's an odd thing to ask, but yes, I do. When I returned from the Manhattan Beach Hotel, my stepfather informed me that she is off visiting her friend down in New Orleans."

Another lie from Mr. Foster, no doubt. He inwardly groaned at the loss of time, needlessly wasted on waiting when Miss Birch had been so close.

"But I have to admit that I thought it rather peculiar, because she has never mentioned a friend in New Orleans, but, of course, we haven't known each other that long, so it's not all that strange, I suppose. Why do you ask? Where do you think she is?" Miss Birch's voice grew concerned.

Bane could see in her features that she had believed what her stepfather told her even as doubt was now clouding her eyes. He ran his fingers through his hair and sighed. "I had misgivings that Mr. Foster would create just such a story to cover his tracks. I prayed that Edyth's absence was because she was seeking legal help without the threat of being found and taken, but I now fear that Mr. Foster did not even give her a chance to hire a lawyer."

"B—but why *wouldn't* Edyth be in New Orleans? And why on earth would she need a lawyer?" She crossed the room and clutched his arm. "Tell me. Is my cousin in trouble?"

He twisted his hat in his grip, the word sticking in his throat. "Yes."

She clapped her hand over her mouth, the blond curls framing her face atremble.

"I have reason to believe from your stepfather's lawyer and from evidence I found in her bedroom that—"

"You were in her bedroom? But you are not engaged to my cousin, unless something has happened since I left?" Her eyes widened. "Is that why you are so worried that she is missing? Did you two have an argument?"

Bane tossed his hat onto a chair and held his hand up, frustrated at the flow of questions. "Please, Miss Birch, cease your interjections and allow me to finish. It doesn't matter that I was in her bedroom, for she was not there. I had to check to ensure her safety. However, what I found there was anything but reassuring. Her room was in utter chaos and held signs of a struggle."

She slapped her hand over her mouth again. "Dear Lord in heaven, you don't think she was kidnapped?"

He nodded. "That is exactly what I think happened. But not for ransom, rather something far more dangerous. After I spoke with your father's lawyer, Jasper Wentworth, two days ago, I've been anxiously waiting for your return to see if you knew anything of her fate. I hoped against all evidence to the contrary that Edyth was not committed to the Women's Lunatic Asylum on Blackwell's Island."

Lavinia clutched the back of the Queen Anne's chair, her perfectly shaped nails digging into the gilded wood. "Where Doctor Hawkins works? Certainly you don't think she is in that wretched place?"

"I found some scribblings on her desk, and from my conversation with Wentworth and the asylum's lack of response, I am led to believe that she is indeed there. I have sent messages to the asylum for the past two days and this morning and afternoon, but no one has answered. I have a suspicion that your uncle ordered that no one be given word of her whereabouts if they are not family. That's the only reason I can think of that they would ignore my messages. And now that I have spoken with you, I will be taking the first ferry to the island tomorrow morning to see for myself.

Will you come with me in order to gain us access to see her?"

"Of course," she replied, sounding a bit breathless as she paced to the window, wringing her hands. "This is terrible. But why have you waited until now to go to the island?"

"As I said, if my messages are being blocked, I fear I have no chance of getting inside. I decided it was better to wait for your return than to alert your uncle that I was making inquiries at the island. If we discover nothing tomorrow, I am hiring an investigator. This has become too much for me to try to figure out on my own." He ran his fingers through his hair with a grunt, muttering, "I'm a fencing master, not a detective."

"Well, there's no need to jump to conclusions. However, from what I've heard from Doctor Hawkins, your guess is correct in that most patients can only have visits from their family. We should have access unless it is in my stepfather's instructions to refuse even me admission, but we can try."

Bane shoved his hands into his pockets and happened to glance out the window and see Doctor Hawkins hopping out of his carriage. "There might be another way to enter should we be barred. Doctor Hawkins can get us inside."

"True, but it might be a little tricky even for him, since he has only just started working in the asylum. But I'm certain if anyone would know anything about our dear Edyth, it would be Roger—I mean Doctor Hawkins." She blushed and corrected herself.

"If that is true, then why wouldn't he have recognized her already and told you about it?"

"Doctor Hawkins told me that it is a large facility that is fairly bursting at the seams with patients. And if my uncle has her locked away, it makes sense that Roger has not seen her yet. But if we can get him to sneak us inside, we can surely save her."

"Save who?" Roger appeared in the doorway in his dinner coat.

She crossed the room and drew him inside before closing the door. "We don't have much time before Mr. and Mrs. Foster join us." And within a matter of minutes, Miss Birch had informed him of Bane's findings.

Roger frowned. "I, of course, will try to take you inside. My shift begins at eight o'clock tomorrow morning. But surely your presence and Mr. Banebridge's is not necessary. I could find out all you seek without you, and then we could formulate a plan."

Hope stirred within him at long last and Bane ached to act. "I know it is not *necessary*, but I need to find her now. I need to see her for myself, or at least try, else spend the day in agony, wishing I had gone."

"I understand, but we must proceed with caution and not deviate from the standard schedule if we do not wish to arouse suspicion." Miss Birch rested her hand on his arm. "We can at least take comfort in the fact that she is being well looked after and is in no danger at present."

"Well, uh, I don't know how well looked after she is if I haven't seen her," said Roger. "There are limits to what the families of patients see at the asylum. And as the newest doctor, they have only shown me the asylum's best floor so far, secretly hoping that I will not be appalled with what I find. Or so Jasper Wentworth has told me. His father works there."

Bane ignored the fact that this man was friends with Jasper and waved him on. "When will you see the other floors of the asylum?"

"That I can answer. One of the doctors will personally be escorting me about the building the whole of next week. I am to see what they call the Lodge, which is the women's violent ward. However, I first must sign some sort of document that states I will not disclose any of the patients' health, the swearing of which is standard for patient confidentiality. But I wasn't anticipating the stipulation that if I discuss any of the conditions or internal workings of the asylum with anyone outside the island, my position will be in jeopardy."

Bane clenched his jaw at the phrase "violent ward." And a vow of silence did not bode well for the treatment of the patients on the island.

"Will you stay for dinner, Mr. Banebridge?" Miss Birch asked, nodding toward the door and alerting them to the turning knob and Mr. and Mrs. Foster's entrance.

"Lavinia, you know it is terribly impolite to invite guests to dine without consulting the hosts. I am afraid that tonight is not convenient, for the staff have only prepared enough for the four of us." Mrs. Foster looked pointedly at Bane while she crossed the room on her husband's arm.

Bane bowed. "I was just departing, ma'am, but before I take my leave, Miss Birch said Edyth has left New York for New Orleans?"

Mrs. Foster's neck grew splotchy. "Yes. Why do you ask?"

"I was wondering if you knew at which hotel Miss Foster is staying? I'd like to send her a telegram."

"Of course. She is not staying at a hotel at present, but I should know by morning which she has chosen." Mr. Foster stumbled over his explanation, making Bane's palms sweat with the thought of Edyth being in trouble.

"Thank you. I'll send her a telegram once you send me her address," Bane replied.

"Do," Mr. Foster growled. He turned, took his wife's arm, and motioned for the group to follow through to the dining room.

His unexpected answer gave Bane pause. Was Mr. Foster simply calling his bluff, or was he actually telling the truth that Edyth was not on the island?

❧

Edyth squinted in the moonlight breaking against the whitewashed wall. She turned her head to find herself in a different room, this one with bars on the inside of the windows instead of outside the windowpanes. A small difference, but one that disturbed her to the core. And then she remembered, her body quaking under her damp gown. They had taken her to the Lodge upon her return. She crossed the room and pressed her ear to the door before a deafening scream of a patient in the hallway sent her scrambling backward. From her position on the floor she caught the continual *tap, tap, tap* against the adjoining cell wall.

"Hello? Is anyone there? Hello?" She scooted to the wall and pressed her arms against it as if embracing the other poor soul trapped in this underworld. The tapping ceased before the patient began pounding, accompanied by a guttural scream that filled the air. The clanging of keys echoed in the hallway, followed by the shouts of orderlies entering the room and then the sound of flesh hitting flesh. Then, nothing but sobs.

"Lord, save me from this place." Edyth huddled in the corner, hugging her knees to her chest and rocking back and forth. How could a place as horrible as the asylum become even worse? She ached for the comfort of scripture. Why hadn't she spent time memorizing passages? She could kick herself for taking the privilege of reading them for granted.

Edyth's focus locked on some scratch marks in the baseboard under the cot. Curious, she crawled under, the cold of the floor seeping into her bones. She made out *E.H.B.* with a little heart carved out followed by the initials *B.B.* She stared at the letters that looked like they had been painstakingly scratched out with someone's fingernails. She ran her fingers over the initials, wondering who they had belonged to. The person in this cell before her must not have been completely out of her mind to carve such a tender memory on the baseboard. Her heart ached for the love that this so-called madwoman felt for *B.B.*

With trembling hands, she began picking away at the rotting wood and carved *E.F. loves R.B.* Seeing their initials side by side made her smile. At least their names could be together. She traced Bane's initials and wished he would allow her to call him by his Christian name. Raoul was a romantic name to be sure, but Bane suited his strength.

The rattling of the keys at her door sent her body to quivering, but she rose, positioning herself in the defensive position Bane had drilled into her. She would not attack them for fear of what they would do to her, but she would not allow them to hit her again.

The wide form filling the door knocked the breath out of her lungs. "Uncle! Are you here to take me home?"

Ignoring her question, Uncle Boris strode into her room as if he owned it. He probably did, for she was certain that he paid for everyone's silence with *her* money. He nodded with approval. "I see you are settling in favorably, Niece, and while it's not the Manhattan Beach Hotel, I'd say this is what a petulant child deserves."

No. Of course he didn't mean to set her free. Why had she even allowed herself to hope? She knew better. She stepped forward, clenching her fists and itching for a weapon, but if she attacked him now with all the witnesses in the hall, she would never prove her sanity. "Petulant child? Because I wouldn't sign over my fortune to you? How dare you. Free me at once, and I will have the judge take pity on you and not have you committed to the men's asylum yourself for your inane scheming."

Uncle Boris threw his head back and gave a short, harsh laugh. "My dear, it is amusing that you honestly think someone would take *your* word over mine. You are never getting out of here."

She felt the bile rise in her throat. "People will soon notice my absence, if they haven't already."

"Yes, I am sure the Banebridge family will miss you, but not for the reason you may think. Rather, they will be sad to hear of your untimely death."

Despite her desperate attempts to maintain control of her emotions, her entire body began to quake again. Surely the man would not have her murdered? Edyth thought of the life that was being stripped away from her, a future with a husband and children. She thought of Bane and the love that was only beginning to blossom between the two of them. Would her uncle be so cruel as to take everything from her, even life itself? She seized his jacket sleeve. "You can have it all. I will sign over my fortune. Release me, and you'll never hear from me again."

He chuckled. "Why would I do that when I have already told everyone that you are away in New Orleans? And while in the French Quarter, which is a dangerous place for a woman to roam about unescorted at night, I believe you will meet with a tragic death and your money will revert to me without even a hint of scandal. Your death will stay any prying questions out of respect for my great loss." He moved out from under her hand and brushed off his jacket, his lip curling at the smudge of dirt she had left from the rotting baseboard. "No one knows that you are here, so I will be free to live my life with my wife and child."

She narrowed her gaze. *Child?* She remembered Mrs. Foster standing on the threshold with her hand on her abdomen, goading Edyth. *That woman is with child?* She swallowed against the bitterness that seeded in her heart that the woman who had locked her away from her future was going to have everything Edyth had dreamed of since her parents died. A husband, a baby, a home where she felt free to be herself without judgement.

She clenched her fists, steeling herself against her rising despair, and gave him what she hoped was a confident smile. "The records are easy enough to access, Uncle. Anyone can look up Edyth Foster and—"

"True, but there is no Edyth Foster in the books at this asylum. Nor has there ever been. Mrs. Foster and I have taken great care in the details."

"What? How?" Edyth's hands fell limply to her sides. How could she be imprisoned here if her name wasn't even recorded?

"Money, my dear. Money."

Bile singed the back of her throat as she curled around her hand pressing to her stomach. All it took was a dishonorable man's word against an unwanted female to get her committed and a bribe to silence the staff of her fate.

"As I was saying, I have rented a room for you in the famous Commercial Hotel in New Orleans, where you will be seen and served before meeting with an accident. The actress I hired was thrilled with the sum I provided. As far as anyone knows, Edyth Foster is in New Orleans, and here, you are just some unfortunate soul that happens to be related to me that I wish to forget." He turned his lips up into a sneer. "And believe me, I will forget you. I informed everyone here on staff that you fancy yourself to be your distant heiress relation and that you call yourself Edyth. However, they are to only call you by nonsensical titles. No one will ever find you. No one."

Nurse Madison's strange words clicked into place. *"Edyth Foster is dead."* Her legs gave away and she fell to her knees on the hard floor.

"Such theatrics will not move me." He snapped his fingers, and the male attendants behind him brought in three large crates. "I have a gift for you to reward you for your little escape attempt. You almost removed yourself from the game for me with that one, and I wholly appreciate it."

She lifted her head, staring at him with blank eyes.

The attendants flipped their crates over, dumping the contents in her chamber. Before she could register what they were kicking about in her cell, the scent of thousands of dead rose petals filled her senses. The sight of them turned her stomach, wrenching her back to that horrible day when she buried her parents and the weeks afterward when the roses in her parents' room were left to rot per her uncle's instructions not to touch their belongings.

"No! Remove them." She turned wild eyes to her uncle. When he didn't budge, she scooped up an armful of the dead petals and bolted for the door, attempting to toss them into the hall, but two of the attendants moved to block the door, sending her sprawling back onto the rose-strewn floor as she shouted, "Get them out. Get them all out! Uncle. Uncle Boris!" She screamed his name over and over, but he left her alone with the reminder of her parents' death. She screamed and sobbed until her wails turned to silent weeping and she curled onto her cot, facing the blank wall, begging God to rescue her.

Chapter Twelve

*Practice what you know, and it will help to make
clear what now you do not know.*
~ Rembrandt

Bane scowled, his gaze fixed on the unreachable island that was veiled in fog. His steps sounded hollow on the dock as a seagull's cry pierced his thoughts along with the clanging of a ship's bell. He marched down the dock and returned to Miss Birch, who was waiting impatiently for Doctor Hawkins while keeping a safe distance between herself and the dockworkers. "The ticket master just informed me that the first ferry left before its scheduled departure time. From what I was able to gather, some rich gentleman paid the captain a preposterous amount, but the man wouldn't officially confirm the rumor even though he has no qualms of spreading it." He gritted his teeth. "We'll just have to find another means of reaching the island this morning."

"This is utterly ridiculous." Miss Birch crossed her arms, emitting an exasperated sigh. "I have never heard of someone hiring an entire ferry. I mean, if it were a yacht or even a small boat, certainly, but a giant, filthy, flea-ridden ferry? Nonsense." She checked her jeweled ladies' watch pin. "Doctor Hawkins should be here soon, but how will we get to the island if there is not a ferry to take us?"

Bane dug his hands into his pockets and fished around for coins, wishing he had enough to hire a ferry himself, or even a boat. Grunting at his stinging pride, he looked at his companion. "Miss Birch? Do you have sufficient funds to hire a boat? Perhaps if we combine our efforts?"

She opened her reticule and withdrew her coin purse, giving it a shake and grimacing at the jingle of two lonely coins. "I don't have much pin money left from my recent shopping trip, but I'm sure if we do not have enough together, the good doctor will be more than happy to oblige."

She dumped the contents of her money pouch into his hand, and they counted out their meager amount before approaching the nearest vessel large enough to accommodate them with a man working it. Miss Birch pressed her lace-trimmed handkerchief over her mouth and nose as the scent of rotting fish grew with every step, but Bane couldn't fault her for it, as he had to swallow to keep his own stomach under control.

The gruff sailor regarded them and hoisted a bucket to the rail, wide-eyed fish heads and guts sloshing to the floor of his boat, causing Lavinia to turn her head and moan into her puffed yellow sleeve, a ridiculous color to wear to an asylum. Was she trying to provoke the inmates?

Bane cleared his throat. "Excuse me, sir, would you be willing to take us to Blackwell's Island in your—" He motioned to the rowboat, searching for the right words. "Fine vessel? The ferry departed ahead of schedule."

"So you think I can drop everything and attend to your needs since you are a gentleman?" He took in Miss Birch's extravagant gown along with Bane's plain suit, no doubt determining the price. He tilted the bucket and sent the vile scum into the East River, the splatter reaching Miss Birch's skirts.

With a shriek, she jumped behind Bane and clutched his sleeve. "Have a care, sir."

Bane murmured through his smile, "Do not offend the man, else we may have to seek passage with someone less to your liking."

"I suppose I could, but it will cost you," the man replied with a rueful grin. He pulled a pipe from his pocket that had bits of tobacco sticking out of the bowl, struck his match on the bottom of his worn boot, and drew and released three puffs.

Knowing they would need funds for the ferry to return home,

Bane kept a small sum hidden in his pocket and offered the man the rest. The old sailor grunted and nodded to Bane's stiff hat. "I'll take that along with your money."

"What would you need a hat like this for?" He nearly snorted, but Miss Birch elbowed him in the ribs, reminding him of the urgency of their mission. "Of course. One hat and a dollar and a half." He poured the coins into the man's hand and handed over his hat, the breeze whipping through his hair.

"There you are!" Roger Hawkins trotted up to them carrying a black leather case at his side and, without questioning what they were about, followed them into the vessel and offered his hand to Miss Birch. The old sailor assumed his position at the oars and stroke by stroke pulled them out of the dock and into the rough, murky waters toward Blackwell's Island.

As they approached the island, its brilliant fall hues and foggy shores evoked an admiration Bane had not been expecting. Devoid of crowded buildings and masses of people, it possessed an eerie calm. Perhaps he wouldn't find Edyth in such a terrible way after all. Maybe Jasper Wentworth had been exaggerating to get to him. He thought of the paunchy doctor whom he fenced with on occasion who worked on the island. Bane chewed the inside of his cheek. The doctor could have been complimentary of the island because he worked at the institution. Bane shrugged, telling himself that he was most likely overthinking things, as usual.

He turned his attention to Miss Birch and Roger, chattering on and on. Wasn't she in the least bit concerned about her cousin? Spotting the brightness in her cheeks and the glint in Roger's eyes, he knew they were taken with one another, but the thought that they were more concerned with impressing one another than with finding Edyth caused him to wonder if Miss Birch was a part of this elaborate scheme. Was he simply a pawn in Miss Birch and her mother and stepfather's game to seize Edyth's inheritance? But, looking at the blond beauty, he didn't see any of the bitterness that her mother possessed. Perhaps her time in Paris had kept her from being poisoned by the woman's greed.

He returned his attention to the choppy waters, studying the shore as the fog began to clear, anxious to see her. *Lord, let me be wrong. I wish to find Edyth more than anything, but I ache at the thought that she is trapped here.* Not knowing what else to pray, he sank his face between his hands and sought to turn his mounting concerns over to God, but he failed miserably. "Trust," he murmured, dredging up the proverb from the cellar of his heart. *"Trust in the Lord with all thine heart; and lean not unto thine own understanding. In all thy ways acknowledge him, and he shall direct thy paths."* He exhaled his anxiety. "Make the path known. Show me the way, Lord," he whispered, his words catching in the wind and drifting away.

They finally reached the island and disembarked, Miss Birch gripping Roger's arm and appearing rather green. Leaving her to Roger's care, Bane hired a carriage that looked like it had seen far better days, but it was either that or a disgusting-looking closed wagon with AMBULANCE in faded red paint on the side.

Passing the alms and workhouses on the right, the carriage turned down a well-kept drive that was surprisingly pleasant, with the beauty of the grounds surrounding them and the vibrant leaves gently fluttering to the earth in graceful dips and sways to find rest in the grass still damp with morning dew. Even if Edyth was here, surely he would find her contentedly working on her paintings. He smiled at the thought of his busy friend. If she wasn't riding, she was painting, or fencing with him. Bane never knew her *not* to be doing something. Sometimes he rather suspected that she didn't like being alone with her thoughts. And if she happened to be alone, she kept her hands busy with the sketchbook and stubby pencil she always kept at the ready in that giant, frumpy reticule of hers. The sketchbook thumped against his heart in his jacket pocket. He hadn't opened it since that day in the museum when he had flipped through it, teasing her. He felt that it was somehow an invasion of her privacy now to open it without her knowledge.

Seeing her closetful of paintings of those three reaching hands for the first time was rather disconcerting, especially the chilling underwater settings, but there were some less disturbing, set in meadows and holding flowers. There were always three, grasping, reaching, trying to touch one another. He would have to ask her why and what they meant. He understood the need for discipline and the power of practicing, but these paintings were bordering on an unhealthy obsession. He shook his head. He knew Edyth. She was not insane. She was only. . .eccentric. But beyond her peculiarities was a woman who possessed a compassion for helpless creatures that sometimes turned to a fierce temper when threatened. He had always admired her love for the defenseless and how she went out of her way to assist the youngest of his students to ensure that they knew how to hold and wield their weapons correctly.

The carriage halted in front of a massive rotunda of gray stone with three-story wings jutting out from the central dome. The building was surrounded by barren trees, their branches reaching out to one another. He shook his head to dismiss Edyth's art from his mind.

Roger paid the driver, and they marched up the stone steps and into the building, their footsteps echoing against the largely vacant hall as they approached the tall desk that was in the front middle of the octagon tower with a small seating area to the side. Behind it, the staircase began at the base of the rotunda and crawled its way around the sides. The stairs accessed the three stories and looked to continue up to the tower's viewing platform of the island with an opulent chandelier hanging in the center, lighting all three levels.

"Good morning, Miss Monroe." Roger greeted the secretary standing behind the front desk, giving her a smile that sent the young woman to giggling and blushing, which Bane noticed sent Miss Birch's brows into a furrow.

"Doctor Hawkins, always a pleasure. Do you have need of

something from me today?" The hope tinting her words brought a glare from the woman at his side.

"I need to inquire after a Miss Edyth Foster who should have been committed in the past week or so," Roger replied.

"Let me see...Miss Foster. Miss Foster." She removed her spectacles from her desk, perched them on the bridge of her nose, and flipped through her ledger to a section in the middle. She scanned the lines with her finger, meticulously murmuring each name starting with *F* to herself when she passed over them. She removed her wire-rimmed spectacles and looked up to him with a regretful smile, blinking her stubby blond lashes. "I am sorry, Doctor Hawkins, but there is no Edyth Foster in my ledger. Are you certain that is her name?"

Bane gripped the top of the desk, his fingers digging into the polished wood. "There has to be some sort of mistake. Would you mind checking again?" His hostile tone made Miss Birch tap his elbow, but he ignored her.

The secretary pressed her lips into a thin line. "There obviously *has* been a misunderstanding, and not on my part. The name Edyth Foster is not written anywhere in my ledger."

"I suppose you never make mistakes, do you? Or were you paid for your silence? Whatever it was, I'll double—"

Miss Birch tugged on his arm once more, whispering, "You are insulting the woman." She sent her an apologetic smile. "You'll have to forgive him. He is in love, and that tends to make even the most reasonable of men illogical. For the sake of his devotion to the maiden, would you mind checking again?"

Miss Monroe's expression lightened a shade, but she still made a great show of sighing and flipping through her work again before shaking her head. "As I said twice before, there is no Edyth Foster listed."

Bane's fingers curled into a fist. He wasn't certain if he should just be thankful or pursue the matter further, but the memory of the slip of paper with *B.I.* scrawled on it festered in the back of his mind. *I need direction.*

"Perhaps she is in New Orleans as Boris said?" Miss Birch whispered to him. "Is that not a good thing?"

"Indeed, it is far better news to discover that she has simply left the city without a word," Roger agreed.

Bane grunted against the facts being presented to him and decided to go with his gut. "No. She would not run from me. She is here. He must have committed her under a pseudonym."

"Why do you assume that my stepfather is so horrible?" Miss Birch's chin went up. "You could be mistaken."

"I held Edyth's note in my hand. The initials of Blackwell's Island was written over and over. Does that mean nothing?" *And she loves me. I know it. She would not leave me on a whim.*

"She sounds just like every other patient we have here," the secretary snorted, and returned to her tea and newspaper, obviously deciding that Roger wasn't worth the flirting.

Bane turned to the doctor. "I wonder, do people ever commit women here without any names?"

Roger scratched his chin. "Well, I hadn't thought of that, but I suppose that could happen." He looked at the secretary. "I've only been here for about two weeks myself. But, perhaps, Miss Monroe, you could do me a tremendous favor by naming all the latest women who have been committed."

She laid aside her paper and clasped her hands, looking up at him. "Doctor Hawkins, I have over thirteen hundred patients here, all of whom are women. You cannot expect me to remember the exact dates of when they were registered."

Bane crossed his arms, scowling. "So what she is saying is that if Edyth *is* here, and they wish to keep her hidden, they could easily do so."

Miss Monroe's nostrils flared. "We are a respected establishment, sir, and I do not appreciate the insinuation of nefarious dealings happening under this roof. We take great care of our patients. Why, we even have the annual lunatics' ball coming up just to make the patients feel more at home and to encourage their happiness. Would an institution who throws a ball for the mentally ill *hide* their patients?"

Roger reached out and patted the flustered woman's hand. "I beg your pardon. He is out of turn and, again, speaks from his passion. I will attempt to remedy his ill manners to you with an olive branch in the form of a box of sweets tomorrow. But would you scan the ledger for the admission dates of this past week to put to rest his concerns? Surely there's not been that many women placed here in that time?" He gave the secretary a grin that clearly agitated Miss Birch, but Bane didn't have the ability at present to worry about her tender feelings.

"Very well," Miss Monroe replied, a coy lilt in her voice. "But only if you promise to lunch with me today, Doctor Hawkins."

"It would be my honor." He gave her a grin and a flawless bow to match.

Miss Birch coughed into her handkerchief until Roger turned his attention to her and proceeded to pat her lightly on the shoulder, but she waved him away, choosing instead to step behind Bane, whispering to him, "He is acting like he hasn't called on me a half-dozen times. I have never been so offended. Imagine a beau of mine behaving like I was nothing more than an acquaintance."

"How old is the patient?" Miss Monroe ran her finger along the desk and brushed it against her thumb, her disinterest in looking again evident in her sigh.

"She is nearly five and twenty," Bane replied, ignoring Miss Birch.

With a hum, Miss Monroe removed a second ledger, flipped to the last page, and turned the ledger so Doctor Hawkins could read it. "This is our appointment book where we keep track of who will be arriving and what day. As you can see—" She slapped the book closed when Bane craned his neck to look as well and scowled at him. "For staff *only*, sir." She cleared her throat and returned her focus to Doctor Hawkins. "There are only eight women marked as young or middle-aged who were committed in the past week. We also have a new set of arrivals scheduled for today."

"Why did she not start with this ledger?" Bane mumbled to Miss Birch, who was still huffing over the doctor's lunch plans.

She folded her hands atop the ledger, looking pointedly at Bane. "However, if you do not know the name of the patient, you may not visit her, *especially* if she is one of the few people here with stipulations in place."

"But we just told you her name is Edyth Foster." Bane's voice grew with his anger.

Doctor Hawkins clamped a hand on Bane's shoulder. "If she is part of the latest group, I shall soon find out." He sent a bold wink to the secretary and earned a faint gasp from Miss Birch.

Bane drew her hand into the crook of his arm to still her from ruining everything like he had nearly done.

"Thank you, Miss Monroe. I eagerly await our luncheon in the dining hall at noon." Doctor Hawkins motioned them to follow him toward the front door. "Look, I will investigate this, and I will find her if she is here. I know what she looks like."

"I want to look with you," Bane replied, unwilling to sit by and wait any longer. He had to do something or go mad.

Miss Birch remained silent with her arms crossed, clearly still upset over the doctor's luncheon plans.

"You cannot, not with the rules as they are, but if I discover that Miss Foster is indeed here under a false name with stipulations in place to protect her identity, I will find a way to sneak you inside." He showed them outside and pointed them down a side path. "The inmates' promenade won't take place until this afternoon, but you can take a gander if you wish of the grounds before the ferry departs."

Even though he hated the idea of leaving without Edyth, Bane adjusted his collar to block the wind and stepped out onto the gravel path. He shoved his hands into his pockets, discontent with having to wait. He was getting nowhere on the island.

Chapter Thirteen

I mean by a picture a beautiful romantic dream of something that
never was, never will be—in a light better than any light that ever
shone—in a land no one can define, or remember, only desire.
~ Edward Burne-Jones

Edyth stumbled into the hallway of the asylum's general ward behind Nurse Madison, rubbing her wrists where the nurses working in the Lodge had tied her to the bedposts overnight to keep her calm. . .or so they had claimed. Edyth had never felt so powerless. For the entirety of her life up until now, all she had to do was say her name and doors would open before her, but now, any mention of her past earned her blank stares and a blow to the cheek. Her fingers traced her temple, wincing at a surfacing bruise. Whimpers bubbled in her throat, and she was tempted to give in to her pain and weep, but after their cruelty last night, she was afraid that if she revealed any weakness, the nurses would say she was becoming hysterical and return her to her bonds.

She had precious little sleep due to the ropes holding her in place and the constant flow of nurses coming and going from her cell in the violent ward every hour to check on her. What did they expect to find with her secured so firmly she could hardly move? Instead of trying in vain to sleep after the second nurse's appearance, Edyth attempted to convince the nurses of her sanity. And time after time, the nurses condescendingly smiled at her or, worse, struck her before bidding her to curb her wild imagination.

One would think I'd have learned by now not to attempt to reason with the night-shift nurses. Edyth crossed her arms and rubbed her hands over her icy skin, desperately trying to regain an ounce of warmth, her toes aching in her thin slippers that never felt dry with the cool floor beneath her feet. *Will they never find me a decent pair of shoes?* She shivered again. In the Lodge, which she now even more firmly believed was a ridiculous name for the violent ward, she hadn't even been given a blanket to stave off the cold. She was thankful to return to the general ward in the main asylum, and she knew that if she wished to stay in Hall Six and have a chance of escape, she would have to find a different means of finding that escape rather than a sympathetic nurse.

Her stomach growled as she rounded the corner and joined the women in the long hall for what she hoped was the line for breakfast. She took her place behind Nellie.

"Edyth! I was so worried they would not let you return," her friend whispered.

"I was too."

"To the benches. No dawdling. Sit down." The nurses herded everyone toward the bench-lined walls.

Edyth's heart sank, her knees weakening. The nurses had purposefully waited to release her, forcing her to miss breakfast. As disgusting and tasteless as the fare was, at least it would coat her gnawing belly. The women slowly plodded toward the yellow, straight-back hardwood benches. Edyth eyed them, not wishing to sit after a night of being tied down. "What about cleaning? Isn't there something we can—"

"It is Hall Four's turn to clean. You clean when *we* say to clean. Shut your mouth and sit. No stretching," came a command from her right, and Edyth flinched as the nurse pinched her arm to get her moving toward the wall. It was a small offense compared to what she had already suffered in the time she had spent under the asylum's care, but Edyth sent her a glare anyway, wishing above all for retribution.

If only I had my rapier, we'd see who would be cowering. She struggled with the growing hatred in her heart that was so consuming it frightened her. She dipped her head and swallowed, clenching her fists and drawing in a long breath, standing a moment longer in rebellion. She looked down the row and didn't see Poppy. She had hoped to sit with her for a chance to read the scriptures to calm her soul. At mealtimes Poppy had kept her Bible open on the table between them, and she had missed that chance this morning. "Where's Poppy?" she whispered to Nellie out of the corner of her mouth.

"They took her during breakfast."

"Took her? Where? Why?" She tried to picture sweet, gentle Poppy doing anything amiss.

"Nurse Sweeney reprimanded her for reading her Bible at breakfast, and Poppy would not close it. Most of the staff, of course, don't dare take issue with it because of her parents and all, but Nurse Sweeney doesn't much care for the Lord and—" Her voice caught, and she swiped her hand over her eyes and drew a ragged breath. "The nurse told her that her father was dead, which sent her into a fit. She kept pointing and saying that he was standing directly behind her. Nurse Sweeney wouldn't stop laughing, so I tried to distract Poppy, and when I finally got her settled, the nurse whispered something so foul to her." She shook her head. "I hesitate to repeat it, but she told her something that sent her into a fit of hysteria far worse than I had ever seen and they dragged her into that room."

Edyth grunted with suppressed fury, not hungry anymore. "The gray one?" She had heard the murmurings about that horrible room.

Nellie nodded, twisting her hands in her lap. "In the chaos, the Bible was forgotten. I hid it inside my bodice to return to her. When they dragged her back from the chamber right before you returned from the Lodge, I saw that she was soaked through, and I. . .I saw bruises on her neck before they locked her away in her room."

Edyth squeezed Nellie's hand and nodded to the nurse marching down the hallway, willing Nellie to be silent. If they were caught chatting, she didn't think she could suffer another blow after what she had heard. She exhaled as the nurse passed them without a second glance. "Was she conscious?"

"Yes, but only just," Nellie whispered.

For the next eight hours, Edyth sat with her back straight lest she was met with Nurse Sweeney's heavy hand, her prayers centered on the poor girl lying somewhere in the asylum, and then Bane, always Bane. She watched as the shadows cast by the sun moved across the walls, willing the time to pass to each meal for eating at the tables gave them the chance to move their stiff limbs.

Taking her seat for her last tasteless meal of the day, Edyth gasped when Poppy took the seat next to her. "They released you!" She touched her arm. "Are you well?"

"I feel much better after a day in bed, and the nice nurse is on staff this evening. Nurse Jenny let me out for dinner if I promised not to cry again," she whispered, her voice hoarse.

Nellie slid the Bible out of her bodice and handed it under the table to Poppy.

"Oh! Thank you." Her voice cracked. She clasped the book on her lap with both hands and rocked back and forth, her gaze flitting across the room to where Nurse Sweeney stood with her hands behind her back. Using her thumb, she flipped the Bible open on her lap and read while she ate.

Edyth's soul was aching for nourishment as much as her body. She squinted and read the small print of Psalm twenty-seven along with Poppy, repeating the last three verses over and over, desperate to memorize them. *"Deliver me not over unto the will of mine enemies: for false witnesses are risen up against me, and such as breathe out cruelty. I had fainted, unless I had believed to see the goodness of the Lord in the land of the living. Wait on the Lord: be of good courage, and he shall strengthen thine heart: wait, I say, on the Lord."*

She had never been very good at waiting, but in this human rat trap, as Nellie so fondly called it, what else was there to do but wait? For once in her life, she was being forced to confront her past, her deep-rooted hurts, for there was nowhere to run or forge ahead on her own. *I will wait, Lord. I will trust You.*

"You best eat because it looks like we are about to be finished with dinner." Nellie's warning broke her from her prayer.

With shaking hands, she dipped the blackened slice of bread into her tea and shoved it whole into her mouth. She managed to take a single draft of the weak tea before Nurse Madison rose.

"Everyone up! It's your hall's bath night." Nurse Madison's shout jarred Edyth into standing with the others as the matron appeared in the doorway, hands clasped in front of her immaculate black skirts while she perused the group.

Women rose about her and stretched. Edyth groaned and pressed her hands to the small of her back. She had inadvertently managed to avoid bathing night so far with being locked away in solitary confinement upon her arrival and in the violent ward after her escape attempt. Now a new dread seized her. "Are uh, there only female attendants, or. . . ?" She hated to even utter her question, but if the answer wasn't favorable, she would claw the attendants' eyes until they were blinded or she was locked away. Whatever came first. "Are we to be—"

Nellie patted her hand. "It's only females beyond this door. But such degradation, I have never before dreamt of until my first night here. I keep forgetting how much you haven't seen yet."

Edyth twisted her lips, chewing the inside of her cheek and picking at her cuticles. "I was taken to my cell right off even though it is apparently customary to bathe the incoming patients straightaway."

The matron clapped her hands and traipsed down the line. "Now, ladies, I expect amenability from you all this evening. We must get you all scrubbed for the ball tomorrow night."

"Ball?" Some women murmured while a few squealed with glee, others simply rocking back and forth either not caring or unaware of the announcement.

"Yes, the annual lunatic ball." The matron's voice lifted so the whole of the group could hear. "We've been having it since we opened to raise the spirits within these walls. Tomorrow, instead of taking your afternoon promenade, you will be prepared for the ball by your very own lady's maids."

Edyth scowled, wondering what kind of twisted plan the matron had up her sleeve.

The matron turned on her heels, her skirt fanning. "Now, I don't want any problems. Everyone must be bathed to enjoy dancing tomorrow. The doctors and male attendants will be joining us to act as dancing partners, so we must look our best."

The women giggled again, eagerly moving as one to the bathing room, but Nellie's dumbfounded expression mirrored her own feeling of disbelief at this unexpected piece of frivolity.

Poppy clapped her hands. "Oh, I do love the ball! I had nearly forgotten about it. I cannot wait to dance with you, Papa." She beamed over her shoulder, catching Edyth off guard.

She had forgotten again about Poppy's peculiar affliction. . .if one could call it that. It did not seem to be an affliction, since she was so happy with her father at her side.

When it was Edyth's turn to step into the room with all females, her breath seized at the sight before her. The two patients in front of her were busy stripping out of their worn gowns as another was getting out of a filthy tub that had obviously not been changed since the first person had stepped inside. Bits of refuse floated in the now murky water, and she cringed at the realization that she was to be plunged under the same water. The duck pond in Central Park was far more favorable.

"Strip down," came the call from Nurse Madison, who was already unbuttoning Edyth's dress.

Edyth stepped back, refraining from slapping the woman's hand away. "I can manage just fine."

The nurse glowered at her and ignored her wishes until Edyth stood shivering from the cool air against her skin. She looked to her right. The nurses had left the windows open. She sighed. What else could she expect from a group of tormenters? With a grimace, Edyth stepped into the freezing water and endured a harsh scrubbing with a filthy rag that reeked of the previous bodies. Three buckets of icy water drenched her one after the other, leaving her senses reeling as she attempted to gasp for air. The nurses dragged her out of the tub and, without even drying her, threw a thin, short nightgown over her soaked body.

Edyth peeled the fabric from her drenched skin and read the large black lettering. " 'Lunatic Asylum, B.I.H.6.' What does the end mean?" she asked the nearest nurse.

"Blackwell's Island and where you are kept, Hall Six." The nurse checked her notes and pushed Edyth toward the door. "Take her to room twenty-eight with Brown."

Edyth's bare feet padded the cold floor that was slippery from the trail of inmates before her, and she struggled to keep her balance on the wet surface as the nurse prodded her forward into the dark hallway to follow Nellie to room twenty-eight. Shivering, she stood dripping on the floor as the door slammed behind her, biting into the back of her ankles. Nellie immediately withdrew a broken pencil and small notebook from under her mattress and sank onto her own cot, soaking wet as well, scribbling away. That was one of the good things about being responsible for cleaning the asylum. The nurses would never check under the mattresses, for fear of the fleas.

A guttural scream in the hallway made them start, but Nellie kept her focus on the page, knowing the nurses would call for bed soon and extinguish the lights in the hall that provided a dim sliver of light through the cracks in the door. Afterward, they would only have the moon for light.

Steeling herself against the piercing wail from the poor soul in the hall, Edyth twisted her hair, the water splattering onto the floor and joining the puddle forming beneath her feet, which were growing numb. Shivering, she eyed Nellie's pencil and paper, longing for some of her own to distract her from her present horror.

Noticing her gawking at the paper, Nellie sent her a tentative smile as if she feared Edyth would attempt to take it. "Do you write?" she asked.

Edyth began plaiting her hair in an attempt to gather it off her shoulders and give her thin nightdress a chance at drying before bed, but it would be another bone-chilling night in any event. "No, but I do love to paint and draw." She wrapped herself in her blanket and nodded to the blank wall of their cell. "I've been longing to turn that hideous reminder of our predicament into something else."

Nellie looked at her notebook and then again at the wall before flipping her pages to the back of the book and pulling out something hidden in the cover.

"What are you doing?"

Nellie handed a red wax pencil to her. "I keep this for helping me edit my notes, but I don't care for the blank wall either. Show me what you can do."

"But the nurses will see. They might confiscate it."

"I have the other half." Nellie shrugged and grinned. "We can give them this stub and say that was it and no one will be the wiser."

Too excited to query about the oddity of editing a journal or even how Nellie had kept this red pencil hidden, Edyth held the stubby wax pencil in both hands as if it were a treasure and stepped toward the wall. Reaching up, she began to draw what she always did, three hands reaching for one another, but this time, set in a field of budding wildflowers.

Chapter Fourteen

Only when he no longer knows what he is doing
does the painter do good things.
~ Edgar Degas

Bane mopped his forehead and slumped into the leather chair behind his desk, breathing hard after a series of extreme bouts with his top students in a desperate attempt to keep his mind off Edyth while Doctor Hawkins searched. His gaze landed on a telegram newly arrived atop a pile of papers. The leather groaned as he jumped up and snatched it, breaking the envelope's seal.

Raoul.

He scowled. Edyth never called him by his first name unless she was teasing him.

In New Orleans at Commercial. Will return in a week. Sorry for leaving suddenly, but wanted to get away after the spectacle at the party. E.

He stepped toward the window, scowling up at the moon. Even though her message did not make any sense, he could not wait a moment longer, doing nothing. He shoved the paper into his pocket and determined to go to New Orleans himself on the last train out tonight to see for himself if she was at this Commercial Hotel and, if so, hear from her lips that she was safe.

With purposeful strides, he trotted to his room that was directly above the fencing club to pack his trunk. He could not ignore this sliver of news. Had his hinting of an impending proposal been too much? Maybe his declaration had frightened her away after all. She did turn down multiple offers the year of her debut, but he never thought she would do the same to him as her other would-be suitors.

"What are you doing?" Bertram appeared in the doorway, tossing his medical bag onto his bed before stripping off his jacket. "You can't be thinking of leaving me in charge when we have classes to teach all day tomorrow?"

Bane sank onto his own bed, running a hand through his hair before releasing a grunt. "I don't know what I'm about! I'm not a detective, so how on earth am I supposed to find a woman who is not meant to be found?"

"Then what are you waiting for? Hire one," Bertram replied, rolling up his sleeves and crossing the room to the porcelain basin atop their shared dresser and pouring fresh water into it.

"The thought has crossed my mind on several occasions, but what if she is hiding from me and I come across as obsessed with her?"

"She has always been obsessed with you and that never seemed to bother you," Bertram mumbled. He soaped his arms, scrubbing his skin to a lather. "You feel in your bones that something is wrong?"

I did before this message, yes. But the knot in his stomach was still there. The message didn't sound like Edyth. Bane wadded up his shirt and pitched it into the open drawer across the room. "Yes."

"Then it is your duty to do everything you can for Edyth. Because if you don't, who will? If you can't go to the police and involve the law, I suggest that you hire a private detective." Bertram rinsed his hands and dried them against his shirt.

If Bertram agreed, perhaps Bane wasn't all that off. Maybe his gut was right, and she was on that infernal island.

"I'm sure Mother and Father could help you with the expense," Bertram continued. "I know you already asked for your share of the inheritance to purchase this place, but this is about Edyth. You know they would move heaven and earth to help that girl if she was in need."

Bane's gaze landed on his prize rapier hanging above the fireplace mantel. He crossed the room and removed it from the wall, stroking the ornate pommel and cross-guard and remembering the victory that had catapulted his career in France before he decided to purchase the fencing club from the previous owner who was retiring, his old instructor. "I will if I need to, but for now, I have another means of obtaining the cash." He gently placed the rapier in a narrow box that he kept for transporting weapons and shoved his arms into his coat, calling a farewell over his shoulder to Bertram before he summoned a carriage and gave the driver the address for the Wentworth household. Jasper had offered to purchase the weapon on multiple occasions over the years, even though Bane had sworn time and again he would never relinquish it. But that did not matter now. He had to find Edyth, no matter the cost.

The Wentworths' maid showed him to the parlor, and he paced the length of the room, waiting while she fetched Jasper from his dinner party with the message of a special sale. A door opening allowed the laughter to fill the hallway and spill into the room where Bane paused with the box gripped under his arm like a walking cane.

"I say, Banebridge, I hardly believed my maid when she told me you were here, but I see now that she spoke the truth." Wentworth waved his dinner napkin dismissively to the maid, who bobbed in a short curtsy and closed the doors. His bright gaze landed on the weapon box that Bane held. Jasper shoved the napkin into his pocket, drumming his fingers against one another. "Dare I ask if that is what I think it is?"

Bane nodded and did not stop to think of what he was about to do. All he could think of was getting enough money to hire a decent detective to find Edyth. "I have found myself in a bind, and I would like to sell."

Jasper took the box and slowly opened it. Lifting the rapier out with a gentle reverence, he turned it this way and that in the candlelight, admiring the weapon. "It is a magnificent piece."

"Why wouldn't it be? I only keep it as a display piece now. Though I dare say it still rivals any new rapier. Are you offering the same amount?" Bane kept his tone on the edge of civility.

Jasper sent him a half smile and rested the piece in the velvet box once again, clasping his hands behind his back and turning to the crackling fireplace. "I see you are rather desperate, and despite what you seem to think of me, I'm a gentleman and I will not take advantage of you."

Bane released the breath he hadn't realized he'd been holding. "That is good of you. Thank you, Wentworth."

"I know I have earned your poor opinion of me. I am afraid that I imbibed too much the night of your party and I behaved like a drunken fool. I've been wanting to extend my heartfelt apologies to you and to Edyth ever since our unfortunate duel."

Bane's brows rose. He had never known the man to own up to his misdeeds, and he wondered what on earth had brought about such a transformation. "I appreciate your apology, sir. And I'm certain Edyth will be happy to hear of it as well."

Jasper pulled his billfold from his coat pocket and removed a large sum. "My mother's friend was in attendance that night, and she told Mother straightaway of my disgraceful behavior. With the threat of disinheritance hovering over me, I've given up the stuff." Jasper counted the bills into Bane's hand. "Anyway, I hope you are not under the impression that I will allow you to purchase the sword back. Once you walk away, this deal is done. Are you certain that whatever you need funds for is worthy of such a sacrifice?"

"I would sacrifice all I have."

His brows rose. "Then it must be a noble cause. Best wishes to you, Master Banebridge."

Without pausing to mourn the loss of his treasured weapon,

Bane stepped into the soft mist of the evening in search of the one Pinkerton agent he was privileged to know. The cab ride over to the man's brownstone took longer than he would have liked, and by the time he reached the second-floor apartment, his nerves were on edge. He refrained from pounding on the door and instead gave a polite knock before stepping back.

"Banebridge? I was just sitting down for the evening to read beside the fire." Agent Thorpe waved him inside, eyeing him as he shrugged off his coat. "But from the looks of you, this is not a social call, is it?"

"I wish it were," Bane replied, pausing in hanging up his coat. "Am I still welcome to join you?"

"A Pinkerton man never sleeps." Thorpe motioned for him to step into the living room. "Have a seat and I'll get us some coffee."

Within a matter of minutes, Bane was seated in a worn wing-backed chair by a crackling fire with a cup of hot coffee in hand, pouring out his tale to his acquaintance.

Thorpe stroked his thick mustache. "I know you are here because you wish to hire a Pinkerton, but I can tell you right now that the price is far more than what your sword can bring. I would love to help you myself, but I've taken on a case recently that has me working far too many hours as it is, and I'd hate not to give your case the attention it deserves."

Bane's stomach dropped. "I have other assets. I can sell my club if I need to or speak with my parents. I'll do whatever is necessary to find her."

"We don't need you to do something as desperate as selling your club. I have another option for you that might be to your liking. I have a nephew whose father—my brother—is a detective for the New York City police, but what my nephew lacks in experience, he has in gumption and instinct. And because he is untested as a lead detective, his prices will be much more affordable."

Bane leaned over, resting his elbows on his thighs, weighing this piece of news, concerned. "Why does he lack experience? Will he be able to find out information about Edyth's whereabouts in a timely manner?"

"In our line of work, we understand that speed is everything. I would not recommend him if I did not think him ready. It's not worth the risk to your young lady." He cleared his throat and scrubbed a hand over his jaw. "But he is untested because he is young, only eighteen."

"Eighteen?" Bane snorted, on the verge of rising and begging his parents for the money.

Thorpe lifted his hand, staying him. "Jude has assisted me in many cases, so I personally vouch for his abilities as a detective. The young man is as smart as they come, and just you watch, he will be famous one day."

Bane rolled back his shoulders and grunted. He would hear the man out, but if Bane did not think the lad capable, he would look elsewhere. He could not afford to be cheap. "What's his name?"

"Jude Thorpe," a deep voice sounded from the other side of the house. A towering, muscular young man filled the doorway with a sandwich in hand large enough to feed three men. "What can I do for you, sir?"

Within the hour, Bane had filled in the young detective and secured his services. Jude seemed competent enough, and as he promised to begin working the case at once, Bane decided to head home. He was a man of action, but nothing he had tried had accomplished anything. It was frustrating to no end, but Jude lent him a sense of comfort that at last he wasn't floundering for an answer by himself.

At the sound of boots pounding the pavement, Bane turned to find Jude jogging up to him. "I'm sorry, sir, but I forgot to ask one thing."

"Yes?" Bane asked, his confidence in the young man wavering.

"Do you have a picture of Miss Foster? From your description, I think I can picture her, but a depiction of her would be most helpful."

Bane drew in a breath and mumbled, "Sorry, Edyth," and withdrew her sketchbook. He had been determined not to break Edyth's privacy by looking himself. . .but wouldn't she prefer the eyes of a friend to see it first before a stranger?

Jude nodded to the worn book. "Is that the lady's?"

"Yes. There may be something in here that can help us, like a self-portrait." Bane flipped through the pages. His heart warmed at a sketch of them together, dancing under a streetlamp that night after Delmonico's, but he didn't see a portrait of her alone.

"Find anything?" Jude asked, shoving his hands in his pockets and shifting from foot to foot as if to keep the cold from settling into his limbs.

Bane turned back to the portrait of them, reminded himself that Jude was his best chance at finding Edyth, and handed it to the young man. "This is the best one of her face."

Jude held it up to the nearby gaslight. "Is it a true likeness?"

Bane regarded the page, his breath catching at the sight of Edyth's eyes looking into his with her raven curls spilling over her shoulders. "Exact," he whispered, his voice rough as his soul ached to be with her again.

"If you don't mind, I'll hold on to her sketchbook for now and will return it to Miss Edyth myself when we find her," Jude said, his tone reflecting the seriousness of their mission.

Bane rubbed the back of his neck and groaned. Edyth would be livid to know her private musings were being studied by a detective, but he was desperate. *Forgive me, Edyth.* "Keep it safe."

"Leave it to me, sir."

Knowing he had a class early the next morning, Bane bid the young man farewell. Once he reached home, he surrendered to his bed, and in his dreams, Edyth was calling to him, her voice muffled as if she were trapped. Her moans echoed his childhood nightmares of lost souls wandering the earth. When dawn's light reached his window, he was eager to begin his class to lose himself in a place where his troubles were not allowed.

Having downed a slice of bread and two cups of coffee to ward off his incessant yawning, Bane trotted down to the great hall to find Bertram had already opened the club. Bane stretched his arms, swinging them across his chest before his series of lunges to warm his muscles, while Bertram started the fire and fetched the water for the refreshment station. With each lunge, his thoughts continued to drift to Edyth. *If Jude is as good as his uncle claimed, I will discover the truth soon enough.*

Bertram laid a hand on his shoulder, and Bane twisted to look at him from his position on the floor. Spotting the dazed expression on his brother's face, he straightened at once. "Bertram? What's wrong?"

Bertram swallowed and lifted a copy of the *World* in his shaking hand. "I just saw this morning's headline and—" His voice broke.

Bane swiped the newspaper out of Bertram's hand, his heart pounding. New York Heiress, Edyth Foster, Dies in Tragic Steamboat Accident.

Chapter Fifteen

I have been here before, but when or how I cannot tell:
I know the grass beyond the door, the sweet keen smell,
the sighing sound, the lights around the shore.
~ Dante Gabriel Rossetti

A scuffle broke out in the corner of the room, drawing their attention to Nurse Sweeney wrenching up a small, sickly young girl, barely a woman. *Poppy.* Edyth swallowed as Poppy pressed her hands to her ears, crying, "Please, stop. Stop. I was only speaking to Papa. Please. Papa, stop her!"

"And I told *you* to quit your yammering," Nurse Sweeney yelled.

"Surely she will stop soon?" Edyth whispered, clutching Nellie's hand. Nurse Sweeney plugged Poppy's nose and mouth, only releasing her grip long enough for Poppy to gasp for air before slapping her again, the girl's screams escalating with each blow. Edyth jumped to her feet, blind to the consequences, and bolted to her friend's side. She grabbed Nurse Sweeney by the wrist and pulled her back as Poppy crumbled to her knees, wailing for her father.

Edyth shoved the woman away from her friend. "She is only a girl. Can't you see Poppy is frightened? Stop it at once. The more you strike her, the more she cries out, you fool."

Edyth knelt down and brushed Poppy's stringy brown hair from her eyes, feeling the singe of her fevered flesh on her fingertips. "You're burning up," she murmured, and twisted around to catch the attention of the head nurse who was still seated at her desk.

Nurse Sweeney seized Edyth by the nape of her neck and threw her to the floor. "And I told you, duchess, that you are nothing here." Pointed boots slammed into her ribs. "You hear me? Nothing!"

Curling into a ball, Edyth wrapped her arms over her head, but the nurse still found a way to scratch at her face and strike her cheeks. All Edyth could do was wait for the beating to be over, knowing that if she fought back, she would be sent to the Lodge, and she couldn't bear the constant moans of the patients, not again. *I will not cry out. I will not.* A kick to her head sent her neck snapping back. *God, deliver me from the will of mine enemies,* she prayed, holding the scriptures close to her heart. *Deliver me.*

She swallowed her groans and imagined herself in her happiest place, with Bane in the fencing hall. The pain threatened to consume her, but just when she was beginning to see the darkness curling toward her, welcoming her into its cool embrace, the bang of a door slamming sent the nurse scurrying back. Edyth froze, not certain she was truly gone, knowing that sometimes the nurses enjoyed teasing their prey.

Hearing firm footsteps coming down the hall, she lifted a swelling lid to find a pair of well-made men's shoes in front of her. She decided to risk it and looked up to find Lavinia's beau. "Roger?" she whispered, her mouth cracking and the taste of copper reaching her tongue. "Is that you?"

His jaw dropped. "Dear Lord in heaven." He ran his hand over his mouth and glanced up as if to ensure that the nurses were far away before he whispered, "What have they done to you?"

She grasped his sleeve. "Poppy. You have to see to Poppy's fever. And—and me. You have to get me out of here or they will kill me and N–Nellie. She is of sound mind. You have to help us."

"Stop your rambling and come now," Doctor Hawkins said, loud enough for all to hear. He hoisted her up and looked to the head nurse. "I'm taking the patient to a medical room."

Nurse Madison glimpsed up from her magazine, as if oblivious to the behavior of her fellow nurse. "But we are about to get this group dressed for the ball tonight, sir."

"I'm certain you can start with the others, and I shall return her to her chamber in ample time once I ensure that she has no broken bones," Roger replied sternly, his tone brooking no argument. He escorted Edyth from the hall, gripping her by the elbow and taking her to the examination room, closing the door firmly behind them both.

Edyth sank onto the long cot that smelled of fresh linen, and moaned. She couldn't resist laying her head atop the clean, crisp bedding and resting for the first time since she had been brought to this wretched hellhole.

Roger crossed the small room and poured a glass of water. He held it out to her, and she downed it at once. He refilled the glass, silently watching her drain it a second time. She used the back of her hand to wipe her mouth, flinching at her cuts and finding streaks of blood staining her hand.

He took a cloth and an amber bottle from the medicine cabinet, pressed the cloth to the mouth of the bottle and flipped it over for a moment before applying the damp cloth to her lips. She sucked in a breath at the taste of witch hazel. She had used it for many a scrape from her antics in the past, but never for wounds of this magnitude. She grimaced as he gingerly touched a gash at her hairline.

He shook his head and retrieved a needle and black thread. "Looks like I'll have to stitch you up. Do I need to call someone in to hold you down, or can you bear it?"

She gave a short laugh. "I think I can manage to bear the pain."

"Very well, Miss Foster." He gave her a pitiable look and removed a pair of spectacles from his pocket, setting them on the edge of his rather large nose before he threaded his needle.

The use of her name shook her, and she gripped his arm, her dirt-encrusted fingernails digging into his sleeve. "Roger, you have to get me out of here."

"Keep still," he chided, his needle hovering over her forehead.

Pain seared to life once more with the pierce of the needle, her eyes stinging at the tug of the thread through her flesh as he pulled, each stitch threatening the contents of her stomach.

"Almost done," he said, and snipped off the end. "There. You did well. Now, I must see to the rest of you." He gently pressed her limbs and rib cage, searching for broken bones.

In spite of her bruises, she kept her eyes focused on his and did not flinch when he applied more witch hazel to her cuts. "Will you help me?"

"Honestly, Miss Foster, if I didn't know you or your cousin, I would assume you are mad." He gestured to her person and shook his head before setting aside the cotton and bottle. "You look positively feral."

She pushed herself off the cot and wobbled. He reached out to steady her, but she shrugged him off and straightened her shoulders, lifting her head. "If I look feral, as you say, it is because I've been kidnapped, swam in the East River in an attempt to escape their treatment here, and have survived many painful blows. I doubt most society women would be standing, much less coherent, after the inferno I've been through."

He thumbed his reddening ear and cleared his throat. "Y–yes, I suppose so. I've only worked here for a couple of weeks, and I've already found at least a dozen cruelties, which I do my best to remedy, but there is only so much that I can change without the rest of the staff behind me. I am the newest of the sixteen doctors on staff, and I'm not sure what I can get away with at present. If you give me time—"

"I have no time to give." Her voice grew rough.

"Surely they will leave you alone for a while, at least until you recover."

"Are you saying that I am only another situation that you are helpless to change?" She tilted her head to one side, her tone void of emotion. She did not dare allow herself to hope any longer. . .not when he had called her feral and treated her like she'd lost her senses.

He rested a hand on her shoulder. "No. I will do whatever I

must to get you out of here. You are in a dire situation that I would not wish on even my great-aunt. And if I would not wish this on her, a most disagreeable lady, I would never wish it on Lavinia's cousin. Besides, I have already begun to help you."

Her shoulders loosened some as the nervous knife in her stomach halted its twisting. "You have? Did you know I was here?"

He did not meet her gaze. "Banebridge and your cousin have been inquiring after you, and they came here with me yesterday morning, but as your name was not in the ledger, I said I would search for you, but of course, I didn't find you until now."

Bane is looking for me. Bane! Edyth's chilled body flooded with warmth. "And now that you have found me, you can tell them, and get me out of here! Why on earth would you say you needed time when you have the help you need at hand?"

"I wish we could have you released at once, but there are legal issues we have to sort out first, so that you are not simply committed again. And besides, if I allow you to escape, I will be dismissed from this position, and I actually *need* this job if I'm ever to secure the hand of a wife like Lavinia."

"Do you think I care about the *legality* of being discharged, or your position?" She rubbed her hand over her face, wincing as she belatedly remembered her cuts and realizing how heartless she was sounding even in her present circumstance. "Listen, if you are fired, I'll make certain you are compensated."

"And how will you do that if you are without your funds, Miss Foster?" He removed his spectacles and patted a handkerchief to his forehead and nose.

She stiffened, her mouth feeling dry despite the glasses of water. "What are you saying?"

"I'm saying that I promise to not linger long in telling Banebridge of your fate. If I cannot legally have you released in a week's time, I will escort you from these doors myself." He held out his hand. "One week?"

"What other choice do I have?" she mumbled, and accepted his hand.

He turned over her hand, studying her palm. "Now, let's see about bandaging this cut." He cleansed the wound and pulled a length of narrow white cloth from the drawer and began to wrap her hand.

"You will tell Bane where I am." She locked her eyes on his, willing him to look at her.

"Of course, in one week's time," he replied, tying off the end of the bandage.

"*Vow* it." Her voice broke from the intensity of her words. She had been lied to her face too many times.

He swallowed, visibly shaken by her savagery as he hesitatingly met her eyes. "Very well. I vow it."

"See to it that you keep it." She jerked her hand from his hold and rose from the cot, her body already aching from the violent onslaught of bruises. Without another word, she numbly strode into the hall, refusing to limp, with the doctor close behind to ensure that she returned to her group. Once she was behind Nellie in the line of women slowly shuffling toward their cells to prepare for the ball, Doctor Hawkins moved along without a word.

"How are you standing?" Nellie whispered. "I feared for your life when I saw how violent the nurse became after your interference."

"Nothing that time won't heal. My body is used to being tested." *But not abused.* "How's Poppy? Have you spoken with her?"

"Shockingly, her spirits are quite high even if she is bruised. She must be a great deal hardier than she appears." Nellie shook her head and sighed. "I don't understand how they could hurt a sweet innocent like Poppy, especially with her being the daughter of martyrs."

"Poppy was the daughter of martyrs?" She thought of the countless times she had found Poppy with her little Bible on her lap and how the nurses did not bother her even though the rules clearly forbade reading at any time. Edyth had supposed it was because of Poppy's high birth. She had considered Poppy her friend, but she had been so consumed with escaping she had failed to learn Poppy's story. Edyth shook her head in disappointment with herself and wondered how much Nellie knew about these women that she had not told her. Nellie had a way of finding out stories. "How did they die?"

Nellie twisted her hands. "They all caught the fever while serving on the mission field. Her mother and father perished, and the fever addled poor Poppy's mind so that she was returned to her mother's people in New York, but they promptly disposed of their unwanted relation here."

"I suppose most of the nurses have enough fear of the Almighty to keep them from hurting a child of martyrs. . .except Nurse Sweeney."

Nellie's wide eyes filled. "That woman should not get away with such cruelties. Does no one here even care? She must be stopped."

"We can only pray that she is released from her position." Edyth looked around. "But where is Poppy now?"

"Nurse Jenny, the kind one, took her away at once to her chamber to calm her and dress her for the ball. I saw her offer Poppy a peppermint, which calmed her instantly."

Edyth shook her head. "I'll never understand the workings of this place. One second they are beating you and another they are dressing you for an inane ball as if that wipes the sins of all the year clean."

Chapter Sixteen

We live in a rainbow of chaos.
~ Paul Cézanne

Bane sank onto the steps of Roger Hawkins's mansion with his head in his hands, waiting for the man to return from the island. With the young detective hard at work sorting out what really had happened to the purported Edyth Foster in New Orleans, Bane had begun to search for a lawyer in the event that she was indeed on the island and in need of absolution. If he had to wait to hear of news, he was going to use his time to legally clear Edyth's name and not dare think of the possibility of the papers being true.

He gripped the newspaper from this morning in his fist. "Blatant lies," he murmured to himself, attempting to calm his hammering heart. He scanned the short article yet again, searching for a speck of truth. *"American heiress, Edyth Foster, was seen plunging headlong off the side of the steamboat. New Orleans police do not suspect foul play, as she was attempting to walk the rail of the boat. It has been conjectured that her skirts pulled her to the bottom at once. Her fortune reverts to her uncle, Boris Foster, and his heirs."* Bane gritted his teeth, swallowing down the lump in his throat at even the thought of her no longer being here with him. *No. Never. I would have felt it if such a sweet soul left this earth. She is not dead.*

But every lawyer he had encountered stated that if she indeed was not dead and had been committed after *several* doctors had examined her, and if Boris Foster had witnesses to support his claims of her eccentric conduct, there was little reason to doubt that medical professionals would forge their diagnosis and risk their medical licenses.

He shoved the paper into his pocket. He had to find a lawyer who would be willing to look into the matter, but so far no one wished to go against Mr. Foster to even test Bane's suspicion that she was alive. One of the lawyers, whom Bane considered as more friend than student, had even said that if Bane was correct, he did not doubt the doctors' diagnosis, given Edyth's odd taste for steel and bizarre fashions. At that, Bane had to take his leave, else risk striking the man. *I suppose I'll have to wait for Mr. Pittman to return my message.*

He gripped his hat. *If only I had a small fortune, enough to entice these lawyers into taking a risk.* He ran his fingers through his hair, regretting his massive loan to the bank for his fencing club and determining that if he did not find someone to take him on by tomorrow, he would use the promise of Edyth's own wealth as payment. And if that promise did not work, he would use his parents' modest savings as his final resort.

A door squeaking sounded behind him as light splayed through the opening, followed by the soft clearing of a throat. "Excuse me, sir?" the maid called from the doorway. "If you wish to wait for the master, why don't you come inside? Doctor Hawkins would not appreciate it if I allowed you to stay outside instead of offering you a more comfortable seat in the parlor."

"I'd rather stay out here." He gave her a small wave of thanks and turned again to the street, searching for the man's carriage, desperately needing the fresh air to keep his mind sharp.

"Please, sir. If you don't, I'll get into trouble, and my position will be at risk."

His brows rose at the weak reasoning. "For such a little thing? Is Doctor Hawkins an unkind man?"

The girl dropped her gaze to her clasped, reddened hands. Her silence was answer enough.

Rising, he whacked his stiff hat against his pant leg, freeing it from the dust of his walking about the city all day, when someone shouted his name. Bane twisted around and saw Jude trotting up to him.

"Your brother said," he panted, holding his side, "that you might be here. Sir, as I suspected, the paper is most certainly misinformed. She lives yet."

Bane's shoulders sagged, and he gripped the column at the front door, leaning his head against the cool wood and drawing a deep breath. It had been the longest eight hours of his life. "I thought as much, but it still caused me"—his voice caught—"caused me great distress."

"But that's not all, sir."

Bane snapped his head up and, seeing the grin on the man's face, bounded down the steps, fairly tripping in his haste. "Tell me."

"I found her." Jude gave a short laugh of disbelief and ran his fingers through his wild hair. "I can hardly believe how fast it all happened."

Bane clapped him on the shoulder. "Praise God. Where is she?"

The victory in the young man's eyes faded. "I followed your instinct and went undercover as one of the staff at the asylum, and as you suspected, she is on Blackwell's Island."

"And? Is she well?" Bane asked all in a rush.

Jude clenched his jaw, pressing his lips into a firm line, and gave a single shake of his head. Bane clutched Jude's arm, steadying himself.

"But she is alive."

Bane straightened as his shock turned into raw fury. Boris Foster would pay for any pain Edyth had endured. "I want to know everything."

The carriage bearing the Hawkins family crest rolled up to the mansion, and Doctor Hawkins hopped out, stilling on sight of the pair at his door. "Bane, good. I was going to send for you. And who have you brought with you?"

"This is Detective Jude Thorpe. He's been helping me on the

case." Bane made the introductions.

Roger nodded his greeting and stuck out his hand, mumbling, "Good to meet you, Thorpe. Glad to have you assisting us in finding our missing acquaintance."

"I've found her, actually," Jude corrected him.

Roger visibly faltered, and the fine sheen above his upper lip grew. "Did you now? Well, Banebridge, that is why I wanted to speak with you in the first place. I have as well."

Bane stepped toward him, eager for any news. "You have? Jude said she was not well. Do you know anything about her condition?"

"Please, come inside. We have much to discuss." Roger motioned them to follow him inside and led them into his study where a roaring fire and a pot of coffee with two cups were awaiting them. Roger took his time in pouring them each a cup, handing one to Bane and one to Jude, and taking a seat on the settee.

Bane stretched his fingers out to the flames, allowing heat to lick his fingers. "For heaven's sake, men, one of you had best spit it out before I go mad."

"You might want to take a seat. It is not a pretty tale," Roger replied, crossing one leg over the other.

"Miss Foster is in a dire way. We cannot wait to obtain a lawyer to secure her freedom," Jude said, mopping his brow with a plain cotton handkerchief and stuffing it into his pocket. "I fear they may soon inflict something worse than a beating."

Roger turned to him. "How would you know?"

"As I told Bane, I went undercover as an orderly and saw how the doctors treat their patients behind the closed doors of the asylum. I must say that the nurses follow the doctors' lead in their cruel games."

Bane's pulse pounded in his ears, but he attempted to keep his anger in check. "Roger, why did you not tell me of this? And if Jude found her within twenty-four hours, how could you have not found her sooner, being on the inside? Are you keeping something from me even now?"

Roger intertwined his fingers, tapping his thumbs together. "I may not have been completely honest about the safety of the asylum, nor exactly when I found her, but to be fair, I only spoke with her for the first time today."

"What?" Bane's voice matched the crackle of the fire, dangerous and low. "Spoke? When did you *see* her?"

Roger jumped up, stepping behind the oversized chair to keep a distance between them, fear passing over his features. "Now, before you lose your temper—"

"Then you had best tell me now." Bane pounded a fist on the mantel, upsetting a porcelain shepherdess.

Roger lifted his hands as if to keep Bane from throwing the antique. "I actually found her yesterday morning."

With a roar, the shepherdess shattered against the papered wall above Roger's head. "Do you know how much anguish I have been in since her disappearance? What on earth could have possessed you to keep silent about such an important matter?"

"I didn't wish to lose my position," Roger answered in a rush. "I wanted us to have her discharged legally. And at the time, she seemed perfectly safe in the Lodge."

"And what exactly is the Lodge?"

"It is where they keep the violent patients," Jude answered.

Bane swallowed, forcing himself to remain still else risk attacking the doctor. "And when were you going to tell me? When she was dead?"

Roger ran a hand over his face and moaned. "I cannot apologize enough for my actions. But you have to believe me when I say that I had no idea they would beat her!"

Bane charged at him, drawing back a fist, but Jude caught him by the elbow. "We cannot argue now. Time is of the essence, Bane. And we need Roger to get into the asylum."

"Fine." Bane shrugged him off and turned to the mantel, taking up his cup again to distract himself.

Jude cleared his throat and resumed his seat. "There is something else you should know. While I was undercover as an attendant today, I discovered a record about another Edyth...an Edyth Hortense Blakely."

The woman in the portrait hanging in Edyth's house? "I believe that was her maternal grandmother. She was on the island?"

"Died there, actually," Jude replied, grim-faced.

His stomach turned. Edyth's grandmother died on the island? She was committed? He thought of Edyth's obsessions and eccentricities...was she showing signs of early madness and following in her grandmother's footsteps? He swallowed back his questions and asked instead, "And this discovery led to finding my Edyth?"

Jude ran his hand over his jawline. "Someone must have a cruel sense of humor. I found some old records and discovered Edyth had been kept in the same cell in the violent ward as her grandmother. I showed Edyth's likeness to one of the elderly nurses, who recognized her immediately as 'Lady Blakely.' She was but a young woman when Lady Blakely was admitted. It was quite hush-hush."

"Her grandmother was committed and died in the asylum? That means—" Bane clenched the fireplace mantel. "That is not important now. Tell me about Edyth. How poorly is she?"

Roger cleared his throat and finally spoke. "I found her in the hallway, curled into a ball on the floor, waiting for a beating to end."

The cup snapped in Bane's fist, the coffee spilling onto the hearth and shards of porcelain biting his hand, blood dripping to the floorboards. He wanted to tear into the man, but if he did, how would he rescue Edyth? "We have to get her out of there. Now."

Jude rose, towering over Roger. "Agreed, which is why I've devised a plan that you two will put into motion tonight at the annual lunatics' ball."

Chapter Seventeen

Living in that childish wonder is a most beautiful feeling—
I can so well remember it. There was always something
more—behind and beyond everything.
~ Kate Greenaway

Dressed in a pale pink gown from another lifetime, Edyth followed the other women from Hall Six to the dining hall where the tables had been cleared out to make room for the festivities and the benches lined the walls to provide ample seating. She snorted, flinching from her bruised ribs. *As if we want to sit after our hours of forced inactivity.* A trio of musicians sat in the corner, preparing their worn stringed instruments, while the women of the asylum stayed on one side of the room keeping away from the doctors and male orderlies on the other, uncertain if they were allowed to mingle.

"I cannot believe my eyes," Edyth whispered to Nellie, taking a place along the back wall. "But I thought they said there were far more patients? I didn't think we'd actually all fit."

"There must be more patients in the Lodge and the Retreat buildings than we thought," she replied. "I heard they moved all of the men to another asylum on Ward's Island awhile back to accommodate the inpouring of women to Blackwell's." Nellie's eyes widened at the sight before her. She shook her head and stroked her ancient gown of yellowing ivory. "Even without them here, I feel as if I have stepped back in time to live in an article I once read in *Harper's Weekly* about how over twenty years ago a ball was held to celebrate the completion of some four-framed buildings on the island. The way they described it, with girls performing impeccable light-toed reels with the male patients and such, it made me feel perhaps the asylum would not be quite as bad as the rumors I heard before I came—" Nellie halted her words, suddenly interested in the decaying lace of her cuff.

"Came?" Edyth chuckled, used to Nellie's random bits of knowledge by now. "You say that as if you had a choice in the matter, but I suppose it is rather odd to find yourself in a place you'd previously read about. Well, hopefully there will at least be food served, right?" She scanned the room but didn't find any indications to warrant this being deemed a ball besides the fact that the women had braided their hair, wound it in simple buns, and were dressed in an array of fashions, most likely taken from the trunks of patients long since departed. There was also the group of three musicians and, of course, the presence of the men in evening attire.

The fiddler tapped his bow and struck a lively tune that had the attention of all, and the atmosphere was transformed into a jovial gathering. As a mass, the women began to sway, some leaping about and hooting while others rocked back and forth, keeping time with the rare gift of music.

A man with a freshly combed beard crossed the room and bowed to Nellie, and with a smile, she accepted his hand and off they twirled onto the makeshift dance floor. Edyth felt herself sway, her eyes filling when she saw Poppy give a pretty twirl, her arms poised as if she were dancing with her father. The joy in Poppy's bruised countenance sparked warmth in Edyth's veins, and she longed to be held by her own father once more. She let the fiddle take her to a time when life was simple, where no one struck her or desired her money more than her happiness.

She lifted her arms and stepped into her memories and began to dance, her skirts swirling as she dipped around the patients, allowing herself to be free from sorrow. Closing her eyes, she twirled with her memories and then, feeling life in her arms, she startled awake.

She blinked at the man before her, shook her head, and halted her twirling, certain that she was at long last weakening as she had seen the other new arrivals do, slowly giving in to the madness surrounding them. "Bane?"

"My darling," he whispered, his gaze holding her as tightly as his hand upon her waist.

"Bane has never called me his darling," she whispered, certain she was seeing things at last.

"That's because you were a friend for so long, but now, you are *my* darling. Edyth, it really is me." He stopped and placed her hand on his chest, the beating beneath her fingertips waking her. "I am here, body and soul."

"Bane!" She threw her arms around him, thankful that the crowd of women about them protected them from the notice of the ever-present nurses.

Bane hated not taking Edyth in his arms and bolting through the doors that kept his sweet girl in captivity. He had never been slow to act when he witnessed injustice. He was a fighter, especially when it came to someone he loved. Even in her gown with its rotting lace trim, with her cut face and matted hair, he found her breathtaking.

He held her to him and kept time with the music, treasuring the feeling of finally having her in his arms. He risked resting his chin on the top of her head, whispering, "Thank God I found you. I've been searching since the morning you disappeared."

"I knew you would. I knew it," she whispered back, lifting her fingertips beneath her lashes and swiping away her tears. "Uncle told me no one could find me, but I prayed and prayed you would find me. But how did you get through the locked doors to the party?" She peeked over his shoulder, dismay flaming in her eyes.

Bane swirled them in a circle and found what alarmed her, two nurses guarding the exit.

"And how will we be escaping with such vigilance?" Edyth whispered.

"Roger was able to sneak me in tonight."

"Roger. He left to bring you back to me?" She shook her head in open disbelief.

"Not exactly," he replied, but now was not the time to explain Roger's role. Bane drew her to the side of the crowded floor, the shoulders of dancers jostling them at every turn, and tucked them in the corner behind three women who were staring at the dancers and running their fingers over their braids and giggling as if they enjoyed the intricate bumps and twists of their bedraggled locks. "I'll explain it in detail once you are safe. But we wanted to let you know tonight that we are planning our escape for tomorrow morning and to be ready for us."

"Not tonight?" Her smile stumbled, her hands trembling.

"I wondered the same, but Roger insisted, quite adamantly, that tomorrow morning the nurses would be so exhausted from this evening that we would have a better chance of making it out unscathed."

"Are you certain we can trust him? Surely the cover of darkness would aid our escape?"

He shook his head. "I thought the same, but I suppose we will have to trust Roger since he's gotten me this far."

The crowd of women cheered as the fiddlers began a Scottish reel, making her start in his arms. Bane stroked her cut cheek, his lips pressing together as he regarded the bruises on her neck and the row of stitches at her hairline. "What have they done to you?" *If only I could return the favor, bruise for bruise to the one who did this to you.*

She turned her lips to his hand and pressed a kiss onto his open palm. "It doesn't matter now. All that matters is that you are here with me. Your presence is enough to dull my pain. How did you find me? Uncle refrained from telling the asylum my true identity to keep the ledgers clear of any record of my being here."

"I hired a detective who managed to go undercover as an orderly and find where you were hidden. I should have hired him the moment you disappeared." He chewed the inside of his cheek, debating whether or not to continue with his confession. By the widening of her eyes, he could tell she was wondering why he had waited. "I'll admit, I almost didn't hire the man, because I was afraid of seeming like a stalker. I thought maybe you had left because I'd startled you with all that talk of commitment and. . . marriage." He paused, knowing it sounded ridiculous to mention marriage while Edyth was trapped under this roof.

She squeezed his hand. "You could never frighten me. You have always been the one person I knew I could spend the rest of my days with until the Lord calls me home."

His brows rose, surprised by her candor and the mention of God. She had always been private about her faith, even with him.

She smiled, recognizing her openness was unexpected. "The only good thing about my time here is that the asylum has felled the walls of my heart, Bane. Outside these walls, I was so busy chasing distractions that I never allowed myself to have time with my thoughts. . .or spend the time I should at the Lord's feet, giving Him my burdens. This place has stripped away the layers of thick skin, and I am raw, for I have had no one and nothing to lean on here but the Lord. I don't think I have ever prayed so much in the past decade as I have in the time I've been here. And my prayers for the future always included you. I know what I want, and I'm going to say it, because life is too short for coquettish games."

He took her hand in his, rubbing her palm with his thumb, aching to hold her. "Your wants are my own, dear Edyth."

A woman whose hair had been pulled from its coil tugged on Bane's arm. "If you aren't going to dance with this handsome prince, I shall," she cackled, her grin revealing a lone tooth as her chin jutted forward through her wiry gray locks.

"No." Edyth scowled at the woman and tugged Bane's arm to lead him away, but the woman howled and grabbed his other arm, her long, curling, yellowing nails digging into his sleeve.

"I do not wish to create a scene, Edyth. Perhaps one dance could not hurt?" Bane suggested. His gaze flickered to the nurses sprinkled about the room who were surveying the group and removing anyone they thought was losing control of herself. He froze at the sight of a middle-aged doctor flirting with a very young nurse. *Jasper Wentworth's father.* If he saw Bane and reported him to Mr. Foster—

"I said back off, Marta." Edyth bared her teeth at the woman and seized his arm, jerking him back and away from the clawing hand of the old woman.

Bane's neck bristled at her feral tone. She had been dancing alone when he came in, smiling as if to someone. He rubbed a hand over his jaw, fearing that this place had truly addled her.

But then, Edyth relaxed against him and sent him a wink. "Sorry. If I didn't hiss at her like that, she would have fought me for you. And I'm afraid I would not have let her win even if she is three times my age, for I want every second of your time while you are here."

"Which is about to be cut short," Bane said through his teeth as a large nurse glared at Edyth from across the room. The women's confrontation must have caught the attention of one of the nurses.

Edyth's voice dropped. "Oh no. Nurse Sweeney. She is the one who beat me."

"She did this to you?" Bane's blood pulsed in fury, but Edyth pressed a gentling hand to his arm before folding her hands and demurely lowering her head.

"Please, don't. It will only make it worse for me if you say anything. Be nice and perhaps she won't hurt me tonight."

He swallowed his anger and forced himself to send a smile to the woman coming their way, hoping she would think all was well and turn back.

But, at the sight of Bane, Nurse Sweeney's scowl disappeared and a coy smile took its place, revealing her mottled rotting front teeth from a lifetime of smoking a pipe. "What a fine guest you have cornered, duchess. Why don't you make yourself scarce while I take a turn with our new doctor?"

"I am actually the new doctor." Roger appeared at Bane's elbow and clamped him on the shoulder, drawing him back ever so slightly. "Nice to see you again, Nurse—?"

"Hester." Nurse Sweeney kept her batting lashes on Bane. "You must be the specialist I've been hearing about tonight."

If being nice helps Edyth. . . Bane gave the nurse a bow, sweeping her hand up to press a kiss atop it as he adopted the part of the specialist. "What a delight to meet you, Hester. Yes, I am Professor Lyons, a specialist Doctor Hawkins brought in to speak with the duchess. I know it's rather odd for me to attend your festive party, but I pressed Doctor Hawkins into returning with me tonight so I might introduce myself to her before our first official session tomorrow. I wish to study her for a series of articles I am writing."

Nurse Sweeney's scowl landed on Edyth, and to his shock, Edyth stepped behind him, betraying her fear of the large woman.

"You need to watch this one." Nurse Sweeney pointed at Edyth, causing her to shrink completely behind him.

Bane felt the quiver of her hand when she discreetly rested it on his back as if seeking to draw from his strength. "Most certainly. I appreciate your warning."

"Ah, Nurse Sweeney, I hate to interrupt, but I believe one of the doctors is signaling to you," Roger interjected, pointing to a rotund doctor who gripped the arm of Marta.

She grunted. "Of course he is. My work is never done. Let me return that one to her cell, but when I come back, let's have us a dance, Professor Lyons, you hear?"

"It would be my honor," he said with a bow, keeping his fingers crossed behind his back for Edyth's amusement. He waited until Nurse Sweeney left to turn around to face Edyth, grasping her hand in his, the world narrowing to only her. "I hate the idea of leaving you tonight."

Roger leaned into their small group so that Edyth and Bane would be the only ones to hear him. "We need to get you out of here at once, Bane. News will spread soon of the specialist's presence, and we cannot have them asking a dozen questions before I can sneak you in tomorrow under the guise of giving Edyth her treatment."

The sheen of tears in Edyth's eyes broke Bane's resolve for their plan. "Are you certain we cannot do this now?" he pressed.

"Are you going to challenge the plan again? Nothing is prepared for tonight. Trust me and wait."

"I trusted you once," Bane muttered under his breath.

Roger narrowed his eyes. "And you will see that I meant my apology. I will not let you down twice."

Bane sighed, his shoulders caving. Roger was right, of course. Nothing was ready, and if they tried to escape and failed, it would be nearly impossible to get to her again. "Very well. We wait."

Edyth's hand immediately gripped his. "Bane?" Her voice was strained.

"I'll come for you." He ached to pull her into his arms and kiss her, but with so many about, they would without a doubt be seen. Even holding hands was a risk.

A tear traced her cheek as her lips trembled. "Goodbye, Bane."

"Until we meet on the morrow," he whispered, his gaze embracing her. He pressed her hand to his heart, wishing he could tell her that he loved her. But now was hardly the place for such a declaration. He stepped back, their connection stretching, and when their fingertips parted at last, a cold seeped into his very bones that was mirrored in her eyes.

Chapter Eighteen

*I put my heart and my soul into my work,
and have lost my mind in the process.*
~ Vincent van Gogh

Edyth floated back to her chamber with Nellie giggling by her side and going on and on about the evening's much-needed distractions from the cruel reality they faced daily.

"Being rather short on partners, one elderly lady, Marta I believe her name is, practically shoved me into the wall to cut in during my dance with Doctor Hawkins. Thankfully, she was only given a warning, but it wasn't long before I saw Nurse Sweeney cart her away. I would have laughed at Marta's dramatic claims to innocence, worthy of the stage, when she was told she was being locked away early after her antics. . .if only it was Nurse Jenny and not Sweeney removing her from the hall." She shook her head and sighed. "I hope Sweeney was at least gentle with the poor dear. What about you, Edyth? I saw you with that specialist." Her eyes sparkled. "Do you have something to tell me? I thought you were in love with Bane?"

Edyth returned Nellie's smile, eager to tell her friend the news once safely inside their room, but when they stepped into the dark, cold cell, she stiffened at the sight of Uncle Boris, standing with his hands behind his back and staring up at the wall she had covered in her crimson sketch.

"Uncle. Did you not have enough amusement at my expense on your last visit?" The rotting scent of the dead flowers was branded into her memory, making her stomach turn. But she lifted her chin. She would not crumble before him tonight.

"I would have thought you had given up this inane little project of yours. I'll have the nurses notified so that it can be scrubbed clean. I cannot have anything interfering with your healing." Her uncle's laugh mocked her as he turned to her, ignoring Nellie, who took a seat on her cot and stared at her hands to give them a semblance of privacy.

"Since when have you ever cared about my health?"

Ignoring her question, he paced the length of their small cell. "They called me down here *again* because of your exhibitions of anger this week and this very afternoon. Your little display will cost you dearly."

She crossed her arms over her chest. "Will it cost me more than their beating me for trying to aid a poor girl whose only crime was reading her Bible?"

His scowl deepened. "I did not care for that piece of news."

Her lips twisted into a smirk. "And why is that, Uncle? Did you suddenly discover a hidden love for me?"

"Because whether or not I like it, you are my brother's flesh and blood. And as such, I will have the most humane treatment made available to you. Since you have become so violent, I have seen fit to have a new type of treatment given to you." He looked pointedly at her.

"What treatment?" She slowly lowered her arms, tilting her head.

Her uncle remained silent, pausing at the window and staring up at the moon through the bars.

"What treatment, Uncle?" she asked again, a cold seeping up from the soles of her dilapidated slippers.

"They will treat you with an immersion therapy and a series of injections of morphine and one other medication designed to help you to forget, starting tomorrow."

She blanched, gripping for the foot of the cot to steady herself. *Bane was impersonating a specialist. . .did he somehow hear about Uncle's plan and has some sort of plan to intervene?* She should have

175

asked him more about the plan. She shouldn't have allowed herself to be swept away by his eyes. *Bane never said what time he would be able to come. . .what if he misses me?* If she was taken straightaway in the morning, how would he know where to find her? Would she still be herself when he did find her? She had seen how the patients who went in for these treatments returned from the chamber. Broken. Some muttering only one word, *gray*. She clenched her fists and stepped toward him. "You cannot expect to get away with this. Doctor Hawkins will not—"

"Doctor Hawkins agrees with me. In fact, he came in person this afternoon after his shift to bid me come to you after your little ball tonight. He was insistent, saying something about you wanting to try to escape again, which, judging from your last attempt, would not end well for you."

Edyth blinked. "Doctor Hawkins. . .he saw you today?" *This must be part of their plan to save me.* Her heart pounded, waking her to the danger of inadvertently giving away her alliance with the man.

Her uncle nodded. "You should thank him for fetching me and saving you from your own violence. In fact, he was the one who suggested the new treatment to help calm your frenzied nerves."

Nellie rose and took Edyth's hand, lending her strength and time to compose her thoughts. "Sir," she said to Edyth's uncle, "you cannot know what you are saying. The people who go in for that treatment, they are never the same when they return. It's as if they are no longer with us."

"Quiet, girl. Do you think I would take the ramblings of a mad girl into my consideration when deciding what is best for my niece? No, she will have the injections starting with her first tomorrow."

Edyth slipped her hand from Nellie's grasp. She collapsed on her knees as if she were truly giving in to her despair, her hands digging at the floorboards like they would allow her to claw her way through, burrowing to freedom. "Please. Have mercy. I repeat my vow that I will give you everything you've ever wanted. I will sign over my fortune. I'll disappear. You'll never hear from me again. Only, please, do not erase my memories." She whimpered, longing again for a weapon of any kind to defend herself against this vile man, but she was powerless. The only weapon she had available to her was deception. Edyth felt Nellie's arm drape over her shoulder. *Good. If I can fool Nellie, I am certainly fooling him. He will not suspect Roger's aid.*

Uncle rested his hand on her wild, matted hair. "It's for the best, dear. You will finally have peace and forget all about those paintings."

She looked up at him, her bottom lip quivering. Even though she was acting, it still cut her that he would go to such lengths to rid himself of her. "Peace about what? I don't need treatment. I am fine, truly."

"Why, the three hands, of course. Surely you know by now what they mean, don't you?"

She drew herself up a little, shaking in earnest. "No. I don't."

He gave her a half smile. "I'm amazed it is taking you so long to remember you were there that day."

"What do you mean?" She pressed a hand to her stomach.

"It doesn't matter now. You'll soon forget I was even here or that I exist for that matter." He turned to the door when it swung open.

Roger stepped inside, his focus on Edyth, his expression void of any hint of hope that she so desperately longed to find. "You can leave her to me, Mr. Foster. We will start with the freezing treatment tomorrow to keep the mania at bay. Rest assured, it is perfectly normal for the patients to become anxious before their treatment begins."

"Then I shall leave her in your capable hands. I shall return tomorrow to see how the first injection takes." He shook Roger's hand. "Now, shall we expect you for dinner tomorrow afterwards, Doctor?"

"I would be honored, sir. Will Miss Birch be present?"

"Of course. Now I really must get home to my wife." And without so much as a glance back at Edyth, Uncle left her.

Edyth lifted herself to rest on her heels to look up at him. She couldn't keep herself from whispering, "Roger? You don't really agree with him, do you?"

His eyes on her, he called out, "Wait for me, Mr. Foster. I have a question for you." And without so much as a reassuring shake of his head to Edyth, he slammed the door in her face, nearly breaking her.

Roger is pretending. Pretending! Remember that, Edyth. He couldn't say anything in front of Nellie. I shouldn't even have mentioned it. Bane will be coming for me tomorrow. She could hardly keep from laughing. She quietly swallowed her mirth and stared at her hands to compose herself. It wasn't that she didn't trust Nellie. But perhaps she was growing paranoid. Surely she could tell her friend, couldn't she?

Nellie grasped Edyth's hands and pulled her to her feet. "Don't worry. My contact should be here by tomorrow morning at the latest."

Edyth rubbed a hand over her swollen eyes and forced herself to maintain a tremble in her voice. "A contact? What on earth do you mean?"

She squeezed Edyth's hand in both of her own. "My contact from the *World*."

"What?" Edyth gaped at her, the idea of madness as an explanation for this outlandish turn of events flickering to the forefront of her mind.

"I know you've seen me scribbling away in my journal each night. That's because I'm keeping careful account of what happens within these walls and taking down the women's stories. My name is not Nellie Brown. It is Nellie Bly, and I am writing an exposé for Joseph Pulitzer, owner of the *New York World*, on the asylum and how the nurses and doctors treat their patients. I've only stayed silent so long to keep my cover. That day when you tried to swim across the East

River, I almost said something to you, but you were so confident in your swimming abilities, I thought maybe you might make it." She twisted her hands as if overwhelmed with guilt.

Hope soared within her as she dared to trust Nellie was telling the truth. They would not perish in the asylum if Bane's plan failed. *Thank You, Lord.* "Do not fret about that day a moment longer. I almost made it." She squeezed her friend's hand, not quite ready to tell of her own plan yet. "So tell me about your idea for an escape, Miss *Bly*."

"I can tell my contact about your case in the morning and he will help me get you out of here before your appointment. I've watched people I met on the ferry ride over here be driven insane in such a short time from the doctors' so-called treatments. It would not rest well with me for the remainder of my life if I stood by and allowed such abuse to befall you when it was within my power to stop it. And when I am released, I plan on helping *every* woman in this pit."

Chapter Nineteen

Look in my face; my name is Might-have-been;
I am also called No-more, Too-late, Farewell.
~ Dante Gabriel Rossetti

Edyth walked stiffly to the benches in the morning before breakfast. She had tossed and turned all night, dreaming that Bane's coming to rescue her was simply a fabrication of her mind. But once her feet touched the floor, the reality of Roger and Bane's plan flooded her being, leaving her feeling quite giddy.

At the nurse's lifted brow, Edyth erased her smile and once again dropped her shoulders. *You are not out yet. Don't give them a chance to find you out,* she chided herself and took a seat beside Poppy, whose eyes were locked on a window.

"Poppy?"

The girl stared, unblinking.

"Poppy, whatever is wrong?" Edyth whispered, feeling the trembling overtaking the girl's body.

Poppy lolled her head onto Edyth's shoulder and moaned. "The nurses. . .they left the windows open last night in my r–room and it was s–so cold."

Edyth pressed her hand to Poppy's forehead and nearly groaned at the heat. She was burning with fever again. She had hoped after seeing Poppy dancing last night that she was on the mend, but that wretched pair of nurses were doing their best to torment their patients into an early grave. She swallowed, wishing there was some way she could free her friend once she escaped today.

"Papa, I will be joining Mama in glory soon." Poppy murmured to the empty air before them. "No, I am not frightened. Why would I be?" She gave the ghost a reassuring smile that soon dissolved into her quivering body.

Edyth bit the inside of her cheek against the pain of watching Poppy surrender. "You will be well, Poppy. Please, you must fight the fever. You cannot let the asylum win." *You cannot die a captive.*

"Fever," she repeated, her gray-blue eyes rolling about in an attempt to meet Edyth's gaze. "I almost didn't survive the first one all those years ago that took my mama and left Papa and me here. I'm not sure I can a second time, and we miss her so. Papa has only lingered this long to stay with me."

"We need to move you to the infirmary and get you well," Edyth insisted, shifting to wave over a nurse. But Poppy's hand stayed her.

"No. Don't fetch the nurse yet. I will be well again, though not on this earth. Jesus will be taking my hand soon, but first, I'm supposed to give you something." With great effort, Poppy unfastened the top three buttons of her gown.

"Whatever are you about?" Edyth nearly stood then to get the nurse but refrained out of respect for whatever Poppy had in mind.

She pulled the small leather Bible from her bodice and placed it in Edyth's lap. "I want you to have my Bible. Keep it hidden. They will not let you keep it if they find it, and I do so want you to continue your reading."

Edyth's fingers stroked the worn cover. "I can't possibly."

"Didn't you hear my papa? He said to leave it with you. I have no need of it anymore now that I'm being called home at long last. Promise me you'll read it? Lean on it?" Her glazed eyes met Edyth's, her voice growing hoarse with the intensity of her need to hear Edyth's vow.

"I promise." Edyth slipped the Bible inside the waist of her gown and gripped Poppy's hand.

"Good." The girl returned her head to Edyth's shoulder. "I've always liked you, Edyth. I hope you are reunited with your love. . . ." Her voice drifted off as her full weight sagged onto Edyth.

No! She picked up Poppy's hand, giving her a shake when the nurse glared in her direction, but at the gentle pulse beneath her fingertips, Edyth could not suppress a little cry of relief.

"Silence," Nurse Madison hissed from behind a copy of *Ladies' Home Journal.*

"Please, could you take her to the infirmary? Poppy has passed out from a fever."

"And that's your expert medical diagnosis?" The nurse crossed the room, roughly throwing back Poppy's head. She pursed her lips and motioned for another nurse to join her. "Help me take her to the infirmary. Nurse Camden, I'll need you to be in charge for the few minutes I am gone. Try not to let them get into any trouble. You are too soft on them."

Edyth rose, staring in horror as the women unceremoniously draped Poppy's arms over their shoulders and pulled her down the hall, Poppy's feet dragging behind them and the door slamming in their wake.

"Return to your seat, please," Nurse Camden called, slowly shuffling to the head nurse's desk where she picked up the journal with withered, shaking hands.

Edyth bowed her head, saying a prayer for her dear friend. *Heal her, Lord, and help me to gain my freedom so I might obtain hers too.* Feeling the book against her stomach, Edyth couldn't keep herself from breaking away from her stiff position on the bench and joining Nellie two benches down. She buried her face in her friend's shoulder and moaned. *When will the cruelties end?*

Mistaking her grief for anguish over the impending treatment, Nellie twisted her hands. "I'm so sorry I don't have any news for you. My contact hasn't come yet, but do not lose heart. He'll come for breakfast. I'm certain of it."

The sound of heeled shoes shuffling alerted Edyth to the ancient nurse's approach. She expected rough hands to wrench her and Nellie apart, but instead, a gentle hand lifted her chin to meet the old nurse's watery eyes and kind smile.

"Can I help you, my dear Edyth?" Nurse Camden stroked back Edyth's hair with such familiarity, she drew in a sharp gasp.

"How do you know my name?" Blinking through her tears, Edyth looked warily at the nurse. Was this another attempt to play with her mind? To pretend to befriend her in order to learn something about her only to tease her mercilessly later?

The nurse lifted her hand, but instead of striking her, she gave her a sympathetic smile and a pat on the cheek before slipping something hard into her hand.

Edyth opened her palm to find a piece of a peppermint stick. She popped it into her mouth before it could be discovered by any of the others on the bench, closing her eyes to enjoy the sweetness. "Thank you," she whispered.

"Of course. Your grandmother used to love peppermint too. It would calm her right down whenever she had a moment." The nurse smiled at her again and shuffled back to her station.

"My grandmother. . . ?" she whispered, her voice cracking. The hard candy turned bitter in her stomach. She could hardly believe it. "Uncle wasn't lying after all."

"Or he merely paid the nurse to say such a thing," Nellie reassured her even as she bit her lip in consternation.

Edyth thought of the scratched initials in the baseboard beneath the bed in the Lodge. *E.H.B. Edyth Hortense Blakely?* And the carved-out heart and second set of initials, *B.B. Beatrice Blakely? Mama.* "Oh, please God, no." She gave a muffled cry and dipped her head, allowing her tears to fall at last, mourning Poppy and her grandmother and herself.

"Edyth, hush now! Please, you are drawing too much attention," Nellie begged her, rubbing her hand over Edyth's shoulder.

Unless it was a clever ruse from her uncle, her future was truly not her own. If her grandmother had been committed when her mother was still a Blakely, Edyth only had a few years left before she too followed in her grandmother's madness. Her own mother had died before the malady had manifested, but Mother had possessed the same oddities as both her mother and, now, Edyth. *Bane, my darling. I am so sorry.* She thought of the children they could have had and how beautiful they would have been with Bane as their father. She could never have a family. . .she would always be alone.

A girl's shrieking from behind a nearby door sent chills down her spine. Edyth grasped Nellie's hand, frightened of her future. "That could be me. Even if I do escape, I will be returned when the madness comes upon me at last. My uncle will have his way and any memory of being loved will be destroyed. I won't remember anything. I won't remember Poppy, my father teaching me to paint, my mother kissing me good night, or Bane. . . ." Her throat caught. She could no longer have the future she had dreamed of with him, but to lose the memory of his lips upon hers? His touch? His strength? *Unbearable. If I can escape and run far enough away from my uncle's grasp, then at least I can have my memories of Bane until my dying breath.*

❧

Roger had not shown up at the ferry to meet him, so Bane continued on with the plan without him and entered the rotunda alone. A nurse at the front desk smiled at him, fortunately remembering him from the previous night's revelry, and waved him through. She didn't seem as exhausted as Roger had claimed she would be since she still took the time to smile flirtatiously and ask him little questions to keep him by her desk. Hopefully, the rest of the staff would be too tired to stop him. He had to get to Edyth.

"Let me take your hat and cane. Since you are a specialist and don't have an office, I can keep your things in the nurses' retiring room."

"Oh, that won't be necessary," he replied, rubbing his thumb over the decorative silver head of his peculiarly heavy walking cane. It had been a gift from Edyth, and he carried it today, thinking it made him appear more professional. He wanted to have something to defend himself and Edyth with if he needed to.

"No problem at all," she cooed, and came around her desk, taking his things, her hands brushing suggestively over his. "You'll find the women of Hall Six cleaning the rotunda today."

Breathing a sigh of relief that the nurse still believed him to be the specialist acquaintance of Roger Hawkins, Bane tugged on his dull brown tweed suit. Hearing chattering coming from above, he watched the asylum women in thin gray gowns cleaning the spiral staircase. His eyes traveled to and from each wild-haired woman, trying to spot his girl. At long last, he found her, mopping the second floor. Her glazed expression, paired with her scabbed, bruised lips, made his heart lurch, pushing him up the stairs to claim her in his arms. Coming up behind her, still undetected, his heart broke at the sight of her trembling hands clenched around the handle of her mop.

"Please." Her voice matched her hands, completely unlike the confident woman he knew. "Please, don't take me yet. Please," she whimpered.

"Take you? Edyth, did they hurt you after I left?"

Her head snapped up, and her gaze collided with his. She gave a small cry, moving forward as if to throw herself into his arms, but he quickly grabbed her arm to still her.

"You are real! You really did come to the ball last night?"

"Of course, don't you remember?" Bane was confused at the haze in her eyes, and he stepped back as a nurse appeared at the bottom of the stairs, looking up at them. "Now, now, miss, there is no need to be alarmed," he said loud enough for the nurse to hear.

"Everything okay up there, Professor Lyons? Bring her down, would you?" A massive nurse joined the other nurse below and crossed her arms, nodding to Edyth. "I was told that if the duchess caused any more trouble at all that she would be sent to the Gray Chamber immediately to begin her therapy."

He nearly froze but managed to riffle through his notebook as if looking for a schedule, which in reality was Edyth's sketchbook that he had recovered from Jude, but she was too distraught to notice. He called down to the nurse, "I believe it is scheduled for next week, correct?"

"I was told it was today, but in any event, I have my orders, and you, begging your pardon, sir, are only a specialist and not Doctor Hawkins. He is personally in charge of the girl's case, and until he arrives to say different, we will keep to his instructions and take her straightaway."

His heart dropped. Doctor Hawkins ordered the treatment for today? If so, he was dangerously close to overplaying his hand in this facade of treatment to assist in her escape, especially since he had not shown his face today.

"Well, I'd like to have that procedure pushed back to December, which would still follow his orders for administering the treatment while giving me enough time to assess this woman's state of mind to write my articles. Could you see to it?"

"December? I authorized for her to have that injection as soon as possible, and it is not in anyone's right to change it," a voice boomed from below at the front doors, footsteps sounding on the stairs.

"Uncle." Edyth's eyes grew wide. She gripped Bane's arm, all thoughts of maintaining a cover vanishing as she whispered, "Bane, he means to wipe my memories. If Doctor Hawkins isn't here to stop them from proceeding, I'll be as a young babe. You have to get me out of here now, else your rescue will be for naught."

Taking her by the elbow, he steered her up the stairs to the third floor of the rotunda, hoping to find some means of escape, trying the doors. Locked. He groaned in frustration.

With a cry, Edyth fell into his arms, dropping the mop she had brought up the stairs in the confusion. Tears streaked down her cheeks. "We are trapped."

"I won't allow them to take you. And besides, Doctor Hawkins only agreed to the treatment to maintain his cover. He wouldn't betray us in such a vile manner. You'll be safe. Roger will help us. You'll see, but you must not give us away now. You must act like you are without hope when he appears."

"And if they proceed without him?"

His heart hammered at the thought. "I won't let them," he whispered and drew her into his embrace as three orderlies and Mr. Foster appeared at the stairway's third-floor landing.

"Let her go, Banebridge," her uncle commanded. "You're surrounded. What did you think could happen by running upstairs? All the doors are locked, and there is no escape. This is a madhouse, after all."

Bane kept Edyth behind him while he scooped up the mop and flipped it around so that the handle was pointing to her uncle, wielding it like a broadsword. "You will no longer hurt her. You have committed her falsely, and now that I can act as her witness to prove her sanity, the asylum will have to release her."

"Are you her husband?" Mr. Foster asked, a smirk forming on his lips as he leaned against the railing, crossing his arms.

Bane drew his brows into a point, knowing where her uncle was leading the conversation as Edyth sidled up to him. "No, but—"

"But *nothing*. In the eyes of the law, she belongs to me. And that allows me to decide what is best for my niece." He motioned to the orderlies. "One of you, go fetch Doctor Hawkins and have him move the procedure up to within the hour."

Overwhelmed with relief that Roger was still in charge of Edyth, Bane fought to keep his guise intact. Edyth's body sagged, and he pulled her up against him as the men approached, aching to save her at once and not wait on Roger. "I will speak with the matron about this."

"And she will side with my uncle." She clutched his sleeve, the desperation in her eyes alarming him. *Doesn't she realize the treatment is a ruse?* "You can't let them take me, Bane. They will erase my mind, and I'll never remember—"

He stepped in front of her again and whipped the mop handle in an offensive maneuver. "Keep back!"

The attendants dove for him as Bane swooped the handle around, knocking both men to the ground before he whirled around to face her uncle and found him gripping her by the nape of her neck, bending her over the stair rail. He had been so focused on the orderlies, he had forgotten Edyth's weakened state. One shove, and Edyth would fall to her death.

"Drop it, or she dies. No one here will breathe a word against mine stating that she tripped in her hysteria."

"And I will confirm the tale," came the raspy voice from a tall, thin woman who appeared as an apparition from the shadows.

"Thank you, Matron." Mr. Foster gave him a grin, a light glinting in his eyes. He jerked Edyth back by her hair. "I can end this all now if you do not comply."

Edyth's arms hung limply, even as her body inclined toward him.

What good was it being a fencing master if he could not even protect the woman he loved? Bane relaxed his stance, stepped back, and threw down his weapon.

"Good," Boris replied, still holding Edyth in place.

"Release her, and we will let our lawyers settle this."

Boris gave a short laugh. "You are trespassing and will be dealt with accordingly. A burglar should not expect special treatment."

"Whatever happens, Bane, I want you to know that I have always loved you." Edyth reached out to him with such tenderness that he felt his heart tear in two at the thought of losing her forever.

"This is not the end, Edyth. I will get you out of here." Several pairs of strong arms wrenched him back as two nurses mounted the top stair and grasped Edyth by both arms. When she was safely away from her uncle, she released a strangled cry and fought against them as she was pulled toward the hallway doors. "Bane! Bane, don't let them take me!"

"Edyth!" Bane tugged against the hold of the men and managed to slip one arm away, but one of the men tripped him, grabbing his leg. He kicked free, rammed his elbow into the nearest man's gut, and sprinted for her, but the door slammed in his face. He heard the shot of the bolt and watched helplessly through the barred glass as they dragged her down the hall, her eyes never leaving his until the men seized his arms again and jerked him back.

"Send for the police!" Mr. Foster shouted behind him.

"It could take awhile, sir," the matron replied, her hands clasped in front of her black gown. "We will need to send a telegram, but the police will most likely wait for the next ferry instead of renting a vessel. It could take a couple of hours for the law to appear."

"Then I suggest you use one of your many rooms here and lock him away until they arrive to cart him off to jail," Mr. Foster growled.

"As you know, we are well beyond capacity here, but we do have a rather large vegetable cellar in the kitchen building available." She waved to the orderlies to pull him along.

Bane allowed them to take him without a fight to the kitchen building, feeling if he didn't struggle he would have a better chance at not being tied up. The men escorted him out the main building and into a kitchen that had seen far better days where a large chef and a few apathetic workers chopped rotting vegetables while several inmates in ragged gray gowns stood washing an endless pile of filthy dishes.

The matron unlocked and swung open a small door with an arched top and the men threw Bane inside, the stone steps biting his knees before he tucked his body and rolled into a mound of potato-filled burlap sacks. The attendants took two small lengths of rope from two sacks and wrapped one around Bane's hands and one around his feet before nodding with satisfaction and leaving him to his own devices.

The grinding lock echoed against the stone walls. Bane twisted to find the source of light and spied a small window at ground level. He didn't find anything of use to saw through his bonds, so he bent over backward and managed to stuff his hand into his pocket and fish out Edyth's pin. He ran his finger over the dull blade and began to saw back and forth across the rope, formulating a new plan to rescue Edyth. *Dear Lord, keep her safe until Roger can save her.*

Chapter Twenty

It is far better to draw what one now only sees in one's memory. That is a transformation in which imagination collaborates with memory.
~ Edgar Degas

Edyth gripped the small Bible to her chest and rocked back and forth on her wretched cot, whispering the name of Jesus to comfort herself. Despite the hope of escape, it frightened her to no end to think that she might forget His name once the madness of her mother descended upon her. "Jesus, save me. Don't let this be my story. Show me what to do."

She laid the Bible in her lap and slowly turned the pages to where Poppy's tattered ribbon marked her last reading. Edyth's gaze rested on the second book of Chronicles. " 'Ye shall not need to fight in this battle: set yourselves, stand ye still, and see the salvation of the Lord with you. . .fear not, nor be dismayed; to morrow go out against them: for the Lord will be with you.'" She bowed her head, almost meeting her knees. "Lord, I will try my best not to be afraid, but I have never felt or have been so powerless. I know You will be with me today as I enter the Gray Chamber. Please let Roger's plan work. Whatever happens, I know You will fight this battle and every one after for me."

The door creaked, sending her scurrying backward and tripping over her back hem.

"It's me." Nellie reached out and grabbed Edyth into a fierce hug, waking her from her panic. "The nurses were distracted with your uncle, so I told a male attendant that it was my time of month, and I needed to return to my cot. He grew uncomfortable and sent me here straightaway. How are you?"

Edyth stepped back to see her friend's expression. "I'm frightened. Did you come to tell me news of your contact? Did you speak with him?"

Nellie shook her head, misery etched into her face. "I don't know where he is. He was supposed to be here this morning at the latest." She raked her hands through her wild hair. "How could he do this? I'll have his hide."

Edyth tried to smile. "His hide won't do me much good now, will it? But there is hope yet."

Nellie seized Edyth's hands. "That's why I'm here. I saw what happened."

"Then you know the specialist is Bane? I should have told you sooner, so you wouldn't be so afraid for me, but—"

"That doesn't matter now. What matters is that Bane knows you are here," Nellie interrupted. "And even if I cannot help you, he will not allow this to happen to you. From what you tell me of him, he will return, charging in here, armed to the hilt. When a man loves a woman, and she is in danger, he will move heaven and earth to see her safe and in his arms."

"Bane is relentless when he sets his mind to something."

"I know it." Nellie gave her a small smile. "I read it in every glance, in every touch. The man adores you. You will not perish in this place, Edyth Foster."

Keys jingled at the door once more, and a giant orderly burst into the room, startling her into dropping her Bible. He grabbed Edyth up by her arms so roughly she screamed.

Nellie darted to her side and slapped the man as he pulled Edyth toward the hall. "Release her at once. Or so help me—"

The attendant slammed the door in Nellie's face and dragged Edyth behind him by her hair as Nellie's cries followed them.

Her blood pounded in her ears as the man jerked her down the hall. *Don't be afraid. Roger is here. He will get you out. Remember what Bane said. Act.* She clawed at his hands, attempting to break his hold. "Let me go! You don't know who I am! I can pay you a fortune if you only let me out of here."

He grunted and tightened his hold on her, ignoring her rant as she kicked and clawed at him. He easily hauled her toward the Gray Chamber, the dim lanterns lighting the way as the island grew dark with a brewing storm, thunder echoing in the hall.

The attendant threw open the door of the chamber, and Edyth dug her heels into the floor and pressed her palms up against the threshold, bracing herself. Using the side of his hand as an ax, the man smacked downward on her elbow, breaking her stance, and heaved her into a room that held two cots with restraints on them, a chair with straps, a board with straps. . . Everywhere she looked, there were restraints. Lightning lit the room, further revealing a crude wooden table that boasted straps to secure the head, arms, hands, legs, and feet. Spread atop was an array of filled needles and metal devices. She shivered at the thought of what they could be used for in the name of treatment. She felt like she was looking at a medieval torture chamber, for there was truly no other word for what this chamber promised for any patients within its belly.

Her gaze rested on a gray metal trough in the middle of the room that was filled to the brim with water, chunks of ice floating on top. Her breaths came in hitches at what stood beside it, a wooden cage the size of a coffin. She whipped her head to the side and bit the man holding her. He cried out and loosened his grip for a second, which was all she needed to bolt for the door and throw it open to find Roger with a short attendant beside him.

Edyth fairly wept with relief as she ceased her flight, the attendants seizing her at once. She was saved. "Roger, thank God. You are going to have them stop this charade of undergoing treatment now, aren't you?"

He kept his lips pursed and stepped into the room, one hand stroking his short red beard as his gaze swept over her. He snapped his fingers and pointed to the floor in front of the trough, the thugs setting her in the spot at once, her back to the door.

"It is time for you to act on your promise of protection." Her gaze fastened on the gray trough awaiting some poor soul. Tearing her attention back to Roger, she forced herself to release a short laugh. "All right, Roger, you've had your cruel amusement at my expense. Now release me so we can all go home."

She had seen the shivering of the disoriented bodies brought out of this room, and she did not wish to find out what it was like firsthand, but instead of answering her, Roger removed a white jacket from a line of white jackets hanging on pegs and tossed it to one of the men, who held it open. Before she realized what they were about, Roger gripped her arms and forced her into the jacket with a series of attached hooks and ties, securing her arms at her sides. The more she twisted, the tighter it became. "Enough of this! Release me, Roger!"

Roger motioned for the men to exit the room, and when the door closed, she exhaled with a shaky laugh.

"You nearly had me fooled, so I'm certain you fooled them too."

He rested a hand on her shoulder, sorrow etching his features. "I am truly sorry, Edyth. When I followed you to report your behavior to your uncle, I thought that, while you were eccentric, you were not out of your mind, and I decided to woo you to secure your fortune, but that all changed when I met Lavinia. She is a beauty. But when Boris realized he had something he could hold over my head, he used it. Your fate now controls mine."

Is he betraying me? She stared unblinking at him, but nothing registered over the roar in her ears.

"Boris told me that I either commit you for a handsome annual stipend and his approval to marry his stepdaughter, or lose Lavinia forever."

Fury flooded her, and she jerked away from his hold, bent her head down, and rammed him in the stomach. Roger fell to the floor, and she aimed her foot for his throat, but he rolled up and lunged for her. She ducked and whirled simultaneously, lifting her heel and butting him in the jaw, sending him sprawling back. She leapt atop the table, intending to dive through the glass of the window that, shockingly, did not have bars.

Roger swung his arm and knocked her legs out from under her, slamming her to the table and taking the wind from her lungs. She pressed her shoulder onto the table, struggling to rise without the use of her hands, but he easily pulled her to the floor.

"I trusted you. *We* trusted you." Her voice cracked.

Roger wrapped his arms around her from behind, his hot breath in her ear. "Hush now. It will be quick, painless."

"If Lavinia finds out that you personally administered this treatment, she will never forgive you. You still have a choice. If you tell her of Uncle's threat, Lavinia will not honor her stepfather. Help me escape, and all will be forgiven."

He shook his head. "If I do not go through with wiping your memories, I risk losing Lavinia if she ever discovers your location and hears the story from your lips." He tapped the cage and squatted. "So, to ensure that never happens, once I'm done with silencing you, I believe there is a specialist who will be having an accident inside the Gray Chamber."

She screamed, slamming her head back into his nose, feeling the crunch against her scalp. "Don't you dare touch Bane!"

Releasing her to cradle his nose, Roger yelled, "Orderlies!"

The men burst through the door and gripped her. Panic seized her as they pulled her forward and proceeded to stuff her inside the wooden cage and shut the top. She pressed her face between the bars, her breath coming in gasps. "Lord!" she cried out. *Protect my memories. Do not let them steal anything else from me.* "Save me, Jesus!"

"Be still. Stop fighting," came the nearly audible command, stilling her at once. *"Ye shall not need to fight in this battle: set yourself, stand ye still, and see the salvation of the Lord with you. Fear not, for the*

Lord will be with you." Tears spilled onto her cheeks, and she gave her trust over to God once more.

She drew a final breath, and they dropped her into the icy waters, stunning her body, but she let herself relax, thinking if she fought she might lose whatever air she had managed to keep. She was a good swimmer. She could hold her breath and fool them into thinking she had passed out. *I will not be afraid. I will not fear.*

The stiffness seeped through her being and, as her breath began to leave her, brought forth a cold from the recesses of her mind, and a memory flickered into life. She was a child again. Happy. She was skating. One, two, three strides and she stopped, her parents calling to her. Her heart stuttered at the vivid color in her mother's cheeks and the concern in her father's warning to stop. She giggled and kept skating. She heard a crack as the ice broke beneath her, and she sank into the freezing depths. Hands plunged into the water and she reached for them, three hands not touching. Then the jagged rim of ice overhead collapsed further, and her parents toppled into the gray water surrounding her.

She felt the cage being lifted, and then she broke the surface, gasping for air. Edyth felt the cool air flowing into her lungs, but she kept her eyes closed and lolled her head to the side, lest the doctor think she had not almost drowned.

"She fainted a lot sooner, Doc. Don't we usually hold 'em under longer?"

I was there. I was there the day my parents died. Those hands I saw reaching were Mother and Father attempting to save me. If Uncle knew that, what else has he been hiding from me all these years?

"Good enough for the first time. Her tolerance is most likely lower. Remove her straitjacket and lay her on the cot for an hour. We will do one last ice treatment before the first injection and then put her to bed directly afterward. Add more ice for the next patient. I'll return momentarily."

Edyth heard his heels click on the floor and the clinking of the ice pick, followed by a splash as the men did Roger's bidding. She dared to open an eye and spied a cane leaning against the one desk in the room, her heart stuttering as she recognized the silver engraved handle of the gift she had given not too long ago. *Bane's.* One of the orderlies must have pilfered it. *Thank You, Lord.* The asylum's greed would be her escape. She gathered her strength and waited for the right moment. Soon the taller attendant left to fetch another patient and the other approached her supposedly unconscious form, reaching for the straps attached to the table. She twisted her body and thrust a powerful kick between the man's legs, sending him to the ground with a groan as he curled into a ball.

"Hussy!" he grunted, attempting to rally, now on all fours.

Evading him, she lurched, her fingers grasping the cane's silver handle. Snatching it up, she twisted the head and yanked, revealing the deadly steel hidden beneath the surface. She swiveled, lifting her rapier, the tip directed at the attendant's face. She whipped the rodlike sheath around, wielding it like a second sword. The man laughed and barreled toward her, but with an expert move, she skirted him, striking him on the head with the sheath while using her blade to slice him in just the right muscle, causing his arm to fall limply to his side as he howled in pain.

Holding the tip of her blade to his cheek, she drew a thin line of blood and commanded, "Your keys."

"You will never make it. Your uncle has told a few of us that if you meet with an accident, there will be a bonus for us." The man sneered as he felt for the keys at his belt using his good hand.

"I'm dead if I stay, and I'm dead if I'm caught. I'd rather take my chances and live with my memories of being loved." *Before I follow in my grandmother's footsteps.*

Edyth snatched the keys from his fingertips, knocked him out with the butt of the cane head, and stumbled down the hall toward the rotunda where she knew she would have the best chance of escaping if she could only garner enough strength to fight her way through to the front doors. Blade at the ready, she checked the door to the rotunda and found it, of course, locked. She tucked the sheath under her arm while keeping the blade en garde and fumbled through the keys on the loop. Her fingers trembled as shouts rose behind her. The first key did not work. With an exasperated grunt, she thrust the second into the lock and nearly fainted at the click of the lock and swing of the door. She bolted through, rounded the corner, and smacked into something solid, knocking her to the ground and sending her weapons from her hands and sliding out of reach.

Chapter Twenty-One

Time is a vindictive bandit to steal the beauty
of our former selves. We are left with sagging,
rippled flesh and burning gums with empty sockets.
~ Raphael

He easily blocked her feral clawing. "Edyth, it's me," he whispered, hoping to calm her.

"Bane," she whimpered, throwing her arms about his neck, her body limp and gown soaked through.

With his arm securely about her waist, he fairly carried her as he snatched up the sword and sheathed it in the body of the cane, perfectly concealing the steel that he had not known existed until now. "Edyth, I need you to rally. We don't have much time." He assisted her down the rotunda's stairs that were miraculously vacant with all at supper. At the main doors, he nodded to the secretary at the front desk, who remained silent and behind her magazine in return for her pocketful of Bane's rent money.

Lightning flashed as they darted down the front steps and into the torrential downpour. His hand gripping hers, they raced down the road, the rain pelting them. If Edyth hadn't been in such peak physical condition before her ordeal, he hated to think how weak the island would have made her, rendering their escape impossible. He had seen the haggard women there and wondered if they were indeed mad or had been driven to madness by the staff. An owl screeched nearby followed by an animal shrieking that made Edyth clutch even more tightly to him. Branches occasionally slapped Bane in the face, and he attempted to keep them from hitting Edyth, but glancing down at her, he saw there were already long, angry scratches marring her lovely face. To her credit, she kept running, her eyes wide and her breath coming in short, rattling pants.

A bell sounded on the island as he leapt over a muddy hole in the road, but she slipped, sprawling face-first into leaves and branches. Bane dropped to his knees, wrapping his arms about her and waiting for her to move, lest he injure her further. "Are you hurt?"

She pushed herself up on her elbows, a soft groan escaping her lips. She sucked her muddied left palm and spat into the leaves before lowering her hand and pressing her lips into a line. She closed her eyes and gave her head a fierce shake, but he could see the wince between her brows when she rubbed her left wrist. "Thorns."

"Take a moment, Edyth. Catch your breath." He stroked her back, grimacing at her sunken ribs under his hand. She had been starved.

"We don't have a moment," she said, pulling herself to her feet.

"Edyth," he breathed, his eyes stinging at the realization that she didn't have any shoes protecting her soles. "Your feet. . .they–they're covered in blood."

"My shoes must have fallen off when I was fighting off the orderlies before Roger—"

"Before Roger what, Edyth? Did he hurt you?"

She nodded, her eyes glazing over. "I can't. Not now."

He pulled her into his arms and rested his chin atop her matted hair, his throat swelling with suppressed rage.

She pressed her hands to his chest, pushing herself from his arms. "We have to keep going. I can fall apart once we are safely away from this place." She held out her hands to him, ignoring the specks of blood blooming on them.

He would wait to hear her tale and then settle the score for Roger's betrayal. He helped her up, and they continued their run beside the East River. It shouldn't have taken them so long, but it was growing more and more difficult to see, and he knew they only had minutes now until the last ferry departed. He could have kicked himself for not hiring a boat for their return.

The dock came into sight, and along with it a wagon rolling straight toward them bearing three policemen inside. Ducking low, Bane drew her to the side of a vacant-looking building and took in her wild appearance. With her thin, torn gown soaked through and her hair that had long since lost its pins and hung in wet, matted strands, she looked entirely wild. He removed his coat and, despite it being soaked as well, wrapped her in it. With a gentle hand, he pushed her hair back from her face, leaving a single curl to hide the stitches. He tucked her long locks under the collar of the coat to hide the worst of the tangles. He pressed a kiss onto her forehead, and with her hand securely in his, he approached the ticket master and purchased their fare.

The ticket master eyed the leaves clinging to their hair and mud marring their clothing and sent Bane a guffawed laugh and a leer toward Edyth. "The bell is ringing. They are looking for someone," he said, his eyes returning to Edyth and back to Bane, his brows spiking.

"Are they?" Bane slid another bill to the man.

The ticket master shrugged. "Guess I heard wrong." He motioned them to the plank leading down to the ferry. The moment they stepped aboard, the captain rang the bell a single time, signaling for the journey to begin, and the ferry slowly pulled away from the dock, leaving Blackwell's Island behind.

Under the roof of the ferry, Bane breathed a sigh of relief and kept his grip firmly about Edyth's hand as her uncharacteristic silence sent a shard of fear into his heart. He prayed that his sweet, bright Edyth would return to him when she recovered from the ordeal. Knowing she would not wish to be trapped, he kept them on the edge of the roofline, not caring if the wind spent sprays of rain into their faces, and watched as the lighthouse scanned the island back and forth and back and forth. The bell still sounded, but they were far from the grasp of the asylum, and the presence of the hidden steel reassured him that if they were accosted again, they could fight their way to freedom. He glanced behind them and found a man keeping an eye on them from under the brim of his hat, so Bane tugged Edyth's hand and darted with her through the rain around to the other side of the ferry and out of sight of the man and the island.

Feeling tremors overtaking her, Bane turned her to him, lifting her chin to catch her face in the moonlight, his heart breaking anew at the bruises and cuts on her face. "You are safe with me. They will never touch you again," he whispered. He once again swallowed his questions. For now, just being together would be enough.

"Thank you. Thank you for looking for me."

"I will always look for you, Edyth. You and I. . .we belong together."

"Bane, I—" Thunder cracked the sky, silencing her reply. Edyth shook her head and lifted a shaking hand to her hair, laughing. "I must look a fright."

"Who cares about that?" He brought his lips down and slowly, carefully, kissed each of the bruises and cuts. His lips grazed her jaw, and seeing the angry fingerprints at her neck, he bent and kissed each mark, her body swaying into his.

❧

His kisses brought a warmth to her bones she'd never known before. She pressed her forehead to his chest, wishing she could stay in the safety of his embrace forever. She lifted her gaze to him. She needed to tell him, but his lips made her thoughts blurred. "Bane, I—I." *I love you.* "I knew you would find me."

"I would have searched for you until my dying breath." He lifted her hand, and she grimaced at the dirt caked under her nails, but he didn't seem to care as he pressed a kiss to each fingertip before stroking her cheek. "I know I'm not the kind of man your father would have wanted for you. I'm not rich—"

Edyth's soul ached. If only she could ignore the truth. . . . She wrapped her arms around his neck and slowly lifted her lips to his, pausing a breath away, and answered, "You are *exactly* the kind of man Papa would have wanted for me." *And as long as I have you, I need nothing else.* She read the hunger in his eyes that mirrored her own, but she couldn't give in to her weakness and kiss him again, not when her secret weighed down on her like a stone. She rested her cheek on his chest once more and sighed. "What do we do now?"

"Well, until we can clear your name in the eyes of the law, you are to stay tucked away in my family's country estate. If anyone comes looking, no one there will give you away."

"But if they do find me and bring the police, they have the law on their side. I will be taken away again, and this time, there will be no escape from my uncle. I need to leave the country. It is the only way to be safe. Well, as safe as I can be on the run."

He grasped her shoulders, moving her to look into his eyes. "There is another way. He will not be able to touch you once you are married and your welfare transfers to your husband."

Her mouth went slack. *He would do that for me?* She shook the stars from her head. *Tell him, you coward. You are not the woman you thought you were before the island.* "Bane. . .it's too much," she whispered, unwilling to shatter their world so soon. She had yet to speak the words aloud. She knew that once she did, everything would change.

"Too much for a man to protect the woman he loves?" He lifted her hand and pressed it against his heart. "I would do anything for you, Edyth Foster. When you were taken away, I realized that the pain of losing you was far greater than that of losing a mere friend. It was the pain of a heart being wrenched away from the one it was meant to love. Because I do love you. And if you allow it, because I know you are a self-proclaimed strong, independent woman, I want to protect you with everything that I am. I love you."

"Being a strong woman doesn't mean I have to live my life alone. There is strength in loving someone." Her eyes rested on his lips and back to his dear face. *Tell him,* her mind screamed over her heart's protests. She tugged her hand away and stepped back, desperate to put a little distance between herself and his alluring scent of leather and sandalwood, then, remembering that she wore his coat about her shoulders, she knew it was futile. "But you don't know what you are saying. I learned something on the island that I cannot forget. My maternal grandmother—" Her voice caught on the thorny words.

"Died on the island in the asylum," he finished for her, taking her hand and drawing her back.

She lifted her gaze to him, tilting her head. "You know? B–but why did you kiss me, if you knew that madness runs in the women of my family?" *And we can never be more than friends?*

"Edyth, your uncle did not tell you why she was committed." He stroked a lock of hair behind her ear. "My hired detective, Jude Thorpe, made short work of finding the answer." His calloused hands cupped her face. "Your grandmother was committed after being accused of adultery brought on by madness, both of which were vile falsehoods created by your grandfather."

"How is that possible?" she sputtered, trying to comprehend it all as her knees weakened with hope.

He wrapped his hands under her elbows to support her. "Your grandfather, Lord Blakely, wished to wed another in order to have the son he so desperately wanted, but the only way that Blakely could get his request for a divorce approved was if Lady Blakely was committed to the asylum on the grounds of adultery brought about by madness. The tale he had spun was all fabrications. Thorpe made quick work in uncovering that Lord Blakely was the real adulterer, but who would believe a woman over her knighted husband nearly fifty years ago? But, as you know, your grandfather did not have any more children, so that fortune went to your mother and now you."

"Then, that means my uncle *lied.* And I believed him like a fool."

She shook her head and gave a soft laugh, never so thankful for a falsehood. She turned to him with a renewed dream in her heart, one with Bane at her side, along with a baby on each hip and her four cats at their feet and a basket of kittens.

"You are and will continue to be as sane as I." He smiled down at her, that rare dimple in his left cheek appearing.

She squealed and lifted her arms to the sky and twirled in the rain, hooting with glee.

He grasped her hand in his and pulled her back under the roof. "So, does that change your mind about marrying me?"

She stepped toward him, a hairbreadth away, her face tilted back to take in his strong jawline in the ferry's lantern light. "If you are certain this is what you want and you aren't saying this to rescue me from a life on the run? Because I can flee to France. I'm certain I could become a respected fencing instructor over there where the sport has been strong for—"

Bane laughed. His deep-throated mirth made her heart dance. "I'm certain you could, but the only problem with that plan is that I would miss you too much. And if you look at it that way, this time it is you who will have to do the rescuing, because there is a peculiar ache in my chest when you are away and I'm afraid you are the only one with the cure. I wish to wed you more than anything I've ever wanted in my entire life."

She traced her finger along his jaw, loving the hint of scruff that had grown since he had come to the island. "I've loved you for so long. I fear that I will wake on the morrow to my nightmare existence on the island and discover this has all been but a dream. Are you truly mine, my dearest Bane?" Slowly, she placed her arms around his neck and rose on her toes and pressed a soft kiss to his lips, melding her mouth with his as he wrapped his arms around her waist and pulled her into an even deeper kiss that banished the storm and summoned the stars to appear.

He pulled back, his eyes bright in the moonlight. "This *is* a dream, but only of the best nature, because it is true. I love you, Edyth Foster, and plan on reminding you every day for the rest of eternity that you are safe and I am yours and you are mine, my sweet bride."

Chapter Twenty-Two

*How different everything is when
you are with the right people!*
~ Kate Greenaway

Edyth fairly ran to take the plank to the dock, but Bane kept a steadying hand wrapped about her elbow as the man who had been eyeing them cut in front of them and trotted off into the night. Bane did not make any eye contact with the crew and, once they had mounted the plank, moved purposefully away from the docks at a clipped pace. Putting two blocks between them and the island's ferry and cutting over one block, Bane could hardly believe that Jude was still there, waiting beside a small coach.

"What happened?" Jude asked, swiping off his hat and politely nodding to Edyth. "I was about to head to the island if you were not on that last ferry."

"Everything that could go wrong did. But now is not the time to explain." Bane tilted his head down to Edyth tucked in the crook of his arm. He settled her onto the worn, tufted coach seat and joined her, returning his arm about her tiny frame while Jude hopped up into the driver's seat.

A soft mist began, chilling them as they drove into the evening. She shrugged out of his wet coat and draped the coach's plaid over them both, snuggling closer to him, the action making Bane's heart lurch. Had he really just kissed her and she promised to wed him? He could sing for happiness but settled for pressing a kiss atop her wet hair, not minding the lingering scent of her time in the asylum. Edyth was here and safe in his arms and had promised to be his. Edyth loved him! He could holler with delight.

The ride to the estate passed in contented, sweet silence as they stayed wrapped in one another's arms, finding comfort at long last. As the carriage pulled into the drive of his family's mansion, he spied an all too familiar carriage that made Edyth sit bolt upright.

She gripped him by the arm as a figure appeared in the doorway, his gaze fixed on their buggy. "The man from the ferry must have been from the asylum, sent to contact my uncle. Bane, he can't reach me. No matter our hopes, if he catches me, all is lost."

"Turn us around at once!" he shouted to Jude.

Jude pulled the reins, directing the buggy into a sharp turn and drawing a protest from the horse as shouts behind them escalated.

"Go. Go!" Bane shouted to Jude, who slapped the reins again, pushing the horse as hard as he might.

Bane held on to Edyth with one arm while gripping the side of the coach with the other, anchoring them as Jude sent them careening down the moonlit road, only slowing as they came to the populated streets, weaving around other hired cabs.

"Bane, I think we should head to your club," Jude called over his shoulder. "It is the nearest, safest place at the moment."

"Agreed." He had weapons enough there and could fight off anyone who dared come knocking.

Edyth shivered under his arm, her teeth chattering and causing her words to slur. "But Uncle will certainly go there looking for me."

He gripped her hands in his and rubbed her icy skin between his palms to draw warmth into them. "We need to get you out of the elements. Besides, I'm hoping Foster will think it is such an obvious place for us to hide, he will search elsewhere first. The moment we make it inside, I'll send Jude for the pastor, and then your uncle won't be able to threaten you ever again."

"Pastor?" Jude twisted back to look at him for a second before turning on the club's street. "You two aren't planning on eloping to beat out the law, are you?"

"That's exactly what we're doing."

Jude let out a whistle through his teeth. "Didn't see that one coming, but if you want to get married, the most efficient way is for me to turn down this road and head to the parsonage."

"Yes, but Edyth will catch her death if we do not get her dry soon," Bane replied, his gaze falling on her blue-gray lips.

Jude shook his head. "I should've considered the lady's health. My apologies."

Shivering once more, she buried her head in his shoulder. "I never imagined much about my wedding, but I thought I'd at least be clean."

He chuckled. "What? You mean you never dreamed of being married in a dress not even fit for the rag pile, much less in a fencing club?"

She turned sparkling eyes up to him. "Actually, the idea of marrying you in the fencing club where I fell in love with you sounds fitting and beautiful."

The carriage halted, and as Bane helped her to the ground, he called to Jude, "Fetch my brother, Pastor Tom Banebridge, and his wife, over at the Baptist church. Do you think you can be back within a half hour?"

"Yes, but I do not like leaving you here without me to aid you."

"Your concern does you credit, but we will be fine. Make haste," Bane assured him.

"Keep alert," Jude called, smacking the reins.

Bane unlocked and held the massive door for Edyth while she slipped inside, her feet slapping the marble foyer, with the only light streaming in the windows from the streetlamps. Setting his cane beside the hall tree, Bane motioned for her to continue inside. She rubbed her hands up and down her threadbare sleeves, shivering as they stepped in the fencing hall.

"We need to get you warm. I'll light the fire," he said, nodding toward the fireplace in the great hall, ready with logs and kindling. "You may have to borrow a gown from one of the women's personal shelves."

"I think I might actually have a fencing gown still stowed on my shelf." She stepped away to change, but he snatched her fingers, intertwining them with his, reluctant to let her out of his sight.

"Allow me to check the room first before you are alone in there." To his surprise, instead of protesting, she gave an appreciative smile.

"Thank you. I didn't want to say anything, but dark rooms no longer seem so harmless after. . ." She dipped her head and focused on their interlaced fingers.

He squeezed her hand and, for good measure, removed a sword from the wall and held it before them as they stepped into the room. No one menacing was lingering in the shadows. He watched while she gathered her striped fencing gown from the closet, her hand stroking the fabric with reverence.

"I never thought I would see any of my dresses again, much less my favorite gown."

He stroked her cheek with his thumb. "I'll be just outside the door. Shout if you need me."

"I have always needed you, Bane."

❧

Lifting the dripping sponge from the porcelain basin, Edyth's hands shook as she slowly bathed her face and arms, freeing herself from the disgusting layers of grime that had been building since she was taken that first night. She ached for a bath but was thankful for even these small ablutions. She reached for the silver comb on her closet shelf, her fingers trembling, knowing it would be hopeless to expect it to make much difference. Instead, she divided her locks as best she could and plaited them in a thick braid. She wound the braid into a bun at the base of her neck and pinned it into place before slipping into her gown that kissed her raw skin.

She turned in the looking glass and sighed at her stitches, cut lips, bruised cheeks, and the dark circles under her eyes from count-less sleepless nights. *Oh well. I never would have been the typical blushing bride even on my best of days.* Spying a vase of fresh-looking crimson roses, she removed five blossoms, snapped off the stems, and stuck them atop her coiffure as she would a jeweled comb, remembering the first night she had done so and had captured her love's attention.

Finding her fencing shoes in the closet with her stockings carelessly shoved inside, she slipped the silk over her legs, sighing with delight at the smooth, rich texture before wincing at the fresh wounds on her soles when they rubbed against the soft leather of her shoes. She took a deep breath, straightened her shoulders, and drew her sash across her body. Wrapping it about her waist for flare, she tied it into a puffed knot at her side and snatched up the remaining roses for a bouquet, wrapping a glove around the stems to protect her hands from the thorns.

"Edyth?" Bane's voice, even from the hall, filled her with warmth. "Jude is standing guard outside, and Tom is here, along with his wife to serve as a witness. Are you ready?"

I've been ready for you for years, my love. For her answer, she joined him, offering her brightest smile. Even though she may not be dressed as a bride, she felt like one.

Bane's brother's eyes widened at her appearance. "Oh my, Miss Foster."

Mrs. Sylvia Banebridge clasped her hands over her ample chest. "My dear, what on earth?"

"It's a long story, which I will tell you *after* the vows have been spoken and the certificate signed. I apologize if I seem rude, but time is of the essence," Edyth replied with a smile, her eyes on her groom.

"Then by all means, please join hands." Tom motioned them to stand together in front of the flickering fireplace.

Edyth basked in the handsomeness of her Bane, hardly believing that after all these years of longing to be his bride, her dreams were coming true.

"Edyth Foster, do you take this man to be your husband?"

"Yes." A shout and the sound of something slamming against the front doors made her clutch Bane, her memory snapping back to the last time someone had broken down her door. "I thought Jude was standing guard!"

"They must have overpowered him." Bane wrapped his arm about her waist. "You will not be taken from me again," he whispered, and then he commanded, "Continue, Tom."

The doors sounded like they were being kicked in, but the pastor kept his voice firm. "And do you, Raoul Banebridge, take Miss Edyth Foster as your bride?"

"Yes!"

"I now pronounce you husband and wife," he concluded in a rush and reached for his wife, tucking her in the crook of his arm just as the sound of glass shattering filled the club.

"The transoms!" Edyth buried her face in Bane's chest. She was tired of being strong. It had been too long since she'd had a moment without the looming threat of her uncle destroying everything she held dear in the world.

"Where is the marriage certificate? We need to sign it at once." Bane looked to his brother.

Tom pulled it from the back pages of his Bible and handed it to Bane.

"We need a pen. Where's a pen when you need one?" Bane grunted, running a hand through his hair.

Edyth ran to a small table by the window on the off chance it held a pen, glancing out and seeing her uncle with the two thugs who stole her away that first night, one threading his arm through the broken glass, attempting to open the door from the inside. "Nothing here, but there will be one at the front desk or in your office."

Hearing shouts in the foyer, they rushed up the back stairs to the second-floor office, pulling Tom and Sylvia along with them up the steps.

Breathing hard, Bane seized a pen, signed his name, then gave the pen to Edyth. She signed the certificate and handed it to Tom and Sylvia to sign as witnesses. Spying a short knife on Bane's desk, Edyth grasped it and slid it into the hidden pocket of her gown as Bane placed the completed certificate in the bottom drawer of his desk and locked it.

"Get the women out of here and fetch the police," Bane ordered Tom, who scrambled to obey, reaching for Edyth.

"I will not leave you!" Edyth gripped Bane's arm. "I cannot bear to be separated again. I would rather stay and fight with you than run anymore." She motioned to the couple to leave without her.

Bane pushed Edyth behind him as Tom and Sylvia moved to take the back stairs. "I'm sorry, Edyth, I should have grabbed a weapon for you as well when I had the chance."

Uncle Boris charged through the doorway, brandishing a firearm that he pointed directly at Bane. Seeing the tension in Bane's muscular form as he held his offensive position, his blade at the ready, Edyth squared her shoulders and lifted her fists.

"You are too late, sir. We are married," her husband boomed, commanding the room with his presence.

"Which shall be remedied at once when the courts have it annulled. You may have delayed her treatment, but she will still have it." Uncle Boris motioned her over with one hand, keeping his firearm trained on Bane. "You will join me, Edyth. However, it is your choice if it is with or without a fatality."

Edyth's stance faltered. Knowing the extent of his cruelty, she would not put it past him to follow through on his threat. She had made the mistake of underestimating him before. She would not do so again. A sword against bullets would not be a fair fight. She had come too far to have her happy ending perish before her eyes, not while she could stop it. "Fine."

"Edyth, whatever are you about? You cannot trust this snake," Bane warned, keeping his sword trained on their foe.

She gave his shoulder a squeeze, silently begging him to trust her. Moving away from the safety of Bane, she dropped her head as if in despair and resignation and slowly approached her uncle, hoping that it wasn't too great of a gamble to expect Bane to understand her intent.

Her uncle directed his gun to her, and she kept her hands where he could see them, all the while moving herself to the best position where she could draw her weapon without him catching her in time. She looked to Bane, widening her eyes at him, hoping he would create the diversion she needed.

"Do not harm my wife, Foster. Our marriage certificate is signed and witnessed. I guarantee that it will hold up in a court of law."

As she had hoped, her uncle returned his attention to Bane. "Then she shall be your widow." Her heart dropped as he directed the barrel to Bane's heart, his finger pulling the trigger. Edyth lunged in front of Bane and sent the dagger flying as a shot split the night.

Chapter Twenty-Three

The door of the human heart,
can only be opened from the inside.
~ William Holman Hunt

Bane watched in horror as the woman he treasured above all shoved him out of the way, her eyes widening as she fell to her knees. "Edyth!"

With Edyth's blade protruding from his thigh, Foster turned his weapon on Bane, an evil glint in his eyes. Bane whipped his blade up and struck the barrel, sending the next shot into the ceiling. With a deft stroke, he disarmed the man and, using his hilt, rendered him unconscious.

Bane sank beside Edyth, her blood pooling into his hand beneath her shoulder. He eased his bride onto his lap, keeping pressure on the wound. "Edyth, my darling. Open your eyes," he whispered, but she remained motionless, her chest barely moving. He jerked off his neckcloth and held it to her shoulder and pressed, praying the blood would cease its flow as he watched her skin pale. "Edyth?" He cradled her head to his chest and took her hands in his. "God, please."

Her hands were too cold, and he could no longer see her chest moving. His breath hitched. "Edyth! You cannot leave me. Please." He lifted her chin, her cheeks bereft of rose and warmth. He folded her into his arms, her head and arms lolling back, her full lips slack. His shoulders caved as his jaw loosed in a soundless moan. He rocked her back and forth, his body racked with suppressed sobs. "No, my dear friend. You cannot leave me. Not when we've only found one another again."

"What has happened here?" Bertram asked from the doorway

in his evening coattails with Jude draped on his arm, pressing his palm to his bleeding forehead. Jude grew a shade paler but kept a respectable distance as Bertram sank to his knees and placed his ear at Edyth's mouth and shook his head. He pressed two fingers at her wrist and then the other.

Bane traced her lips with his fingertip, numb. "She sacrificed herself."

Bertram exhaled. "Her pulse is weak, but it is there, Brother. She lives yet, praise God."

Alive? Bane pressed a kiss to her forehead before lifting his gaze heavenward, tears trailing down his chin. *Thank You, Lord.*

"Let me fetch my medical bag. Keep pressure on that wound! I'll be back directly."

The room around him faded as he clamped his hands over her wound and prayed for her life, his throat swelling at the bruises on his sweetheart, a vivid reminder of her abuse. "Hold on, sweet girl."

Bertram trotted back into the office and knelt beside her, and with a deft slice from his scissors, he cut her gown from her wound and gently turned her. "She has an exit wound. It is a miracle that the shot did not shatter her collarbone or strike anything vital. I'll sanitize her wounds and stitch them up, but we should send for a physician once she is stable and pray that she doesn't fall victim to an infection."

Foster shifted, groaning as he awoke and moving as if to heave himself to his feet.

Bane snatched up his blade. "If it weren't for her kind soul, Foster, I'd run you through, you heartless—" The man made a lurch for the knife in his leg, and Bane flicked his blade in warning as Jude crossed the room and secured the man's hands with rope. "I warn you to stay down, sir, or a knife wound will be the least of your worries."

Jude pulled the rope taut before shifting Foster's leg to examine it, which made him grunt with pain.

"Have a care, man!"

"I do, which is why I need your shirt." Leaving the blade in place, Jude ripped off the bottom of Foster's shirt, his ample waistline providing a generous tourniquet for the man's upper thigh.

Foster spat on the rug at Edyth's feet, skewering Bane with his narrowed gaze. "You *thief*. How dare you interfere!"

How dare he? "You threw her into a pit, leaving her there to die while you stole her future from her." Bane kept his voice low, wishing he could strike the man, but he wouldn't leave Edyth's side until she opened her eyes.

Boots sounded on the stairs, and Tom returned with two policemen in tow. "My apologies for having to abandon you during the scuffle. Sylvia is safe, and I've brought the authorities." His words faded at the blood-splattered room before him.

Bane's gaze returned to Edyth, as bits of the argument around him came through the haze of his friend's. . .wife's pain. He stroked her brow that furrowed with every stitch of Bertram's needle.

"Officers, this man abducted my niece and has been holding me against my will," Foster called to the policemen from his place on the floor, clutching at his leg. "And I need medical attention. The girl threw a knife at me!"

One of the officers nodded to the blade stuck in Boris's thigh. "That the one, sir?"

"Obviously. Seems they don't pay you for your powers of deduction over in the police department. That boy refused to remove it, and I am certain I lost more blood because of his stubbornness."

The officer nearest him knelt and examined the wound. "We best get him to a hospital before bringing him in to the station. But I suggest you mind your words. That boy, as you call him, is the son of one of the finest detectives in the city, and he probably saved your life by not removing it until we can get you to the hospital."

"Bringing me in? Are you out of your mind? What did that pastor tell you? Well, he may be a man of the cloth, but it is all a lie."

His lips curled into a sneer.

"And the bullet through the lady's shoulder would be a lie too?" Bane replied, never looking up, waiting for Edyth to stir in his arms, anything to let him know that she was going to live.

"It was meant for you in defense of the abduction of my niece, a child."

Jude scratched his chin. "How can a man abduct his own wife, a grown woman of nearly five and twenty years?"

"Your wife? She's only been out of the asylum for a couple of hours." Bertram looked up for half a second before snipping away the ends of the thread and retrieving bandages from his bag. "Good work, Tom."

Jude returned his attention to the officers. "Boris Foster broke into my client's place of business and shot his bride."

Tom nodded. "Even though I did not see the shot itself, I witnessed his attempt at abduction. My wife is still shaken from the ordeal."

"Your word and Jude's is good enough for me, Pastor. Boris Foster, you are under arrest for breaking and entering and the attempted murder of Mrs. Banebridge." The officers pulled Foster's arms behind his back and, with their hands on his shoulders and forearms, propelled him toward the exit, despite his wound.

"I want my lawyer," he shouted.

"Better hope he's good," Bane growled. "Or I fear you may languish in a cell much like the one you placed your niece in. Perhaps it would be a mercy to send you to the men's asylum instead of prison? What do you think of that, Officers?"

"Sounds a little cracked to shoot a defenseless girl who is a close relation."

"You thieving—!" Foster's tirade was cut short as the officers dragged him from the room and down the stairs.

Bane kept careful watch as his brother finished dressing Edyth's wound. He massaged her hand, hoping to bring warmth to her chilled body. "Why hasn't she awakened yet, Bertram?"

Bertram rolled his soiled instruments into a cloth. "The shock of it must have caused her to faint, and then, followed by such blood loss, it's natural she has not gained consciousness yet. But she is resting quietly now. I could wake her with smelling salts, but I don't want her to jar her stitches and risk reopening the wound. Now, we can't rightly keep your bride on the floor until she wakes. What's your plan, Brother?"

❧

Edyth grew aware of a burning sensation. *What new torture have they found?* Sitting up, she groaned at the pain radiating from her shoulder. She reached to find the source of the pain, but someone grasped her hand, stopping her from touching it. The pressure on her hand was not a hostile one, not like any nurse in the asylum, besides Nurse Jenny and Nurse Camden.

"Sweetheart," Bane whispered, the timbre of his voice calming her as his arm tightened about her waist. "Don't move just yet. You were shot but are on the mend."

Memories came flooding back with the tug of stitches against her skin. She was safe. She was married! "Bane?" She lifted her gaze to his, squinting in the lambent candlelight. "Where are we?"

"At my family's estate. You have been given a draft every few hours that has been keeping you still for a few days while your body heals. We've been feeding you soup whenever you have awakened. Though you have been pretty incoherent, which is understandable given the medicine. But the doctors are now tapering off your doses, so you should begin to remember soon."

She looked down and found herself in a clean nightgown, her nails scrubbed free from dirt, the scent of lavender coming from her skin. She rubbed her fingers together, finding the silky texture of cold cream. Her cheeks warmed. "Who—?"

"Mother's lady's maid." He dropped his gaze, his cheeks also tinting.

His heightened color made her want to giggle at the thought of Raoul Banebridge feeling embarrassed.

A throat cleared from the darkened corner of the room and Mrs. Banebridge approached the bed carrying something white in her arms. "My dear girl, we were so worried about you. We didn't know what had become of you when you disappeared. I thought Raoul would fret himself mad."

Edyth gave a weak smile. Mrs. Banebridge had always treated her as another daughter, and now, Edyth could hardly believe that she actually was by law.

Mrs. Banebridge leaned down and handed her the tiny, mewing fluff.

"Michelangelo?" She nestled her nose in the kitten's fur and sighed, her heart mending just a bit as the kitten licked her chin. "I thought my aunt would have disposed of you right away."

"She tried, but I snuck inside and fetched him, Leo, Raphael, and Edgar out in time."

She reached for his hand. "It seems I will have an endless list of thank-yous to give you."

"Oh, there's more where that came from." He grinned. "And I plan on telling you the moment you are ready to hear everything I've done for you. Including, rescuing your sketchbook." Bane pulled it from his coat and rested it in her free hand.

"It's so warm," she replied, stroking the worn cover.

"I've kept it with me constantly, *except* for a brief time when I lent it to Jude. No telling who he showed it to."

"What?" She sat up, her wound protesting.

Mrs. Banebridge laughed. "Raoul, don't tease her. Now, I'll send up the soup. You two sit still and rest." She rustled out of the room, closing the door behind her.

Edyth's stomach rumbled to life with such a vengeance, it frightened the kitten. She was starving.

Bane lifted her palm and pressed a warm kiss onto it. "The

doctors said that despite your ordeal, you are strong and will heal quickly. They must have said at least a dozen times that it was quite the miracle that the bullet passed through without doing more damage or that you did not incur a fever as a result. We are lucky."

"Well, I don't know about lucky. My uncle was never a very good shot." She sent him a wink to ease the creases between his brows. "But in all seriousness, I am thankful the Lord saved me once more."

A knock at the door sounded, and slipping from the bed, Bane opened the door enough to take the tray from the maid. He closed the door with his boot, the dishes rattling in his unsteady hands.

Edyth smiled at her husband's balancing the tray as he carefully crossed the room and set it on a side table with a clatter.

"You most likely don't remember, but I fed you soup for the past few days, even though you clamored for cherry pie."

"Pie sounds lovely, especially with a little browned crumble on top." She licked her lips that were no longer chapped. She would have to thank the maids for their attentiveness.

"But soup will do for now," he said, giving the folded napkin a snap and tucking it under her chin.

Sitting up, wincing slightly at the stitches pulling again, Edyth moved to take the bowl from Bane, but he clicked his tongue and lifted a spoonful, blew on the liquid, and brought it to her lips, the rich broth bringing life to her weary body. The soup dribbled onto her chin, but Bane reached out and wiped it with his handkerchief with such tenderness that it made her stomach do a strange flip. She brushed the tips of her fingers along his jawline, loving the ruddiness of his unshaven skin and reveling in the fact that it was not improper for her to wish to do so any longer.

Bane caught her hand in his and lifted her fingers to his lips, sending her pulse to pounding as the gravity of what just happened pressed on her. She had married the man she longed to for years and wed him with the stench of the asylum upon her. *He must really love me.* Despite the throbbing in her shoulder and her weakened state, Edyth was truly happy. She was free—for now—and that thought threatened the contents of her stomach. "What happened to my uncle? Is there any reason to believe they will take me again?"

"Don't worry." He pressed another kiss along her fingertips before returning to the soup and lifting a spoonful to her lips. "You are safe, and I am hoping to take you away as soon as you can speak with your lawyer. Mr. Pittman will be here in about an hour and a half."

"Mr. Pittman? I haven't seen him since I was a girl." *After my parents' death,* she added silently.

"Mr. Pittman was quite disheartened to hear of your ordeal and thinks we have a strong case, especially since Wentworth had too much to drink again at his dinner party last night and told him enough to get himself suspended from practice if reported." He shook his head. "He won't be, of course, because of his old family name, but it gives us rather an advantage."

"I'm eager to speak with Mr. Pittman and put this behind us, but uh. . ." She glanced down at her frilly nightgown. She would have to dress. She lifted the covers to her shoulders, giving a little shiver to disguise her shyness, the shiver costing her as the stitches tugged yet again. Would she ever be free from pain? "I think I am well enough, but you may have to carry me down the stairs."

"Any excuse to hold you is fine by me," he replied, giving her a roguish grin.

Now it was her cheeks that warmed at this new side of her dear friend. "I don't think I mind you holding me either," she admitted, dipping her head.

He leaned in and pressed his forehead to hers and waited for her to meet his beautiful jade eyes. "Mrs. Banebridge, if you *did* mind, I think we might have an issue, with us being married and all."

Giggling, she set Michelangelo on the pillow next to her and lifted the covers. She attempted to move her legs but found them to be shockingly weak. It was rather disturbing how quickly one's body could deteriorate.

"Let me help you," he said, moving aside the rest of the quilt. With gentle hands, he lifted her bare ankles and helped her twist so her legs were hanging off the bed. "Would you like to try to stand?"

"I don't trust my limbs at the moment, but with more food, I should be wielding my sword soon enough." She gave a soft laugh to hide her displeasure over the state of her hard-earned muscles.

"Let's get you back down," he said, and slowly lowered her to her pillow, placing her legs on top of the comforter this time. "I would prefer for you to wield your paintbrush for the next few months. However, the doctor said you could attempt a few light exercises in four to six weeks to help you regain your strength before you attempt to return to your full fencing lessons. Now, you have three bites left, Mrs. Banebridge." He lifted the spoon to her lips, her portions coming quickly now as if to stave off any protest.

"Because you are my husband, I suppose I should agree with you. . .at least until I regain my strength. For now, I will be content to be doted upon." The bowl empty, she leaned back, surprised to find herself exhausted from the effort of eating such a small meal, but her stomach still rumbled. "Did the doctor say anything about pie? I long for a flaky crust with a sweet cherry filling." Her mouth watered as if it were before her.

He laughed and rose. "I can see what he has to say about that. Is there anything else you wish for while I relay the message?"

She felt the color rise in her cheeks. "Well, I'd love to have a bath drawn before I see anyone. I appear to be clean enough now, but until I am aware of the scrubbing, I don't think I'll ever feel clean."

He scooped up the kitten, holding it in one arm. "Certainly, but the doctor was very clear that you are not to get your dressings wet. Rest a moment, and Michelangelo and I will send two maids in to help you from the bed to the tub."

Within a half hour, Edyth found herself in a luxurious bath with bits of lavender and scented soap. A soft moan escaped her at the clean water against her skin, but when it was time to do her hair, she found her heart pounding at the thought of plunging her head under the water. But instead, one maid positioned her hands over Edyth's wounded shoulder as the other slowly poured the warm water over her tender scalp. She then applied the luxurious soaps to Edyth's hair, removing every trace of Blackwell's Island with a precise and gentle hand.

Wrapped in a pink silk dressing robe borrowed from Bane's mother, Edyth did not possess the strength to sit up at the vanity. Instead, she sprawled atop the tufted settee as the maid combed through her hair as gently as she could manage while another worked on her nails, shaping them into perfect ovals before rubbing Edyth's arms and feet with cold cream, murmuring over the state of her poor bruised skin. Pity radiated from their touch and words, but they treated her with such kindness, Edyth did not mind. Had it really only been days that she'd been trapped on the island from Hades?

She glanced into the gilded looking glass as the maid formed a braided coronet with her damp locks. Her cheeks were so sunken that she appeared to have been trapped on the island for months. But she supposed starvation would do that to anyone, and with the thought of food, her stomach sparked to life once more.

The maid splayed a hand over her chest. "Oh miss! Forgive me, I was supposed to ring for a tea cart with sandwiches and pie once you were out of your bath." She crossed the room and pulled the bell, murmuring her apologies until the cart appeared.

Pie consumed, along with a few sandwiches, and dressed in a corset-free satin gown of her favorite color, Edyth spread her crimson skirts on the settee and picked up her sketchbook while she waited for her husband to join her.

❧

Bane stood in the doorframe with his arms crossed and studied his wife as she sat with her feet propped up, sketching away. "I can't believe I'm married to such a stunning woman."

"Oh!" She started, dropping her pencil. "Well, being clean can improve anyone's looks. . .even when one is as battered as I."

Crossing the room, he knelt and returned her sketchbook to the side table before wrapping her in his embrace and gently sweeping her in his arms, her skirts trailing down over his arm.

She studied him, tilting her head as she bit her lip.

"What is it? Does this make you feel uncomfortable?"

"I must say I have always wanted to do this." She reached out and, with both hands, raked her fingers through his shoulder-length blond hair. "Your hair is meant to be adored, good sir, and often."

Bane grinned at her and nestled his nose into her hair. "And I this, now that you have finally bathed. Your matted hair kept reminding me of that time when you went weeks without washing after our fencing bouts."

Her jaw dropped as their passionate spark sputtered into laughter at his teasing. "For your information, I was on *strike*. If my mother and father did not discharge that horrible governess who rapped my knuckles every time I uttered a word out of turn, I would not bathe. It took a month, but my stench at the dinner table, after our lessons, wore them down eventually." She shrugged and added, "And who knows, I may have to pull the same stunt if you get out of hand and start demanding I turn in my rapier. You should know that while I consider homemaking to be one of the most noble professions, it is not in my nature to wait upon you at home while you work."

He threw his head back and laughed. "You keep mentioning your sword. You should know me well enough to know that I'm not the type of husband who would demand you stop doing what you love."

Edyth stroked his cheek with the back of her hand before returning her fingers to his hair. "I'm sorry. It's an old worry of mine."

He kissed the tip of her nose. "I knew you chose not to marry all those years for some reason."

Edyth laughed and rolled her eyes. "The reason, my dear, was that I was waiting on you to notice me."

He rested his forehead on hers. "Thank you for waiting." He sighed. "And as much as I would rather stay tucked away up here with you, we best be on our way, Mrs. Banebridge, to speak with Mr. Pittman."

"I suppose. The sooner we do, the sooner we can be alone," she replied, leaning her head on his shoulder.

Bane carefully maneuvered the stairs with her in his arms, relishing the closeness of her. He didn't wish to share her with anyone, but the moment they got this business out of the way, they could take their extended holiday for her recovery. Watching Edyth sleep for the past few days had been difficult, the weight of not knowing her full story pressing on him. He wasn't even certain she would be ready to share anytime soon, but in the meantime, Bane hoped she would enjoy the trip he'd planned for her.

"Edyth, thank the good Lord you are well." Lavinia didn't wait for Bane to set her down before pulling her into a gentle embrace, mindful of Edyth's healing wound. "I was so worried, and I couldn't bear the thought that you might be under the impression I was secretly helping Boris and Roger. Bane and I had been searching and when we couldn't find you—" Her voice cracked. "I was sorry to learn of Roger's unfortunate choices. You could have been spared a great deal. And I want you to know that I have, of course, broken it off with him. He was ever so repentant, but I did not and will not relent in my decision. The man is a fiend."

Edyth took her cousin's hand and patted it. "I know you were innocent in their games. How else could I explain your helping me capture the heart of the man I now call husband."

Lavinia's lips parted and she whipped her gaze up to look at him and back to Edyth. "Husband? You're married? But how? When?"

Bane chuckled and slowly lowered Edyth to her feet.

"I'll tell you all in good time," she replied, leaning on him as they drew toward the fire, stretching her fingers out toward the flames.

His brother Tom and Sylvia joined them, along with his mother and father, followed by four maids carrying silver trays of covered food that they placed on a card table in the corner of the room.

Edyth sniffed the air. "Are those biscuits I smell? And bacon?" She turned to her husband, beaming up at him. "You ordered breakfast for dinner for me, didn't you?"

"Of course. Nothing but your favorites, but only until you are well. We cannot have you turning into a tyrant."

"I thought I was already a tyrant?" She winked at him.

"No one could ever accuse you of being a tyrant. Eat your fill, my love," he whispered, keeping his arm around her, offering support. "Ah, it looks like your lawyer will be joining us for our meal." He motioned to the gentleman in the hall, inviting him into the parlor.

At the sight of the lawyer, Edyth stiffened and grabbed his hand at her waist. It felt strange to be so intimate with her in front of others, but she was his wife, and they could take each other's hand whenever they pleased. Leading her to the settee with the most cushions, he saw to it that she was settled in comfort before retrieving a plate for her. Today was not a day to enjoy a meal at the table.

"Good evening, Mr. Pittman. Please, have a seat. We are picnicking instead of dining at the table, for my wife's comfort."

The lawyer greeted them all in turn, and Edyth returned his greeting with a weak smile and a nod.

"Miss Foster," Mr. Pittman began and stopped, shaking his head. "I mean, Mrs. Banebridge. Please forgive me for not hearing of your predicament sooner."

"How could you have known, Mr. Pittman. Please, fill a plate, and we can begin."

Edyth did not inhale her food as Bane imagined she would, but instead, she was the picture of propriety. She ate silently while the lawyer asked the group his questions, only pausing to answer his direct questions. Mr. Pittman listened to their accounts, stoic, while Lavinia openly wept into her handkerchief and Bane's mother gingerly patted her on the shoulder. His father sat, grim-faced, no doubt imagining his only daughter in the place of Edyth as he reached out and took Mother's other hand.

Bane had refilled Edyth's coffee and plate once more before Mr. Pittman closed his folder and rested his clasped hands on the documents and looked to Edyth. "Well, Mrs. Banebridge, you were obviously wrongfully imprisoned on the island, and from the marriage certificate produced by Mr. Raoul Banebridge and the verification of Tom Banebridge's testimony, your marriage is legally binding."

She blushed at the mention of the validity of the marriage, but Bane squeezed her hand, hoping to provide her with a small measure of comfort.

"And for my final question before I depart, do you have anyone willing to testify of your treatment on the island and of your sanity on your behalf?" Mr. Pittman gestured around the room. "Besides those present here today, of course? Someone from the asylum, a nurse perhaps?"

"I know just one. She's a patient who goes by Nellie Brown in the asylum. She should be free from that prison within days, if not already. Miss Nellie Bly has been undercover researching for an exposé that she is writing for Joseph Pulitzer of the *New York World*."

The lawyer's eyes widened. "You don't say? Well, that should prove most helpful." He tucked his folder under his arm and, taking one last draft of coffee from his cup, rose. "I will get to work on this right away. Don't worry about a thing. It is my job to do the worrying. You focus on getting well."

Lavinia was the first to stand. With a smile and tinted cheeks that Bane recognized as admiration, she offered to show Mr. Pittman to the door. With the lawyer's departure, the family gave them some privacy, his mother closing the doors behind them.

"Thank goodness that is over. Mr. Pittman seems kind," Bane said, returning to his seat beside her.

"Yes, he is, but it has been years since I've conversed with him." Edyth slumped into her pillow, her exhaustion plain.

"Did his being here bring up memories of your parents' accident?" He rubbed his thumb over her palm, still shaken from hearing her gruesome account of her days at the island and the final treatment she received before she was rescued.

"Yes, but since my revelation on the island, the pain is beginning to pass, leaving behind the memories of my parents that were previously shrouded in my grief." She met his gaze. "I'll tell you about it soon."

"I'll be patient until you are ready." Bane scooted next to her. He drew her to him and kissed the top of her head. "I'm proud of you. It could not have been easy to relive such inhumanity. . .depravity." His voice caught, and Edyth seized his hand.

"Don't," she whispered, her own voice growing rough.

He pressed onward, needing to confess the burden that he had been carrying since the day he found her. "I cannot help but think that if I'd found you sooner, I would've spared you—"

She pressed a hand over his mouth, her eyes flashing. "Stop that at once. Do you hear me? I should have paid my uncle's threat greater heed, but I was foolish in my misplaced trust of the man. I should have sent for you. *I* should have done anything else rather than shut myself up in my chamber like a child. We could both go on and on blaming ourselves, but it's done. We must place our doubts, our burdens, where they belong, in God's hands and *leave* them there." She raked her fingers through his hair, gripping the back of his head. "Promise me you will stop blaming yourself. You found me. *You* did not give up on me." She pressed her forehead to his. "Promise?"

He closed his eyes and exhaled. "Yes."

"Good. Now we won't have to talk of that or of lawyers anymore, right?"

"No, not for a while. Mr. Pittman has what he needs from you, but I want you to know that if the only way to keep you safe is to move to a foreign land, I'll do it in an instant."

"You would sacrifice your club that has taken you years to establish?" She shook her head. "I—I couldn't ask you to do that."

"You wouldn't have to ask, my darling. I love you." He wrapped his arms around her and she melted into him. "Shall we leave all this behind and take our wedding trip? The doctors said you could travel as long as the journey was short and, above all, tranquil."

She shifted herself to look up at him with wide eyes. "Our wedding trip? Where?"

"Well, you always talked about how your happiest memories were of your summers spent at your parents' estate in Newport. So when Mr. Pittman discovered that the mansion was the one item your father left to you without any conditions in place, I thought that it was high time we go there for a relaxing holiday. I've already alerted the staff in Newport, and they are preparing for our arrival tomorrow evening. If you wish it, that is. We will have to take the steamboat as your aunt and uncle have your yacht secured until your fortune is released to you."

She rested her head on his shoulder and gazed into the fire. "I haven't gone back to Newport since my parents' death. The memories the house holds were all too dear to taint with my sorrow."

He drew her chin up, and along with it, her gaze. "Will it be too painful of a place for you to recover?"

She smiled, stroking his cheek, his chin, his lips. "No. With you by my side, I will create new memories and honor my parents by remembering them. It is time I stop running and face my past. . . with you as my present and future."

Chapter Twenty-Four

The pain passes, but the beauty remains.
~ Pierre-Auguste Renoir

Edyth paused on the shore, eyeing the gangplank, her chest constricting. And it wasn't because of the very loose corset Sylvia had encouraged her to wear in public. She smoothed down the front of her jewel-blue traveling gown and exhaled. *I can do this.*

"Sweetheart, what's wrong?" Bane asked, leaving the bags with the Wickford Landing crew to load aboard the steamboat, *Eolus*, for their short journey to Newport.

"I know it is silly, but the idea of being on any kind of boat again after my ferry trips makes me remember." She clenched her skirt in her fists. "I'm not running from my past, truly, but it—it sparks my anxiety, and I'm afraid of what may happen if the spark turns into a wildfire."

He drew her hand through his arm. "It's not silly in the slightest. You are still recovering from a traumatic time. You have to give yourself time to heal. If you're not ready, we can find another place for you to recover."

He was right, of course. The facade of strength that had taken her years to build had tumbled in only days in the asylum, and she was left vulnerable. "Tell me again what's in Newport to propel me onto this steamboat."

He pressed a kiss atop her hand and grinned. "Well, it's not crowded, most of the reporters will not follow you, and there will be nothing for you to do but rest and paint and do all of your favorite things. There is also that pie shop in town you've been dreaming of for a decade that we can go to every day if you wish."

"Every day?" She wet her lips, her gaze flickering to the plank again. Could she do it for the sake of Miss Penny's Pie Shop?

His grin faded into a furrowed brow, and he lowered his voice. "Certainly, but in all seriousness, I do not want to push you into doing something that you aren't ready to attempt. It could be counterproductive to your healing. I can always send for pie to be delivered here. You do not have to do this."

"No, no. I can do this. I want to do this." She squeezed his hand and they stepped aboard. The plank was the worst part, but once on the promenade deck of the steamboat, the luxury of the boat banished the ferry from her mind and she began to feel herself relax.

"So, what would you like to do first when we arrive?" Bane asked as they leaned over the rail to watch the rest of the passengers board.

"Stop at Miss Penny's in town on the way to Blakely Manor. And if her pie shop is closed, given the hour, we will pay her as much as it takes to get a pie," she replied without hesitation. When she summered in Newport, her family would purchase a whole pie every Saturday and eat it in place of dinner. She grinned, thinking how their weekly trips to the pie shop were most likely responsible for her plump waistline as a girl.

A hand touched her shoulder and she jumped back and into the present, lifting her hand as if to block a strike. But she dropped it at once at the sight of the regal woman peering down at her.

"My apologies for startling you, but are you not Edyth Foster?"

Recognizing the society matron, Edyth dipped into a curtsy. "Mrs. Finley. What a surprise."

Her brow arched. "Yes, so it would seem. Who is this charming gentleman with you?"

Remembering the woman's abrupt manner from that fatal season six years ago, Edyth cleared her throat. "This is my husband, Mr. Raoul Banebridge."

"Mr. Banebridge of the New York fencing club?" Her eyes sparkled. "I never thought you would marry, what with your nose always stuck in that club, otherwise I would have presented my own daughter to you."

"Well, that's what businesses require these days," he replied, taking Edyth's hand in his.

Her lips pursed at his remark and intimate action. "In any event, I was not expecting to see anyone from the old families heading to Newport with it being the off-season there and all. You must join my husband and me for dinner at our residence in Newport tomorrow night."

Edyth pressed her fingers into his arm. *No.* Mrs. Finley had made her debut season miserable, and as she was no longer forced to subject herself to the society matron, she did not feel compelled to humor her now.

Bane sighed and shook his head remorsefully. "It is with our deepest regret that we must decline. This is our wedding trip."

"Which is why I am being so kind as to extend you an invitation, despite my past interactions with your wife. I'll expect you at seven o'clock."

"We cannot attend you. I apologize," Bane replied, his tone reflecting only the barest hint of his agitation.

Mrs. Finley's mouth fell open before she corrected herself. "Why on earth? No one else on the island is aware of your arrival, and you surely do not have plans, as I know all who are worth knowing on the island."

"We plan to be by ourselves, actually," Edyth interjected.

Mrs. Finley's cheeks tinted. "Excuse me for saying so, but anyone would be happy to dine with us, since we are in the elite Four Hundred, a most coveted position, as you *very* well know. If you were to dine with my family, your standing would be greatly increased, and I'm sure the sins of your past would be wiped clean, dear Edyth, which is why I am offering this as a wedding gift to you."

"I beg your pardon for any disrespect, Mrs. Finley, but I'm not sure you understand why I declined. It's our wedding holiday and we wish to be by ourselves. I doubt we would even consider dining with the queen of England." He looked at Edyth with mischievous eyes and swept her lips into a passionate kiss, blurring the world.

"Well, I never." Mrs. Finley whisked her skirts behind her and continued down the promenade.

Edyth broke the kiss and ducked her face into his shoulder and giggled. "You are positively wicked, Raoul. But thank you."

"My pleasure." He winked at her and continued their walk, in the opposite direction that Mrs. Finley had taken, enjoying the brisk afternoon air. "I say, wasn't Mrs. Finley the one hosting that party where you—"

"Yes, yes! She was the hostess at the party where my society debut season died, but shall we make our way to the main cabin for tea? I haven't dined on the steamboat in a decade, but I remember their fare being rather tasty, and it will help pass the hour to the port."

Entering the long main cabin, Edyth took in the familiar grandeur of the *Eolus* with its opulent molding and four chandeliers across the length of the room. The waiter showed them to a small round table in the corner of the room, but not bothering to look at the menu, Edyth gave her order for high tea, intent on enjoying herself even if high tea was beyond the fashionable hour.

"Are you ever going to tell me what happened?" Bane asked, his eyes sparking as the waiter left.

Edyth grunted. "You are not going to let that one stay unaddressed, are you?"

He grinned, leaning both elbows on the table and cupping his chin in his hands as if he were a boy and she was about to tell the most delightful story.

She sighed and squeezed her eyes shut. He would find out the truth eventually. "Fine. Many years ago, I read an article about a petticoat duel between two women. Even though it was with pistols, it led to me researching about other female duelists."

Bane blinked and sat back in his chair. "I beg your pardon?"

"You should know about them since you are such an accomplished fencing instructor. There was a pair of women who dueled with swords only last year. It was in all the papers! Didn't you read about it?"

"I seemed to have missed that article." He chuckled, shaking his head.

"I don't know how, given your vocation, but anyway—" She waved her hand dismissively while fully intending on finding said articles and sharing them with her husband. "Not long ago, women would duel just as men, and well, with that parcel of history fresh on my mind—"

"Oh Edyth, please tell me this isn't leading where I think it is?" He ran his hand over his mouth, his shoulders shaking with mirth.

She sucked in through her teeth and charged ahead to the awful truth that she had kept from him for years. "As I was saying, that snippy Heather Finley, who is a miniature of her mother, made a few choice remarks on my dress and the reason why a certain gentleman wasn't giving me the time of day and—"

"Certain gentleman? You don't mean. . ." Bane's jaw dropped.

Her cheeks blazed. "Yes, you dear. Even at that age, I carried a torch for you. Well, Miss Heather Finley told me she was interested in you enough to hire you as her private instructor and goaded me by saying that you seemed to be interested in her, which you weren't, correct?" She looked pointedly at her husband.

He shrugged. "I must admit that I have only a dim recollection of a Miss Heather Finley."

"Good, because, well, Miss Finley insinuated you had kissed her." She crossed her arms, one brow lifting.

"What! I never—" Bane halted as his voice had drawn the glances of travelers about the room.

"I know, which is why I defended your honor against her accusation that you had kissed her, promised marriage, and then jilted her."

Bane threw up his hands. "That is utterly ridiculous. What could she have possibly gained from telling you such a falsehood and bringing herself such unnecessary embarrassment?"

"Because she was planning on forcing your hand into a match or seizing your assets in recompense of a breach of promise. So I did the only thing I could think of to challenge her outlandish claims."

"Don't tell me. . . ." He grimaced.

"Jasper Wentworth was not the first I have challenged to a duel and beaten," she muttered under her breath, relieved that the tea had arrived along with the tier of sandwiches, miniature quiches, and little cakes.

Bane nodded his thanks to the waiter, but the moment the man departed, he returned his attention to Edyth, his brows rising in expectation. But Edyth began pouring the tea, refusing to return to the subject at hand. The unexpectedly heavy pot made her shoulder ache, causing her to slosh the tea into one of the saucers, and she quickly set it down.

"Let me." Bane filled their cups, and she again felt eyes on them as he handed her one. "And I am assuming that duel was the nail in your society coffin?"

She nodded and took a tentative sip of tea. "Excellent deduction. The Finleys, of course, never allowed the tale of the duel to leave the family, but they spread a rumor that as a parentless debutante, I lacked certain manners to be welcome in that elite circle, despite my fortune and heritage."

Still laughing, Bane finished off his finger sandwich. "Only you, Edyth. Only you."

"But I'm not the only one. Women duelists are a real thing," she protested.

He rolled his eyes. "I would have heard about this long before, if that were the case."

She snatched up a petit four and stuffed it into his mouth, staying his argument.

"I hope you don't mind, but I'd rather leave the master room vacant," Edyth whispered to Bane as she stared at the massive chamber where the maid had escorted them.

Bane turned to the maid. "Thank you so much for your preparations, but I think Mrs. Banebridge would prefer her old rooms instead of the master."

The maid kept her expression smooth and bobbed into a short curtsy. "Of course, sir. It will take the staff about a half hour to prepare, but please call or pull a bell cord for anything, should you have need."

Edyth gripped his hand and pulled him along for a tour of the house, showing him the ballroom, library, and finally the studio, which overlooked the ocean. He turned and saw the paintings from young Edyth. None of them were a study of hands.

He picked up a sketch of a fencer that was partially painted. "This is rather impressive for such a young artist. Why, I think I recognize this young fencer as me?"

She smiled. "I had forgotten all about it. It was meant to be a gift for you, but I left it here by mistake and then, well, I lost my courage to give it to you, and when my parents died, I never thought of it again."

He took in the lines, admiring her work at such a tender age. "You were talented even then."

"My father thought so, but I always thought he felt that way because he was my father."

"May I keep it?" he asked, lifting the painting in question.

"It's always been meant for you." She propped both hands against the windowsill. "I'm feeling rather dizzy from all the traveling."

He was by her side in an instant and wrapped his arm around her waist. "I'm sorry. I should have had you sit while they made up the room."

Edyth leaned into his arm in a way that let him know how

exhausted she must truly be. "It's no one's fault but my own. I did too much."

He swept her into his arms, his boots clicking on the marble floors as he carried her to the beautiful peach-colored room of her childhood. At the sight of them, the three maids straightened from their place at the side of the bed, fixing the fresh linens. "We are almost done, sir."

He looked about the room. All the furniture had the white dustcloths removed, their trunks were standing open in one corner, the fireplace was roaring, and a vase of fresh crimson roses was on the nightstand. "I'm afraid Mrs. Banebridge is feeling poorly, so if you all could finish up in the morning, that would be better. Can you send up a tray of tea and that pie we brought with us?"

The women curtsied, and the head maid with mousy brown hair, who earlier had introduced herself as Sally, answered, "Certainly, sir."

"And if one of you wouldn't mind assisting me, I would love to get out of this wretched corset and into my robe," Edyth said, pulling at the top of the corset confining her.

Sally motioned the other maids out as she retrieved the needed items from the trunk and Edyth stepped behind the dressing screen. Bane kept his back to the screen, focusing instead on the fireplace until Edyth reappeared in a lilac dressing robe and sank onto the bed as the tray arrived.

Throughout their small feast atop the comforter, Bane noticed Edyth's rattling, wearied breathing but refrained from commenting on it.

"The pie was even more wonderful than I remembered!" Edyth yawned behind her hand, sinking further into the pillow.

"And I fully intend on purchasing another as soon as it's gone," Bane agreed. He stood and gathered the tray, setting it in the hallway and closing the door. "If you don't mind, I'll sleep on the settee as I did at the estate. I'd hate to accidentally hurt your shoulder in my sleep."

"There is plenty of room for the two of us in bed," she protested, her ears turning pink. "I think it is ridiculous for you to lose sleep on account of my shoulder."

"Well, you'll find out sooner or later, but I'm what's called a thrasher. I don't sleep in one position all night. As boys, my brothers all refused to share a bed with me after I inadvertently gave each of them a clawed eye or bruised cheek on multiple occasions."

A hint of a smile appeared in the corners of her lips. "Very well. I would offer you a room nearby, but. . ." Her frightened gaze slowly moved to the window and back to him as if she were ashamed.

"I don't mind sleeping on the settee or even the floor if I grow uncomfortable with being curled up. I'd rather be near you."

She caught his hand. "I appreciate it. Good night, Mr. Banebridge."

"Good night, *Mrs.* Banebridge." He grinned, bent down, and kissed her forehead, pulling the covers up to her chin before he curled onto the settee and drifted off to sleep.

Edyth's screaming jarred him to his core. Nearly falling off the narrow settee, Bane crossed the room to her bed in an instant, seized her hand in his, and cupped the other to her cheek. "Edyth? Wake up. You are safe!"

With a whimper, she sat up, her cheeks still wet with tears. "Bane, I am sorry. I was having a nightmare." She gave a shiver and moaned, clutching her shoulder.

"Do you need anything?" He stroked back her hair, wishing he could bear the pain for her. "Perhaps the medicine the doctor sent to help you sleep?"

"No. It makes me feel like I am drowning. Just a cup of water, please." She pressed a hand to her throat. "I'm always parched these days."

He poured her a glass from the pitcher on the nightstand and held it to her lips.

"Thank you," she whispered, wiping her mouth with the back of her hand as he set aside the glass and settled her back onto the pillow.

"I'm worried about you, Edyth."

"Me too." She bit her lip. "Would you mind staying with me?"

"I am." He gestured to the settee three yards away.

"No, I mean beside me. If I can feel your warmth, I won't be so afraid. I was never warm in the asylum, and with you beside me, I will know it's only a bad dream keeping me captive and not reality. Would you mind terribly?"

For his answer, Bane sat on the bed beside her and slipped his arm around her, allowing her to rest her head on his chest, her breathing evening out. "Better?"

"Much. Bane?"

"Yes?"

"Thank you," she whispered.

"We will get through this, Edyth. One day you will wake up and feel better, I know it, but it will take time. We can't expect that your heart is healing at the same pace as your body."

She lifted her lips and grazed his chin. "You make it easier. God knew what I needed when He sent you."

Chapter Twenty-Five

My wish is to stay always like this,
living quietly in a corner of nature.
~ Claude Monet

The gulls cawed overhead and the wind rippled through her hair as she stood on the back lawn of her mansion in Newport, her easel facing out toward the ocean. Bane lay under the willow tree on a plaid blanket with the kitten crawling over the back of his legs, reading to Edyth from Poppy's Bible, fulfilling her promise to the dear girl to read it every day. Her uncle hadn't cared for her expressing her thoughts about God because he thought church was only meant to be attended on holidays when it was fashionable. . . but it was so much more. Poppy had shown her what it was like to truly have an unashamed thirst for God and His Word. Without Poppy sharing the Word, Edyth knew she could have easily despaired on the island. "Read those last few passages again, won't you?" she asked her husband, lingering in her strokes.

Bane cleared his throat and read again, his rich voice bringing further life to the psalm that she had taken for granted before the asylum. " 'He sent from above, he took me, he drew me out of many waters. He delivered me from my strong enemy, and from them which hated me: for they were too strong for me. They prevented me in the day of my calamity: but the Lord was my stay. He brought me forth also into a large place; he delivered me, because he delighted in me.' "

Her throat swelled as she paused in her depiction of the lone ship on the ocean. How well she knew those verses now. The good Lord had spared her again and again. While she did not understand why it was she and not her parents who lived, she now knew the truth of what really had happened that day, and she would never paint from that obsession or sorrow again. She would paint the words the Lord placed on her heart each day. And so she painted the ocean before her to remember how He had drawn her out of its depths and breathed life into her weary soul, giving her a new hope and a new future with Bane.

"Mr. and Mrs. Banebridge!" The head maid came trotting toward them from the house. "You have a visitor, Mrs. Banebridge."

"On our honeymoon?" Bane grumbled, rising and scooping up the kitten. "Who is it, Sally?"

"It's a lady reporter, a Miss Bly." Sally bent over, clutching her side as she reached for the kitten. "I—I tried to put her in the parlor, but she is in the foyer, saying she didn't wish to take up too much of your time and was only here to give you something. I'll fetch some tea though, unless you want me to send her away?"

"Oh no, please make tea." Edyth set aside her brushes at once, wiping her hands on her drop cloth. While she was aware that Nellie had begun releasing her articles in the *New York World*, Bane had thought it might be best for her anxiety to wait to read them until she had healed a little more emotionally, physically, and spiritually. And she had willingly agreed.

"Are you ready to see her?" Bane whispered, taking her hand in his as they crossed the green.

Edyth paused at the bottom of the back steps, breathing heavily. "It will take time for the memories to stop throbbing, but my fears of being taken away are slowly abating." She took both his hands into her own. "I know my future does not belong to anyone but God." She shook her head and released a little laugh. "I wish it were possible to offer a onetime prayer to God and my anxiety would disappear, but for me, it has been a slow healing, and I must offer up my burdens to Him every time I open my eyes."

"And I'll be here for you, as long as it takes for you to be free from this anxiety."

She kissed the top of his hands. "Then let's take the next step by confronting the past head-on. No more running."

They entered the house and found Nellie standing in the gilded marble foyer, her hands clasped around her ever-present notebook. Edyth left Bane's side and rushed to embrace her friend, wincing slightly from the pressure on her still-healing wound.

"Nellie! How is Poppy? I had my lawyer inquire, but last I heard, she was still ill."

Nellie squeezed her hand. "That is partly why I came in person. I wish I could bring you news of her health, but Poppy is in a better place. She is with her father and mother at last."

Edyth swallowed. She had feared as much, but to her surprise, she felt a modicum of relief mixed with her sorrow, for now her dear friend was with Jesus and her beloved parents. "At least we know that she is happy and at peace."

Bane came to her and rubbed his hand gently on her back, offering her strength at the news.

Nellie looked at him and dipped into a short curtsy. "Bane, I mean, Mr. Banebridge, I feel as if I know you already. It is a pleasure to formally meet you."

Bane bowed. "The honor is mine to meet the woman who comforted Edyth when I could not."

"Knowing that Edyth was safe in your hands despite my poorly executed efforts that last day in the asylum has helped assuage the guilt I felt."

"Guilt?" Edyth asked.

"I cannot tell you how I regret not summoning my contact sooner for you, Edyth. I was fully intending on having you leave with me. I didn't think they would actually subject you to the Gray Chamber before then."

Edyth squeezed her hand. "Let us not speak of the chamber or of guilt. Tell me, how are your articles being received?"

Nellie's eyes filled as she gave a short nod and paused to draw a breath before answering, "That is the other reason why I am here. I wanted to give you this in person since it is as much your story as mine." She pressed a stack of newspaper articles into Edyth's hands. "The installments of our story have all been released and have already caused quite the stir. People are outraged."

The first headline read in bold lettering BEHIND ASYLUM BARS. Shaking slightly, Edyth's fingers grazed over the title, memory's knife sticking her anew, but before she could look at any of the others, Bane took the stack and set them on the foyer's gold-leaf table.

"My editor wishes to turn the articles into a book! People are clamoring for answers, and so I was summoned for the grand jury's investigation."

Edyth gasped. "An investigation?"

"Yes, and there are rumors flying about the city of a million dollars to be donated to the asylum for the benefit of the patients," Nellie added.

A million? That would go a long way to helping the patients. . . but only if the staff, namely Nurse Sweeney, was dismissed. "And of the staff? Will the guilty parties be held responsible?"

"All are being evaluated individually. Most of the doctors will be dismissed as will, I'm certain, the nurses. The new staff is to be supervised in order to provide accountability for the treatment of the patients." She clasped Edyth's hand. "We did it."

"*You* did it," Edyth whispered, in disbelief of how much a series of articles could change the lives of hundreds in the present and thousands in the future.

"You helped me learn and be a part of the stories of others. *We* have given a voice to the voiceless. Poppy's death will not go unnoticed. Her story has touched the city."

Her tears welled for Poppy, for herself, and for the countless others on Blackwell's Island. They would all have a better life. She buried her face into her hands and wept as Bane wrapped her in the safety of his arms.

Edyth stood on the cliff's edge, arms spread wide, allowing the ocean's breeze to flow over her as Bane held her securely by her waist. "I never want our wedding trip to end."

Bane kissed her lightly on the cheek. "I feel the same, my sweet wife."

She sighed, turning around to face her husband. "But, I suppose with Uncle's looming trial, we really should be returning."

"Actually, I wanted to discuss another option for you. Your uncle's attorney, Jasper Wentworth, sent an offer to settle outside of court to avoid further scandal."

She frowned. "But why would Jasper suddenly wish to give up?"

"Because of Nellie's articles. I read them while you were napping this week. It is harrowing. New York is in an uproar, and our lawyer is elated. Mr. Foster immediately confessed his part of the scheme and has relinquished any and all control as your guardian. You are a free woman, and with our marriage, your fortune has been released to you, my love."

She threw her arms around his neck. "We are safe! Part of me worried that it was all too good to be true and that the courts would have our marriage annulled due to my supposed insanity."

He pulled her into a kiss. "And what will you be doing with all of this newfound freedom?"

"First off, I shall have my lawyer look into each patient's admission into the asylum and secure another round of testing for every single woman there in order to free anyone who was falsely committed. Then, I will arrange an annual stipend to be donated to the asylum."

He pulled back, his brows furrowed. "That's very generous of you, but aren't you afraid any testing will be a farce and funds given will be squandered, especially after they so wronged you?"

"With Nellie's story, the doctors and nurses will have been thoroughly interviewed by now and the bad ones weeded out. And, if I allot funds, I'll have the power to say how they are used. My funds will hire not only a cook to prepare decent meals fit for a lady, but also give the women an outlet by allowing them to have music and painting available to them, a small measure of comfort in their trials. It's not right that I live in luxury after meeting those souls on the island and not do anything to ease their lot in life dealt to them by their own relatives."

"I am so proud of you." Bane squeezed her hand, his voice rough.

She lifted a smile to him. "Then you'll hopefully be doubly proud of me with this next announcement."

"Oh?"

"I sent word to Mr. Pittman a few days ago to see that your fencing club loans are paid off and that the deed is sent to you the moment the funds are mine."

His jaw dropped. "That's too much."

She tapped her finger to her lips and tilted her head. "So, you would risk your life for me, marry me without hesitation to protect me and fight for my freedom every day, but somehow my paying off your loans is too much?"

He shook his head and laughed. "I love you, Edyth Banebridge."

"I love you more," she replied with a wink.

He sighed. "I'm afraid that is not possible." He pressed a finger to her lips, staying her protest. "And before you argue, I suppose now is as good a time to ask you what I was going to ask you when we returned to the city."

Her eyes grew wide, having not the vaguest idea of what he meant.

"I want you to be the first female fencing instructor at the club and take over the female students."

"Bane!" She squealed as he gently spun with her in his arms. She leaned her head against his chest, thankful for a man who not only cared for her but cherished her. It had been so long, but now her eternal winter was over. She was safe, loved, and protected at last. She lifted her lips to him.

His brows shot up and he grinned, that tantalizing dimple appearing in his cheek. "What's this? I suppose you're asking for a kiss?"

"That would be most agreeable, sir."

"What are the odds that I would find it most agreeable as well?" With a roguish grin, Bane pulled her into his embrace and whispered, "I am yours and you are mine, Edyth Banebridge."

"Forever," she whispered, allowing herself to be swept away in his kiss that day and every day for the rest of their lives.

Author's Note

While Edyth Foster is a fictional character, her tale of being committed in order for her family to seize her wealth is inspired by a true story. Grandmother Blakely's account is also inspired by true stories. In my research, the grounds by which the institute would commit women to the asylum were shocking. I read stories of women being committed just because they were immigrants who were unable to speak English, or because they suffered from postpartum depression. In far too many cases, the woman held no power and had no way to prove her sanity.

The *New York World*'s exposé, *Ten Days in a Mad-House*, written by Nellie Bly, or Nellie Brown as she was known in the asylum, did wonders for the patients on Blackwell's Island where the so-called treatments included plunging the patients into cold water until they lost consciousness in order to calm their "frenzied" state and injecting their patients with copious amounts of various drugs such as morphine and chloral, driving them into madness. Many nurses at the asylum did indeed beat their patients, strangling them to the point of almost fainting and "teasing" the patients to make them lose their tempers so the nurses could further pinch and torment them before sending them to the Lodge for solitary confinement or to the Retreat for their "treatments."

In my research of the asylum and its many buildings, there was a reference made to a closet room in the main asylum, or Mad-House as they called it, where they would take patients to nearly strangle or drown them in tubs of water. It is from this closet that the idea for *The Gray Chamber* was born.

For the sake of my story, I did take a few liberties. I took the "treatments" used in the Retreat and placed them in the Gray Chamber to make Edyth's escape coinciding with Bane's rescue more fluid. And while there was a "Lunatics' Ball" held at the asylum, it did not occur during Nellie's time there, so I chose to adjust the actual dates to fit it into the story. It was interesting to note that by 1871, all the male patients on the island were transferred to Ward's Island to accommodate the overflow of women patients, so that is why there were no male patients at the ball. Also, reading was not permitted in any form in the asylum, so Poppy's Bible was my addition.

After Nellie's articles were released, there was a grand jury investigation where Nellie swore to the validity of her words. The staff were examined as well as the treatments, facilities, and food given to the patients. And, despite the asylum attempting to put on an exhibit of their perfectly baked bread and clean kitchen, the jury saw through the asylum's farce and sustained Nellie Bly's account, advising for her proposed changes. Because of Nellie's exposé and the ruling, provision for a million dollars was allotted to aid the patients inside the asylum's walls.

To read Nellie's firsthand account, check out her book *Ten Days in a Mad-House*, which is the horrifying true crime story that inspired this novel. Look for Jude Thorpe's story in *The White City*.

Acknowledgments

To my husband, Dakota, I love you more, and since this is printed in a book, it is true.

To my little boy, you are my heart. I love being your mama.

To the future Doctor Madden and Mrs. Madden, thank you for your expert medical advice and for allowing me to shoot dear Edyth and stab Uncle Boris with confidence.

To my favorite Doctor of Jurisprudence and ole partner in crime, Charlie, thank you for correcting my "lawyer" scenes and saving me from certain legal demise.

To my wonderful betas, Theresa and McKenna, thank you for your guidance and encouragement.

To my family, Dad, Mama, Charlie, Molly, Sam, Natalie, and Eli, thank you for all of your support and for babysitting while I write!

To my fantastic agent, Tamela Hancock Murray, I could not imagine writing without you on my side. Thank you for all that you do!

To Becky, Shalyn, Liesl, Laura, and the Barbour Publishing team, and Ellen, thank you for believing in me and coaching me. You are all wonderful!

To the reader, thank you for getting to know Edyth Foster and Raoul "Bane" Banebridge. I hope you enjoyed their story of friendship blossoming into love.

And to the Lord for His steadfastness and constant, overwhelming love. You are why I write.

Grace Hitchcock is the author of *The White City* and *The Gray Chamber* from Barbour Publishing's True Colors series. She has written novellas in *The Second Chance Brides*, *The Southern Belle Brides*, and the *Thimbles and Threads* collections with Barbour Publishing. She is a member of ACFW and holds a Masters in Creative Writing and a Bachelor of Arts in English with a minor in History. Grace lives in southern Louisiana with her husband, Dakota, and son.

Visit her online at GraceHitchcock.com and sign up for her author newsletter for behind-the-scenes book news and exclusive giveaways.

Books by Grace Hitchcock

The White City – True Colors Series

"The Widow of St. Charles Avenue" from
The Second Chance Brides: A Novella Collection

"Miss Beaumont's Companion" from
The Southern Belle Brides: A Novella Collection

"The Bridal Shop" from
Thimbles and Threads: A Novella Collection